Katherine Hall Page's

FAITH FAIRCHILD
MYSTERIES

"[Page's] young sleuth is a charmer."
New York Times Book Review

"Katherine Hall Page has found a great recipe
for delicious mysteries: take charming characters, mix with ingenious plots, season with
humor."

Nancy Pickard

"An expert at the puzzle mystery."
Fort Lauderdale Sun-Sentinel

"The author writes with grace and gentle wit,
expertly weaving all her material together into a
satisfying whole (and throwing in a few tempting
Down East recipes as well)."

Denver Post

"Forget about your diet. It's time you sampled
this author's marvelous treats."

Jackson Clarion-Ledger

"Skillful sleuthing . . . Bon appetit."

Tampa Tribune

Faith Fairchild Mysteries by
Katherine Hall Page
from Avon Books

KATHERINE HALL PAGE

THE BODY IN THE LIGHTHOUSE

A FAITH FAIRCHILD MYSTERY

AVON BOOKS
An Imprint of HarperCollinsPublishers

This is a work of fiction. Names, characters, places, and incidents are products of the author's imagination or are used fictitiously and are not to be construed as real. Any resemblance to actual events, locales, organizations, or persons, living or dead, is entirely coincidental.

AVON BOOKS
An Imprint of HarperCollins*Publishers*
10 East 53rd Street
New York, New York 10022-5299

Copyright © 2003 by Katherine Hall Page
Excerpt from *The Body in the Attic* copyright © 2004 by
Katherine Hall Page
ISBN: 0-380-81386-6
www.avonmystery.com

First Avon Books paperback printing: April 2004
First William Morrow hardcover printing: May 2003

Avon Trademark Reg. U.S. Pat. Off. and in Other Countries, Marca Registrada, Hecho en U.S.A.
HarperCollins® is a registered trademark of HarperCollins Publishers Inc.

Printed in the U.S.A.

10 9 8 7 6 5 4 3 2

To
Tom, Trevor, and Valerie Wolzien,
who love "Sanpere Island"
as much as we do

Acknowledgments

My thanks to Ethel and Stanley Clifford for all their help, and for answering what often must have seemed like extremely odd questions. I'm particularly grateful to Stan for supplying the proper term—a *no'theaster*—to describe that fierce storm; I'll never say *nor'easter* again. Thanks also to Paul and Corinne Sewall for the information pertaining to life as a fisherman and Paul's insider information on how to win a Wacky Rowboat race. Thank you, Hubert Billings, for setting me straight on the moose lottery and some other things. Once again, Dr. Robert DeMartino supplied medical information, and culinary expertise was provided by Kyra Alex, Lily's Café, Stonington, Maine. And, as always, special thanks to my editor, Jennifer Sawyer Fisher, and agent nonpareil, Faith Hamlin. Finally, a special bow to the Sunshine Dance Club.

. . . one fire burns out another's burning;
One pain is less'ned by another's anguish.

—WILLIAM SHAKESPEARE, *ROMEO AND JULIET*

THE BODY IN THE LIGHTHOUSE

One

Sawdust and nails covered the floor. A piece of plywood had been set on two sawhorses as a makeshift counter. It bowed slightly under the weight of an ancient microwave, power tools, containers of coffee, and doughnut boxes. Mold was floating in the congealed cream on the cup Faith Sibley Fairchild had picked up, intending to heave it at her husband, Tom, who was smiling sheepishly at her from the doorway—a doorway Faith had thought was supposed to be the site for a fireplace. She put the cup down, grabbed a desiccated doughnut from the hand of her seven-year-old son, Benjamin, snatched an iridescent beef jerky stick from the lips of her three-year-old daughter, Amy, and spoke in a carefully measured tone. A very carefully measured tone. Each word enunciated. Each word weighing several tons.

"*Sweetheart*, I thought you told me that the house was almost finished. It doesn't look almost finished to *me*."

She had been driving for five hours from the Fairchilds' home, the parsonage in Aleford, Massachusetts, to their summer cottage on Sanpere Island, off the coast of Maine. Five hours in a car with two children well below the age of reason or ability to retain liquids; children who required not only frequent pit stops but constant stimulation in the form of Raffi tapes. Ben, a curious soul, also needed to pepper his mother with questions, answerable and unanswerable: "Why is it called the Maine Turnpike—'cause it's in the state or 'cause it's main?" and "Why are they always working on it every time we drive to Sanpere?" Faith had often thought of offering her services as a consultant to the Massachusetts Department of Correction. Locking miscreants up in cells displayed a certain lack of imagination when it came to sentencing. Most parents could reel off dozens of alternatives, with no possibilities for recidivism.

"Honey," Tom said, "I know how it looks, but, believe me, it really *is* close to the end. We've got the punch list. Mostly, what you're seeing just means painting, a little cleanup, and a few trips to the dump." In contrast to his wife's words, Tom's rushed out in a torrent, and he tested the waters by moving a few steps closer to her. Clutching a child firmly at each side, she was standing as rigid as Niobe after the gods got to her.

She held up her hand, and Tom stopped in his tracks.

"There are no cabinets, as far as I can see," she said, starting to tick off items with one finger, "nor counters, except for that." Pointer went down as her gaze swept over the plywood, virtually igniting it. "I see you have apparently decided on a different location for the fireplace." Another finger joined the others. "And . . ."

Before she made a fist, Tom strode over and put his arms around his family.

"Okay, okay. It's not as far along as we'd hoped, but I was sure you'd want to be here, want to be a part of it, make decisions—and besides, I missed you guys."

Tom, the Reverend Thomas Fairchild of Aleford's First Parish Church, had been making the long commute to Maine whenever he could steal some time. The Fairchilds' cottage, a simple one-story square built before Amy was born and Ben reliably ambulatory, had been in desperate need of remodeling. From the beginning, the project had been dear to Tom's heart, and he'd spent the previous two weeks away from his family, nail gun in hand, having a ball. Caterer Faith had obligations and was, truth to be told, just as happy to avoid the mess. Yet she had missed Tom, too. She looked into his deep brown eyes. He had sawdust in his hair and was wearing a carpenter's apron from Barton's Lumberyard jauntily tied low on his waist, a badge of honor. She scrutinized his shirt to make sure it was well tucked

3

into his jeans—front and back. That other badge of honor, revealed when a workman bent to his task, and known locally as "The Sanpere Smile," was safely out of sight.

"It will be wonderful when it's done," she admitted, returning his hug and looking through the three large plate-glass windows at "the view." People in Maine prized their views, or, if they didn't have much of a one, drove or hiked to one. The Fairchilds' view would have been "Worth a Journey" in any Michelin guide. The tide was still coming in and the late-afternoon sun had turned the water's surface to gold. A heron was perched on a granite ledge in the cove. The tip of a long sandy beach, one of few on the island, curved to an end at their property. Sea lavender, grasses, and bayberry grew in abundance above the high-tide mark, giving way to a small meadow surrounded by tall pines and slender birches. A few sailboats dotted the expanse of water that extended as far as the eye could see—Swans Island and Isle au Haut distant on the horizon, large rounded shapes like slumbering beasts.

"Come on, let me show you the rest. You're going to love it!" Tom enthused. "And don't worry about dinner. I've got everything under control." His relief was palpable—and contagious. Faith doubted the dinner part, but, after the initial shock, she could see that the room was going to work, and she began to feel happy. They'd gutted the original house, leaving the tent ceiling with its Adirondack-like bead board intact. She noted that under the debris, the hardwood pine floor had been installed. This one large room, with all its windows bringing the outdoors in, would serve as kitchen and living room area. There was an island divider in place, waiting for the drop-in stove, and their refrigerator had been enclosed in its new location.

"Home Depot's delivering the cabinets and counters tomorrow. It won't take long to install them. Lyle's hired some extra crew members to help. But all the electrical work is finished, and most of the plumbing. See?" He proudly led them through the dining area, which connected the "old" house with the new addition, and flung open a door. The bathroom tile they'd picked out looked better than Faith had hoped, and all the fixtures were in place. Ben was hopping up and down. Maybe he was excited, maybe not.

"Ben, you go first," Faith said, ushering the rest of the family out.

Downstairs, there were three bedrooms, one for each child and the third for guests. No walls had been painted, but windows were in place. All the new furniture—most of it still in flat IKEA boxes—was in the garage, which the original builder, Seth Marshall, had insisted the Fairchilds build, despite their protests that it was almost as big as the cottage.

"You have to have a shed for stuff. Make it a garage, even though you'll probably never have room for a car in it," Seth had told them prophetically.

Seth had moved up to larger projects and given them Lyle Ames's name. Lyle didn't build new houses, preferring additions and remodeling jobs to what he called the "million-dollar mansions" that had started to invade even remote Sanpere.

Children drained, they climbed to the second floor, its master bedroom overlooking the water. The high, sloping ceiling echoed the pitch of the roof on the original half of the house. There was a large alcove to the rear for Tom's study, and a master bath with an extra-long tub. Tom Fairchild liked to stretch out and soak. So did Faith. At the moment, the tub was filled with scraps of wallboard, not rubber duckies. It was Amy who noticed that it, as well as the sink, lacked faucets. All of them plainly noted the missing toilet.

"We can certainly make do with one bathroom," Faith said, deciding not to scream until she found out whether Tom had put a bottle of Chardonnay in the fridge or not. "But where are we going to sleep—and eat? How am I going to cook?"

There had been an odd assortment of chairs—most certainly from the "take it or leave it" at the dump—in the living room/kitchen. Besides the microwave oven, she thought she might have spied a hot plate, but three meals a day for a family of four? Faith considered roughing it a nonconvection oven and no Cuisinart.

"Didn't you notice I've set us up downstairs? The kids are in what will be Ben's room, and we're in Amy's."

Faith led the way to inspect the accommodations. The reason she'd missed them previously was that she'd assumed the sleeping bags spread out on thin, very thin, mats were drop cloths left by the workers.

"It will be fun," Tom said in earnest. He was a born camper. "There's going to be a gorgeous sunset tonight, and the picnic table is where it's always been. We can eat there, then put the kids to bed and . . ." Faith knew what the "and" was. It had been two weeks.

"These mats look mighty comfy to me," she said. "Now, how about you find me a drink? Anything. Quickly."

With no shades on the windows, the little Fairchilds were up with the sun. Her back stiff and limbs aching, Faith was pouring milk when the carpenters showed up at 6:00 A.M. Another item Tom had forgotten to mention: work hours. For a while, the traffic in the cottage was straight out of a Marx Brothers movie as large men moved large pieces of wallboard and other objects past small children in various stages of undress and one very weary mother coming to terms with the fact that she wasn't going to get to shower. One of the carpenters, younger than the others, tall, skinny, and with little more than peach fuzz over his upper lip, blushed fiery red at the sight of Faith still in her nightgown. A very decent nightgown—the others were at home, stowed away for the rare occasions she and Tom were sans children. Her nightclothes were further obscured by a long sweatshirt. She glanced at his left hand—no ring, a blackened thumbnail moving toward the blue spectrum. He stood frozen in his tracks, clinging to the bundle of molding strips he was carrying, until Lyle called, "Kenny!" and the spell was broken. It would have been funny at, say, nine o'clock in the morning.

"I'll take the kids with me to the IGA, then drop them off at day camp," Faith told Tom, who nodded absently, eyes glued to the level before him, his expression similar to the one he wore when approaching the altar.

The day camp, relatively new to the island, ran from 9:00 A.M. until 3:00 P.M. and served both natives and summer people. Faith had viewed it as a godsend, but now she wondered what she was going to do all day without the kids to tend, and the house unfit for habitation. Long walks—definitely not long swims in these frigid waters—read all the books she'd meant to read since college, and . . . Her closest friend and neighbor from Aleford, Pix Miller, who had lured the Fairchilds to Sanpere in the first place, was away for the month. The oldest Miller, Mark, had graduated from the University of Colorado, and since they were all going to be out there, they had decided on one long, grand family vacation to celebrate. They'd be camping their way across the Rockies, into the Pacific Northwest, returning through Canada. Faith had thought a grand tour meant Paris, London, and Rome, but the Millers were not cut from the same cloth.

It was a perfect Maine day. Warm, but not too warm. Blue sky, clear air, which seemed to bring everything into sharp focus, and the sea, always the sea. Route 17, the main road that encircled the island, was never far from shore, and every turn brought a glimpse or flat-out breathtaking vista of Penobscot Bay. Gulls, crook-necked cormorants, and one regal osprey flew overhead.

The IGA didn't offer too many choices, so Faith was counting on the small stands set up by local gardeners in their front yards to provide fresh produce. You selected your tomatoes, then left the money in a jar or coffee can, making change as need be. There was one on the way to day camp.

"I won't be a moment, chickadees," she promised, thinking of panzanella—that simple Italian salad of ripe tomatoes, rough cubes of bread, a little salt, pepper, olive oil, vinegar, and fresh basil—a one-dish meal, as she stopped the car by the side of the road and got out.

The cupboard was bare. Or almost. A few sad-looking cukes lay next to a zucchini the size of a baseball bat. Try as she might, she hadn't been able to convince the island growers that bigger was not better when it came to squash. Spying the proprietress deadheading her tuberous begonias, Faith called out, "Any tomatoes today?"

"No, nor none likely. Lettuce, neither. Guess you've been away. We haven't had a drop of rain since early July. Don't want the well to run dry, so the only things I've been trying to keep going are my begonias." She walked out toward Faith.

"For the fair, you understand," she explained. *Fair* came out as two syllables, not unlike *ayuh*—a Maineism Faith had yet to hear.

Disappointed, Faith returned to the car, fervently wishing this particular gardener had been after a blue ribbon for veggies at the Labor Day weekend Blue Hill Fair, and not prize blossoms. Still, there were other stands, and every Friday morning, there was a farmers' market in the parking lot of the Congregational church. In addition to locals, it drew purveyors from the mainland, who might have deeper wells. With a short growing season anyway, the news of the drought, further limiting supply, was depressing. Faith's aunt lived in New Jersey. As she drove, Faith fantasized about getting some Big Boys. Aunt Chat—and the rest of the state—claimed Jersey tomatoes were next to none, and Faith tended to agree. How would ripe beefsteaks do in the mail? Cheered by the image of love apples by post, she dropped off the kids at camp. Neither of them had ever displayed any separation anxiety whatsoever, a fact that pleased Faith—her kids were secure, adaptable, ready for adventure—and ever so slightly displeased her. One small hesitant backward glance, a hastily whispered "Mommy, I'll miss you" wouldn't kill them.

Kids settled, she left, and soon after, she pulled up to the cottage. Toting her groceries, she was surprised to see the entire crew, Tom included, sitting outside the house. Coffee break? Except no one seemed to be drinking any.

"Hi, what's up?" she called out.

One of the older men answered succinctly. "Skunks."

"Skunks!"

"Yup. Skunks in your crawl space. Elwell went down the hatch in the bedroom closet and stepped on one. Came up like salts through a goose. Thinks it's a mumma and a few babies."

"Elwell doesn't even take to dogs," said Lyle. He was smiling, although Faith couldn't see there was much to smile about. "He was out of here in no time. Said to call him when they're gone."

Amazed at the inactivity before her, Faith stated the obvious, "Well, shouldn't we be getting rid of them *right away*?" It was a miracle the mother hadn't sprayed the house when Elwell, whichever one he had been, had made his inauspicious discovery.

"That's what we're out here studying to do," Lyle said. "Want to keep an eye peeled for the Home Depot truck, too. Can't put the delivery in the house now."

"Tom!" Faith wailed. She had been looking forward to the month of August since the last snowstorm—in April—had unpleasantly arrived in Aleford, bringing power outages and leaving sooty ice-encrusted remnants well into May. She'd dreamed of Sanpere. The house would be done, the kids would be at camp, and she'd have Tom all to herself—time together. Or when he was working on his book, a study of the impact of chastity on Western thought, she'd have time for herself. Both kinds of time were as rare as unicorns.

She had reluctantly given in to the blandishments of her husband and the Millers that first summer some years ago and agreed to a rental on Sanpere, instead of in the Hamptons or on the Vineyard. One thing had led to another, and now the Fairchilds were home owners. She should have been firmer to start with. If she had, they wouldn't be in this predicament. Sure, there were skunks in Edgartown and East Hampton, both the two- and four-legged kinds, but there were solutions easily at hand. It went without saying that there were no exterminators on Sanpere, no service that could be called. No little man to take care of everything. She sat down on the grass, took out a bag of store-bought cookies, Pepperidge Farm Milanos, grabbed one, and passed the rest around. She'd known she wouldn't be baking in the next few days. She hadn't known she might not be baking—or cooking—for weeks.

"Anybody have any ideas?"

Many alternatives later, her husband emerged from beneath the house and declared triumphantly that all they had to do now was wait. The skunks had entered through a small open vent under the deck, a space that Lyle had not closed in yet. It was too high for them to get out the way they'd come in; ergo, all they had to do was provide a means of egress, along with bait. They'd slid a board loaded with bits of Milanos embedded in sticky peanut butter at intervals through the vent opening. Lured by the treats, the skunks would literally walk the plank and scamper off to tell the tale to their forest friends.

"They'll be gone before morning," Lyle said confidently, getting into a pickup Faith couldn't help but notice was brand-new and loaded with extras. He charged by the hour, and she wondered if the skunk conferencing had been billable. "You can move around in the other part of the house; I'd try not to go directly overhead. They'll come out tonight when it's dark."

Goody, thought Faith, glancing at her watch. What with finding space in the garage for the Home Depot delivery and providing haute cuisine for the skunks—they'd added banana slices in peanut butter at the last minute for the fruit lovers—it was almost time to pick up the kids.

"Guess we'd better bed down in the living room," Tom said. "I'll move our stuff. And we'll go to Lily's Café to eat. I don't want you to have to bother."

Faith had not intended to bother. She'd already called ahead to find out what the specials were, planning to get to Lily's early. She'd also called the one motel, one inn, and one bed-and-breakfast on the island, only to find, as she'd expected, that all three were booked through Labor Day.

"I'm sorry," said Tom. His cheek was warm from the sun as he pulled her close. "Someday, we'll laugh about all this."

"Soon, I hope," Faith said.

"Soon. They'll be gone by morning—and I don't think we'd better mention anything to the kids. You know Ben. He'll want to go down and make pets out of them."

Faith did know Ben. He was exactly like his father.

Again, the kids were up early. Again, Faith ached in joints she hadn't known she possessed. But there were no early-morning workers. And the skunks were still in residence. Tom had bravely flashed a light down the hatch in the closet.

"I can see their eyes, and the plank is as clean as a whistle. I think they like it here."

Faith didn't need this evidence. She'd heard the sound of tiny feet scratching all night. So had Ben.

"I think there's an animal under the house, Mom. I'd better go look."

"No, you'd better not. You don't want to be late for camp."

"It could be hurt. It could need our help!"

Seven is a passionate age, Faith thought. "Dad and I will investigate while you're away. Don't worry."

"But I *am* worried. Very worried," Ben mumbled.

Tom left with the kids, and Faith sat on the deck with a second cup of coffee. A lone gull flew overhead. She'd planted some perennials in front of the house last July, with Pix acting as overseer, and added some very rich loam to the claylike soil. The result was gratifying, spectacular for a nongardener like Faith. The scents of the old-fashioned flowers—phlox, delphinium, a rainbow of daylilies, Shasta daisies, and *Rosa rugosa*—wafted toward her, mixing pleasantly with the smell of her strong coffee. Then the scratching began again, and she tucked her legs up away from the edge of the deck. She sniffed once more. Only coffee and floral scents. So far so good.

But she was very worried, too.

"Mothballs will do it."

Faith had picked up the phone on the third ring, racing in from the deck.

"Mothballs. I hear you have skunks."

"Ursula, is that you?"

"Of course it is. And why are you staying there anyway? Your house is far from finished. You'll come here to the Pines."

Faith didn't know which subject to approach first, but it was clear that Ursula Lyman Rowe, Pix Miller's redoubtable octogenarian mother, had the Fairchilds' life under control. Ursula's grandfather had built the Pines in the late 1890s, when the journey from Boston took two days by steamship. Ever since, the family had spent part or all of each summer on Sanpere.

"That's very kind of you, but we're managing fine here, except for the skunks." Faith had no desire to descend on Ursula with two lively children, although Ursula was used to the Millers' progeny and dozens of nieces, nephews, and their offspring. The Pines had spawned the Birches and the Balsams, creating a family enclave on a large point of land jutting out into Eggemoggin Reach on Little Sanpere, an island attached to its larger kin by a paved causeway. You hit Little Sanpere first after crossing the bridge from the mainland. The bridge had been a WPA project, and there were still a considerable number of Sanpere residents who lamented its construction—and a considerable number who had not been across it more than a few times in their lives, if at all. "Never had to," Fred Sanford had told Faith the previous summer. "Everything I need is here, and if it isn't, I don't need it."

"Nonsense," Ursula said firmly. "It's no bother. I'm rattling around this ark of a place until Arnie and Claire come at the end of the month, and you'll be settled in your own house by then." Arnold Rowe, Ursula's son, was an orthopedic surgeon. He and his wife, Claire, lived in New Mexico. "You could go to Pix and Sam's, but they gave it to my cousin's granddaughter and her new husband to use for their honeymoon."

Faith knew this. The Millers' house wasn't far away. She'd taken the kids to the beach and woods in the opposite direction yesterday, loath to intrude on the couple's first weeks of connubial bliss. Besides, they might be planning to be parents themselves someday.

"Go to Barton's and get a couple of boxes of mothballs. Then go down to Island Supply for some bait bags, or get Freeman to give you some, though his might smell too high. It's easier to clean up after the skunks are gone if you put the mothballs in the bait bags. And don't get moth flakes. You'll never get rid of the smell. And be sure you have flour."

"Flour?" Faith poured another cup of coffee. The caffeine suited her mood perfectly.

"They hate the smell of mothballs, so they'll go. But if you want to be absolutely sure they're gone, you sprinkle the flour outside the opening. Then you'll see their tracks."

Of course.

"Now, I'll expect you for dinner. Or why don't you come with your things when you pick Benjamin and Amy up at camp?"

Faith hadn't mentioned any plans to Ursula. Had not, in fact, seen her or spoken to her for weeks, yet apparently Faith's life was an open book. It was pointless to ask how Ursula knew about day camp, just as it would have been to question how she'd heard about the skunks and state of the Fairchilds' remodeling job.

"I'll talk to Tom about it," Faith conceded.

"Good, it's one of Gert's days, and she's making pies. Lemon meringue is his favorite, isn't it?"

Gert Prescott "did" for Ursula several days a week and had probably carried the news from Ghent to Aix, now that Faith thought about it.

"Yes, it is." She knew when she'd been licked.

If it hadn't been for the skunk problem looming over them, it would have been a wonderful morning. Tom returned with boxes of mothballs, beer, and a garden preparation called "synthetic dried blood." He'd been deluged with suggestions when he dropped off the kids at camp. Then, when he'd stopped at Barton's for a tube of caulking, everyone there had had an opinion, as well.

"Len offered to come over and shoot them, but I was able to convince him that we just couldn't take the chance of a bullet ricocheting off a wall and hitting him, crouching down as he'd have to be to get into the space. I knew the notion of the slaughter of innocent creatures wasn't going to do it, and I was right. I emphasized the word *crouching*, so the picture of where the bullet might end up was what probably did the trick. After he left, Velma—you know her, the nice brunette at the counter—told me Len gets a little antsy when it's not hunting season, especially lately. Seems he lost the moose lottery last year; thought he'd had it all sewed up."

Tom was beginning to sound like a native, Faith reflected. But even she knew what the moose lottery was. Tourist draw that they were, the moose population could outnumber the camera-toting gawkers if it wasn't checked, and hunters with visions of a really big set of horns to hang on the wall entered the lottery. You could only enter once, but a family member could enter his or her name with you as the designated hitter, so to speak. Len had a big family, and his wife, a transplant from Aroostook County, had an even larger one. Len had been in on the moose shoot every year since its inception, until last year. He was firmly convinced that some skullduggery in Augusta was to blame. He planned to travel off island and make the ninety-seven-mile trip to be there in person at the statehouse when they drew the names this year. The state auctioned off twenty-five of these golden chances to the highest bidders, but Len said he couldn't get a foot in the door that way—too rich for his blood—and added a comment or two about money always talking. A damned shame, too.

Faith was more concerned with small game at the moment.

"We have to get bait bags. Ursula called and gave me precise instructions on how to proceed, down to capturing their paw prints in flour, should we be missing any valuables in the future."

They spent a pleasant morning driving to Granville, the largest of the two main villages on the island. Away from the unfinished house, and uninvited guests, Faith relaxed and allowed herself to feel like a vacationer. They ate fish chowder at the Harbor Café, which Tom followed up with Grape-Nuts pudding, one of his favorites. "Cereal is cereal," Faith told him as she dug into it, nevertheless, savoring the rich real whipped cream piled on top. Tom had asked for two spoons. He was very good about sharing food, which was Faith's number one criterion in evaluating a candidate for marriage. Forget communication, compatibility in bed, solvency, et cetera. Will this potential partner for life give you a bite—or say something like "If you wanted it, you should have ordered it"? It was a simple, easy test, one that answered all the other questions. Selfish with food, selfish with . . .

Back at the cottage, Tom pitched the mothball-laden bags gently into the crawl space while Faith packed up their things for the stay at Ursula's.

"They're nocturnal, so we won't know until morning if they're gone. I told Lyle I'd call him before six. Everyone's ready to get back to work once they get the all clear."

Faith felt oddly reluctant to leave. It was so beautiful—and it was theirs. The evergreens, birches, bayberries, even the invasive alders—and the view. She wanted the crew to finish as soon as possible. If the mothballs didn't work, they'd try the other stuff. Beer? Get the skunks pie-eyed and trap them? Dried blood? Gross them out? And then there was always Len . . .

How could she have hesitated for even one second before deciding to come to the Pines? Faith wondered as she finished cleaning up the kitchen after dinner. Gert had left the pie, also fresh haddock, which Faith had pan-fried in one of the iron skillets that hung on the wall. They ranged in size from one just right for a single fried egg to a behemoth that took up two burners. She had also steamed some new potatoes and added them to the pan when they were soft, letting them get crusty in the sizzling butter. Pix and Ursula had put up dilly beans last summer, and these completed the meal. Neither kid had spilled milk at dinner, and in general, they had behaved beautifully, as was always the case when it was not their boring—or worse—same old family alone. Tom had taken them to explore the tide pools and the old lighthouse farther up the beach while Faith got dinner. Ursula had set the table, then come into the kitchen to keep Faith company. Now she was playing Chinese checkers with Ben while Tom put Amy to bed. It was all like something out of Gene Stratton Porter. And there were plenty of her works, as well as those by everyone from Will Shakespeare to Louise Dickinson Rich, lining the bookshelves all over the house. It was one of those houses where nothing that came in ever went out, unless consumed, and vintage Lincoln Logs cohabited happily with LEGO Technics on the shelves devoted to children's amusements. That's how Ursula had referred to them, turning the kids loose. "These are the shelves filled with children's amusements." To amuse themselves, the adults had the books, of course—and jigsaw puzzles, board games, flower presses, shell collections, material to make a quilt, knit a sweater, embroider a tablecloth, build a model boat, carve a bird, and paint or take a picture. The efforts of a number of generations decorated the house. Faith thought of the apartment in Manhattan that had been her childhood home, where her parents still lived—a prewar duplex on the Upper East Side. Suddenly, she would have traded its tasteful appointments—Jane Sibley had exquisite taste—for a wall hung with odes to the woods scrawled in childish hands and framed by birch bark, as well as with photographs of everyone lined up on the front porch, the uncomfortable wicker and Bar Harbor rockers in the same places as they had been when Faith had walked up the stairs that afternoon—only the photo was from 1925. Was this what mid-thirties meant? The chronological age, that is? Was she suddenly going to start a fern collection, save *all* the kid's drawings, not just the best ones? Was she going to become hopelessly sentimental, in the name of posterity? Maybe.

"It was built a long time before I was born and has been there ever since," she heard Ursula say. Faith hung the dish towel up to dry and went into the living room to join them at the big round table that served for playing games. A small rectangular table by the window had a puzzle on it—as always.

"What's been there?" she asked.

"The lighthouse. Ben was asking me about the lighthouse."

Ursula's silver hair, cut short and slightly wavy, glistened in the light from an oil lamp that had been electrified. She was still a beautiful woman.

"I can remember when it was manned—you can see what's left of the keeper's house in the field, a few bits and pieces of the foundation. It burned to the ground twenty years ago. Some summer people owned it and left soup on the stove while they went sailing.

"The last keeper was Franklin Pomeroy. He

and his family came from Rhode Island. They were a lighthouse family. When the Coast Guard would automate the one they were in, they'd move on to another. I was friends with all three children, but especially Marcy, who was exactly my age. We were born on the same day, and until she passed away five years ago, we always sent each other a card. Marcy wanted to be another Abbie Burgess."

"Who was that?" Ben asked excitedly.

"Abbie's father was the keeper of the light out on Matinicus Rock. A more isolated place you can't imagine, but wonderful if you want to see puffins. When Arnie—that's *my* son, Ben—comes, we'll get him to take us out in his boat. Anyway, Abbie lived on the Rock in the mid-1800s with her family. Captain Burgess didn't have anyone to help him, except his son. Later, the Lighthouse Service realized it was too dangerous a job for one person and kept a whole crew stationed there. At that time, Matinicus's light had two towers, so that meant keeping the oil lamps burning in both. This was before electricity, you understand. One January, Mrs. Burgess got sick, and the family was running very low on food, besides. Captain Burgess rowed over to Matinicus Island, about six miles away, intending only to be gone a few hours. As the day wore on, his son realized a storm was coming and went after him. The storm hit, and neither could get back to the Rock for three weeks."

Ben's eyes were as round as Andersen's fairy-tale dog guarding the tinderbox. "What happened? Abbie kept the lights burning, right?"

"Abbie kept the lights burning, took care of her mother and two younger sisters. She even rescued the hens, so they'd have eggs to eat, though she almost got washed off the Rock while she did it. That's what they were doing when her father and brother finally got home—eating scrambled eggs and some cornmeal mush. Abbie was fourteen, and at the same age, Marcy kept hoping *her* father would go off and she'd get to be a heroine. Of course, this light was built much later, so it was electrified and had a Fresnel lens." Seeing the question form on Ben's lips, Ursula said, "And I'll explain about that another time. There are plenty more lighthouse stories, including some about ours—I'm not sure whom it belongs to these days. It's been through a lot of changes. No light or foghorn even, not anymore. We still consider it our very own lighthouse. It's as much a part of the landscape as the rocks below it and the trees behind it. It was made from local granite, and that's why it's never needed much upkeep. Didn't have to be painted. We don't have a ghost, like some—I guess it isn't old enough." She sounded disappointed.

Ben sympathized. "That's too bad, but maybe one will move in this summer. Maybe Abbie's. She's dead, right?"

"Yes, she is. Abbie Burgess's ghost. Now, that would be interesting," Ursula mused.

Although the conversation had certainly taken an unusual turn and the two soul mates at her side seemed one step away from table turning and a Ouija board, Faith realized it was getting late, time for Ben to go to bed. His protest was stillborn as Ursula put a large molasses cookie in his hand and told him firmly to sleep tight.

"I wonder what happened to Daddy?" Faith said as they mounted the stairs.

She and Ben both stifled their laughter at the picture Daddy presented—sound asleep, while Amy was placidly turning the pages of *Good Night Moon* and "reading" to herself.

"Tom," Faith whispered to her husband, gently shaking his shoulder. Getting no response except a snore that sent both kids into peals of laughter, she repeated his name more loudly and the gesture more firmly. He woke with a start, took in the scene, and said, "Guess I'll go to bed."

After tucking Ben in and turning off the light in the tiny room under the eaves that he had chosen, Faith was almost glad they'd had to vacate their new house. This was turning out to be a wonderfully suspended time out from all the cares of her everyday life. Tom could get up at the crack of dawn and do whatever it was he was doing at the new place. She'd take the kids to camp, hang out with Ursula, read, and cook up a storm. The Pines kitchen sported not only a recent-model gas stove (circa 1965) but also a fully functional wood-burning Wood and Bishop, perfect for Saturday-night baked beans. Gert kept the behemoth blackened, its Victorian metal trim gleaming.

From the window at the hall landing, she had a

fine view of the lighthouse. It was in good shape, except for the tangled mass of weeds and wild rosebushes that surrounded its base, creeping up the proud column in disorderly abandon. What was it about lighthouses that was so captivating, so romantic? People loved them, eagerly learned their histories, made pilgrimages to the famous— and not so famous—collecting these destinations the way others did the fifty states. West Quoddy Head, Minots Ledge, Cape Blanco, Barnegat, Manistee North Pierhead, Bolivar, Castle Hill. Much had to do with the tales of the people who had lived there, people like Abbie Burgess, and their many acts of courage. Keepers kept the lights burning, but they also rescued mariners, often at great peril. Perhaps the allure was the notion of perfect isolation—and isolation with a purpose. Or perhaps it was that the buildings were so beautiful—the perfect simplicity of their design, beacons of light jutting up into the sky from a rocky shore, a sandy beach, or some tiny outpost in the midst of the sea itself. They'd certainly given rise to a whole world of collectibles and home decor. You'd be hard put to find a home on the Maine coast that didn't have at least a pot holder with one of these noble edifices brightly stamped on it—and more likely would find a lamp, lawn ornament, bedspread, and a bank calendar to match. Faith herself had succumbed to dish towels and a key chain.

She went downstairs to say good night to Ursula, who had told her when she arrived that there were no fixed rising or bedtimes at the Pines. Faith was relieved to hear she wouldn't be expected to accompany Ursula on her early-morning swim, a family tradition that no one had had the good sense to break. Pix had explained it patiently to Faith. "We never thought it was cold water. It was just water, and the only water we ever swam in, so it always felt fine. If you're not used to it, the trick is to jump in at once and swim like hell to get your blood flowing; then it's warm as toast." British toast, Faith surmised. The kind they put out in those toast racks, until the slices are the consistency of Stonehenge. She had never followed Pix's advice, taking the kids instead to a small lily pond, the only freshwater swimming hole on the island—and considerably warmer than the ocean.

Ursula was reading, but she closed the book as soon as she heard Faith enter the room.

"You must be tired after the day you've had. I'll be going up soon myself, although I don't sleep the way I used to. I've always heard old people needed less sleep, and I suppose it's true."

Old people? Ursula didn't often refer to herself as old—or anything else age-related, and it was a slight shock to hear her do so now. Looking closely, Faith thought Ursula seemed as if she could use a good night's sleep. There were faint shadows under her eyes and both lids drooped. For a moment, the two women sat in silence; then Ursula broke it.

"Something is very wrong on Sanpere this summer."

Two

Ursula sighed and pushed her chair away from the table. "It's late. I shouldn't have said anything. We can talk in the morning."

"Oh no we can't," Faith said, pulling her own chair in. "It's only nine o'clock. It just seems like the middle of the night because it gets so dark here." Both in Aleford and on Sanpere, Faith had suffered terribly from light deprivation when she'd first arrived from New York after her marriage to Tom. Neither the Massachusetts nor Maine locale went in for streetlights, and porch lights went off early. Apparently, it was assumed one would be snug in one's trundle or up to no good—and the less illumination the better. Plus, there was the issue of good old Yankee thrift. Accustomed to bright lights, big city, Faith had complained bitterly, and still did on occasion.

"I'll make us some tea, cocoa, or whatever you want and you can tell me all about it."

What Ursula wanted was a snifter of brandy, and Faith joined her. They moved to the overstuffed easy chairs in front of one of the windows that looked out at the Reach. The moon was almost full and streaked across the water toward the lighthouse like its missing beacon.

"I've never gotten used to seeing the lighthouse dark—and silent," Ursula said. "Loran and GPS and all those other fancy things put our light out of business. It was never even automated, although that might have been a blessing. The one over at Mark Island aimed right at Harborside and was so loud in the beginning that no one could hear themselves think until the Coast Guard finally fixed it."

Faith waited.

"It's nothing I can put my finger on directly," Ursula said slowly. She obviously wasn't talking about lighthouses anymore. "It's a lot of things— feelings I've been getting here and there. Mostly, it's change, I suppose. That's the hardest part of all . . . change." She took a sip of her brandy.

Change. The word was anathema to the entire Rowe and Miller clan when it applied to Sanpere, and Faith was fast becoming a convert. Like Pix, she'd bemoaned the influx of gift shops and galleries on Granville's Main Street. That they had replaced the small stores and offices serving Sanpere residents—stores and businesses unable to survive the long touristless season, when Sanpere's resident population halved to about fifteen hundred people. In the past—well after the time of Champlain's sojourn, which had given the island its name, a corruption of Saint Pierre—the year-round population had been much larger than the seasonal invasion. Now, the granite quarries, fish cannery, and other means of employment were fast becoming distant memories; the tourists put the cash in the till. Tourists—people in need of balsam pillows, moose T-shirts, and caps with lobster claws; people who, in order to experience the "real" Maine, had to eat one steamed lobster, see one live moose, and meet one authentic Down-Easter, who would hopefully tell them, "You can't get there from here." Two of the three were possible during the summer months on Sanpere. For the moose, you had to head north and inland. The only time moose were sighted on the island was during the hunting season, when a hardy soul or two would swim over to escape the barrage of ammo on the mainland, only to find themselves looking down the selfsame gun barrels. It always caused a lot of excitement, these moose sightings—for the moose, too.

"You don't get the paper in the wintertime, but Pix may have told you about some of the trouble."

Ursula and Pix subscribed to the *Island Crier* year-round, reading it with the same intensity others brought to the *Wall Street Journal*'s stock reports. They both read "Real Estate Transfers" first, as did the rest of the island, then the "Public

Notices" column, with its agendas of Planning Board and selectmen's meetings. If your neighbor was trying to sneak a deck on his house, smack in the middle of your view, that's where you'd find out about it before it was too late. Then Ursula read the obituaries and Pix read "Police Beat," mostly a brief sentence or two about kids cutting rubber on the cemetery road or an occasional DUI. Both skimmed "From the Crow's Nest," which carried the news from each section of the island: Sanpere Village, Granville, Harborside, Bonneville, South Beach, Little Harbor, and Little Sanpere—"Margery Sanford's brother, Fred, and his family are visiting from Bangor"; "Hiram White is at Blue Hill Hospital and would appreciate cards"; "Annie Marshall gave a birthday tea for her sister, Louise, but neither woman is saying which birthday it was." "The Fisheries Log" reported the prices seafood was fetching: "Clams— $1.80 per lb. Pretty good dig now and then"; "Halibut—$4.24 per lb. Not too exciting." Faith read the paper when she was on the island in the summer, yet her passion didn't extend to the rest of the year. She had to admit that Pix had not told her about any trouble on Sanpere. Faith hoped it was true and that she hadn't forgotten it.

She hadn't.

"Last winter, some year-round residents started a group called Keep Sanpere Sanpere, or KSS.

Faith breathed a surreptitious sigh of relief. *This* she would have remembered. KSS!

"You know that for the last few years, people have been buying any shore frontage they can get their hands on and building houses that are . . . well, not like any we've ever had here before. You can see them best—though that's not the word I should be using—from the water. Deep water. Millionaires have yachts—can't moor one on a clam flat."

"Mansionization," Faith said. "It's happening all over the country. Even in Aleford. Remember that sweet little Cape on River Street? Now it's a six-bedroom, six-and-a-half-bath Colonial on steroids, with great room, gym, home theater, and wine cellar."

Ursula nodded. "Fortunately, I haven't seen it, but I know about it. The town quickly passed a whole set of new zoning restrictions, although I understand they are being challenged in court. Anyway, that's what KSS wants—zoning."

"You mean there's no zoning on Sanpere?"

"There's never been a need. The state has a very comprehensive set of regulations for shoreland property, including a seventy-five-foot setback from the spring high-tide mark for new building, all of which Sanpere enforces. KSS wants a greater setback, a limit on the size of dwellings, and a ratio of house size to lot size. Oh, and they want to make it impossible to build too close to an already-existing structure. There's much more, like the number of trees that can be removed."

"But you can't take trees down on waterfront

property." Tom and Faith had been scrupulous about clearing, sticking to the complicated point system in the Shoreland Zoning Ordinance, measuring the diameters of the trunks of the trees they wanted to take down and calculating the percentages. Faith had heard the jokes about the air being filled with "The Sound of Chain Saws" after a storm as people got rid of trees that had ostensibly blown down in the no'theaster. The same liberal interpretation of the law was often applied when it came to what was dead and what was alive in the seventy-five-foot setback from the shore.

"People go ahead anyway, clear-cut even, then pay the fine. It's not that much money to the kind of people building these places."

This was something Faith hadn't known.

"That's terrible! They shouldn't be allowed to get away with this. Are you a KSS member?" Faith had to stifle a giggle at the sudden image of Ursula in face paint and rocker regalia.

"No, I'm not. Although I agree with many of their points, I don't agree with the way they're going about it all. For one thing, they've accused the selectmen and the Planning Board of favoring the builders and developers. It's true that many are related, but it would be hard not to be on this island. KSS says they've been making secret deals during executive sessions. It's all become quite ugly. There's so much shouting at meetings, nothing can get passed, which I suppose is the point."

"But aren't the Keep Sanpere Sanpere people

cousins or whatever, too? You said they were year-rounders."

"They're year-rounders, and many have lived here for a very long time, but they're not natives."

"Oh, people from away. Why didn't you say so in the beginning? It's all clear now."

"Clear as mud," said Ursula, sounding slightly indignant. "They don't get it. That's the problem. And it's this divisiveness on the island that has me so worried. I can't recall a time when the groups have been so stridently defined. There have always been summer people, of course. I'm one and you're one. You can rent for two weeks and be one, or own a place for almost a hundred years, like my family, and you're still one. The short-termers, and tourists who come down from Bar Harbor for the day, don't have much impact on island life. We long-termers have a bit more, but we're not really from here—we don't have to worry about heat in the winter or where to get the money to pay our taxes, for example. Natives are natives. Born here, bred here since Noah. They know who they are. But the year-rounders who aren't from here *don't* know who they are. I'm not saying this right." She paused.

"You mean they think they should be regarded as natives because they live here, too? Everybody all together in one big chowder pot."

"Yes, and in theory, that would be lovely, except it's just not the way it is or ever has been. The problem I have with the KSS people is their attitude that they know what's best for this island,

and the people who have been here for generations don't."

"Well, they must have done something right, if all these people want to come and live here."

"Exactly. Sanpere is a paradise, supposedly, but it's going to go to hell in a handbasket if KSS doesn't take charge."

Ursula must be very upset, Faith mused. Mrs. Arnold Rowe seldom swore.

"People on this island don't like to be told what to do. They may not be happy about these huge places going up, but if someone pays his money fair and square . . . well, the land is his and he can put up what he wants, so long as he doesn't break the laws that are in place. I hate these houses, especially the fact that most aren't going to be used for more than a month or so each year, but people probably hated the Pines when it was built. And yes, I'm upset that taxes on shore frontage have risen so high that local people are forced to sell. But on the other hand, this money coming into the island has given us a fine new school and a whole lot of work."

"So what's the problem?" There was always some kind of turmoil on Sanpere, yet Ursula had been suggesting something more, something worse.

"Since last spring, several of the building sites have been vandalized. Slogans spray-painted in green—"A sea of fish, not a sea of houses"; "Every day is Earth Day." That sort of thing, and arson. Ironically, the worst fire did more damage to the surrounding woods than clearing for the new house had."

"Ecoterrorism! The Earth Liberation Front? Sounds like their work. Then there was that guy Sands in Arizona. He was setting all those movie star–type homes on fire outside Phoenix. He started because his favorite jogging trail was being destroyed! Ended up getting off on the whole arson thing. Do you think KSS and maybe ELF are behind this?"

"After the first incident—some spray painting—everyone thought it was kids. You know the problems we have with not enough for them to do here. The nearest movie theater is in Ellsworth, and a lot of the teenagers and adults in their twenties drink too much on the weekends and act foolish. But then more and more places were struck, and people began to suspect KSS. I don't know about ELF; no one has mentioned a connection. KSS issued a statement deploring the actions, but the whole island believes otherwise. It's quite horrible. At the Fourth of July lobster dinner at the Odd Fellows, everyone sat apart. You could have drawn a line down the middle of the room."

"Sounds like a junior high cafeteria."

"The Fish 'n' Fritter Fry is coming up, and I hope we don't see more of the same—or worse. You can't imagine what I've been hearing around the island, from both sides. Thinly veiled comments about the effects of inbreeding over time, and remarks like 'Why did they have to come to our island in the first place?' Then, to make matters worse—and give the KSS members more fuel for their theory that locals are semisavages—we have a full-scale lobster war going on."

"Lobster war!" Faith had a sudden vivid image of catapults loaded with scarlet crustaceans.

"The Hamiltons and the Prescotts. It started when one of the Prescotts accused one of the Hamiltons of poaching his territory; then traplines started to be cut. And now neither family is talking to the other. Supposedly some of them are keeping guns on board. It *is* true that shots were exchanged one night off Long Point. Someone on land was watching, trying to catch someone on the water in the act of sabotaging a trap. A lobster war is a serious thing. There've been the ones with Canada over fishing grounds, and then our own internecine ones for as long as anyone can remember. These days especially, fishermen have to make enough money during the season for the entire year. There's been a boom these last few years, but nobody expects it to last forever, and I hear catches are already starting to go down. So people get worried—and maybe desperate. There's always a lot of stress. Fishing sounds romantic, but that's the rod-and-reel kind. Groundfishing, including lobstering, is the most dangerous occupation in the world. More so, even, than being a fireman or policeman.

"Now, we do have to go to bed. I'm talked out, but it's helped. Things go in cycles, and perhaps we're just in a downward one here at the moment. Maybe I'm overreacting."

Faith reached for Ursula's hand. It was warm and smooth, the skin so thin, she could feel the outlines of slender bones and veins without the slightest pressure.

She tried to sound reassuring, "Feuds are hard to deal with, but usually someone from each camp decides she or he has had enough and then things get resolved. But I'm not so sure about the KSS people. I know the type, and these people have a 'My way is the only way' perspective. I feel sorry for them, though. Their children will be Mainers, but *they* won't. Just as I'll never be a New Englander."

"You don't want to be, dear," Ursula observed shrewdly, and accurately. "These people do. Help me turn out the lights and I'll tell you a joke."

This is enticing, Faith thought, wondering if it would involve a lobsterman, a rabbi, and a priest.

"A Down East man and his pregnant wife are visiting in New Hampshire, when she goes into labor. He bundles her into the car and they drive as fast as they can to the Maine border, but it's no good. The baby is born before they can cross it. The same day, another baby is born somewhere on the Maine coast. As soon as he can travel, his parents take him to the Orient, where he lives for the rest of his life. The other baby lives a long life, too, but he never leaves the state again. They die at the same time. The *Ellsworth American* runs both obituaries: "Local Man Dies in Singapore" and "Man from New Hampshire Dead at Eighty-one."

Faith laughed, getting the point.

Upstairs in their room, Tom was sleeping soundly—and silently. Faith got ready for bed and sat on the window seat before turning in. The sky was so clear, even clearer than in Aleford. The stars were bright and seemed close enough to touch. Her husband moved slightly, and she turned her gaze toward the man for whom she had given up the Great White Way for the Milky Way, as well as the three *B*'s— Bergdorf's, Barneys, and Balducci's—and reliably good haircuts. She missed the energy and diversity of the City, but she had never regretted her decision. She still wasn't used to the move— and hoped never to be—yet there hadn't really been any choice. She'd met Tom at a wedding reception she was catering, unaware that he'd just performed the ceremony and changed out of his vestments. Daughters and granddaughters of clergymen, Faith and her sister, Hope, one year younger, had sworn never to marry into the fishbowl existence that was inevitably parish life. Hope had stayed the course, presently engaged to Quentin, another urban warrior on the Street, almost as successful as she was; Faith had been diverted from the path—decisively. Love has a way of doing that.

She stood up and reached to pull the shade down. She wanted to be outside, looking up at the sky. Her religious beliefs were somewhat eclectic, and tonight she thought she might be a Transcendentalist. What other name could there be for what was before her than the Oversoul—reaching out to pull her into one great, grand Universal?

In the morning, she'd talk about it with Tom. Tom, her beloved. She pulled the shade and noticed that some trick of starlight was making it seem as if a lantern was moving about the old lighthouse. Maybe Ben was right. Perhaps Abbie Burgess's ghost, or that of some other long-ago lighthouse keeper's daughter, was taking up residence. She pulled the shade back up again and dismissed her whimsy. It wasn't the stars. It wasn't a ghost. It was definitely a light.

No one had pulled up the shade, yet the strong sun pierced through, dappling the bright patchwork squares on the quilt Faith had pulled over her shoulder when she'd gone back to sleep after Tom had gotten up. It had scarcely been light then and she'd barely been conscious. Now, she realized with alarm, it was late. After eight o'clock. She had to feed, clothe, and get the kids to camp within the hour. Throwing on her own clothes and pausing briefly in the bath, complete with lion-pawed cast-iron tub, she raced downstairs, fearing the worst. Normally, she would have been awakened much earlier, at least by Amy jumping on the bed. Where were her children and what were they doing? She stopped short at the kitchen door. The scene was straight out of Norman Rockwell. Amy, not only dressed in a top and shorts that matched but with her silky blond hair

41

in two tightly braided pigtails, was drying a fork with a voluminous dish towel. She was standing next to Ursula at the sink. Ben, similarly well turned out, was in the rocker by the woodstove, reading out loud from Harry Potter. One of the cats was curled up by his feet.

"Good morning, Faith dear. There's a stack of pancakes keeping warm in the oven, and the coffee's hot," Ursula said.

Kissing her children, as much from affection as to make sure the body snatchers hadn't paid a nocturnal call, Faith kissed Ursula, too. The woman should be bottled.

Ben resumed his reading after casting a stern look at his mother for interrupting. Then they all prepared to leave.

"The skunks must be gone," Faith said. "Otherwise, Tom would have come back. Or maybe not. He might be trying something else."

"They're gone. Don't worry. He called about an hour ago."

"That's wonderful." Faith was enormously relieved. "I think I'll go see what's going on over there. We should be able to move back now."

"Nonsense," Ursula declared. "Your house isn't ready, and it's a pleasure to have you. Besides, it will go faster if you're not underfoot."

Admitting to herself that she had been hoping Ursula would say something like this, Faith offered to take her over to the house to see what progress had been made.

"Not today. It's Sewing Circle at Serena Marshall's. Vera Hamilton's taking me. The fair is coming up, and we aren't nearly ready."

The Sewing Circle, or, officially, Sanpere Stitchers, was a group of island women who got together periodically to sew and chat. During the winter, they made quilts for the Ronald McDonald House and other worthy causes. All year, especially in the spring and summer, they made items for their annual fair in August, the proceeds of which went to the Sanpere Medical Center. The fair usually sold out in an hour. Faith was glad of the reminder. Ursula had been knitting a beautiful deep blue pullover with a chain of tiny white starfish at the neck, which would be perfect for little fair-haired Amy. The Sewing Circle. Ursula might be a summer person, but she was in a category all her own, the only nonislander to be invited into the select group.

"Serena is Seth Marshall's mother, isn't she?"

"Yes, and I understand he has more work than he can handle. Booked for two years from now."

"Well, tell her to say hi from us. He did a wonderful job on the original part of the house, and we're grateful he recommended Lyle."

After asking whether Ursula needed anything, Faith added that she would be handling the meals from now on, even breakfast. Ursula told her that would be a treat and to get going; otherwise, the children would be late for camp. It was hard to feel like a grown-up at the Pines, no matter what tack you took.

When Faith arrived at the cottage, she was

happy to see that no one was sitting outside. A steady sound of hammering was issuing from inside, reverberating in the warm summer air. Very warm for Maine. She eyed the cove. The tide was going out. Pix claimed the best time to swim was the second tide—when the water came back in over the sunbaked mud and rock. Faith shook her head. What could she be thinking of?

"Tom," she called, going into the house. "Did you see their footprints?"

He emerged from one of the bedrooms.

"Hi, honey. Yup. They were as plain as day. Lyle has put in the vent, so there won't be any more return visits from these guys or all the relatives who will have heard by now of the fine cuisine we offer."

"What's happening today?"

"We're starting on the counters and cabinets. Kenny's finishing the upstairs ceiling."

"Is he the young one? Tall, skinny, crew cut, not used to women in dishabille?"

"Sounds like Kenny, except he must have seen his mother plenty. He's Persis Sanford's son, never married and lives at home with her."

It was at moments like these that Faith especially missed Pix, who filled in all the blanks for her, both in Aleford and on Sanpere. It was slightly galling to have her husband so much more in the know than she was, but Faith was feeling generous. The skunks were gone. All was right with the world.

"So tell me, who's Persis Sanford?"

"She's a real estate agent, local, as you might guess from the name. Also Grand Marshal of the Fourth of July parade not once, but twice, and general mover and shaker on the island with a finger in every pie."

"Mixed metaphors aside, how do you know all this?"

"Oh, the guys talk, and when Lyle said he was hiring Kenny as extra help, I heard all about Persis. Apparently, she was quite a hot ticket in her youth."

"But Kenny's not in the business?" Now that she thought about it, Sanford Realty sounded familiar, although Faith couldn't recall seeing any signs dotting front yards or along the roadside. What did adorn local front yards this summer were black plywood silhouettes of bear cubs, granny in a rocking chair, gramps with a corncob pipe, and everything in between. They'd replaced the ornaments of yesteryear, the Smurfs and bloomer-clad fat ladies bending over.

"Kenny's not in the business. He's a very good carpenter. Period."

"Slightly dim?"

"Not that. Just not all that bright."

Faith nodded; she understood the difference. He wasn't slow, simply wasn't burning up the road the way his mother seemed to be.

"Well, he has time. He could be a late bloomer. What is he, twenty-two, twenty-three?"

Tom laughed. "For an astute observer, you're

way off on this one. Kenny's in his early thirties. About our age. But he does look like a kid—as do you," he added charitably, and truthfully. Faith was wearing a white T-shirt and khaki shorts. She'd let her thick blond hair grow longer over the winter, and now it was pulled back in a scrunch. Like the rest of the family, she was slender, and despite heavy applications of sunscreen, her skin had acquired a light tan.

"I didn't get that good a look at him," Faith said, defending herself. "Now, do you have what you need for lunch? I'm going to Blue Hill to do a big marketing. After that, I'll pick up the kids and bring them here."

She realized she hadn't mentioned her conversation with Ursula—or her own late-night Emersonian thoughts.

"Maybe we can get some time to talk after the guys leave," she added. "Ursula was telling me that some pretty disturbing things have been going on this summer. Sanpere's own version of ecoterrorism, and a lobster war."

"I've been picking up some of this, but both topics are pretty off-limits. Especially the lobster war. Elwell is a Hamilton and Lyle's sister's son is married to a Prescott. As for the other, they pretty much think it's this nutty group and want nothing to do with any of it."

"It's more complicated than that. KSS, I mean. I don't know about the Hatfields and the McCoys."

"KSS?"

"Keep Sanpere Sanpere."

"I hate it already," Tom said as Faith got into the car and set off for the mainland.

Feeling guilty for shopping off island but needing to stock Ursula's larder for a family of four at Trade Winds, the large Hannaford in Blue Hill, Faith had almost finished her list when she narrowly avoided ramming her laden cart into Jill Merriwether's. Jill owned the Blueberry Patch, a combination bookstore/gift shop in Sanpere Village. Jill, who had been raised by her grandparents on the island after her parents' deaths, looked as guilty as Faith at being caught outside the aisles of their local IGA.

"Earl's coming for dinner and I wanted to get one of those big porterhouse steaks he likes so much."

Earl was Sgt. Earl Dickinson of the Maine State Police, responsible for patrolling Sanpere. After years of patient persistence on his part, he'd finally gotten engaged to Jill. The wedding was planned for the Saturday of Labor Day weekend. Jill would make a beautiful bride. She had straight dark brown hair that grazed her shoulders in a shining curtain, and deep brown eyes to match. She was tall and had a serious, quiet air about her. Faith had known her for a long time before Jill had spoken to her with the ease they now shared. Perhaps it was being raised by her grandparents, growing up in a taciturn household. Perhaps it was learning loss at such an early age. But Jill was beaming at the moment, her generous mouth, the feature that most broadcast her warm nature, curved in a big smile.

Faith gave her a hug.

"It's wonderful to see you, and your groom deserves the best. Are you very, very happy and very, very crazed?"

"Both, and more. I wanted to elope somewhere or just go up to Ellsworth and get married in the courthouse, but Earl says he's only doing this once and wants to do it right. I was down in Portland for the final fitting of my dress. I do love the dress, but I hated to close the store when the island is filled with tourists. I haven't been able to find anyone to work for me. It's the same all over the island. They're offering dishwashers eight dollars an hour at the inn. I could make more money there!"

Faith had noticed that Jill's store was closed and had wondered where she was.

"If there's anything I can do to help, you know you can call me. We're staying at Ursula's. The house isn't anywhere near finished, so I have plenty of time."

"There is a God!" Jill exclaimed.

While assuming that Jill held such a belief—after all, she *was* getting married in the Congregational church, with Tom assisting—Faith was surprised by the outburst and wasn't sure whether to respond, "Praise be!" or "Are you okay?" She said nothing, waiting for a further cue.

Jill grabbed Faith's arm excitedly. "I've been

desperate. You know we've been working on a production of *Romeo and Juliet*—an updated, Down East version—as a fund-raiser for the swimming pool project, right? Pix must have told you; she's been involved from the beginning."

This was one of the things Pix had mentioned, and Faith had been amused at the prospect of Romeo and Juliet in bright orange oil pants and hip boots. The swimming pool fund-raising had been going on for years. There were swimming lessons at the lily pond every summer, but only a few children took them. In the winter, there was more free time, but no place to go either to practice or to learn. The nearest available indoor pool was over an hour away. Most adults couldn't swim, and every year there were tragedies, especially among the fishermen, who regarded their life jackets as an impediment. Faith had also heard the fatalistic view that when your number was up, it was up, so why bother? The Fairchilds had supported all the fund-raising efforts for the planned indoor pool, and now Faith got her checkbook out to buy tickets or be a patron—whatever Jill wanted. Surprisingly, Jill waved Faith's checkbook away.

"We don't need money. I mean, of course we do, but that's not how you can help the most right now. Pix is gone for almost the rest of the month and the woman who took her place has had to leave to take care of her mother, who lives in Paris."

Faith correctly assumed Jill meant the decidedly non-Gallic Paris, Maine. The state had a penchant for keeping foreign travel close to home. Norway, China, Lebanon, Poland, and other distant destinations were all well within its borders. This had occasioned one of Ben's imponderables: "What do they call people who live in China, Maine? Chinese? People who live on Sanpere are called Sanpere Islanders. So what are these people called?" Faith made a note to ask someone, but not Jill, who was in the full flow of conversation about the play.

"Since you have some time on your hands, you can step in." Jill said these last words as if offering Faith not simply an opportunity but a very special gift. "You don't have to learn any lines; they didn't have roles, just production work."

"But I don't know anything about the theater. I've never been involved in putting on a play," she protested, watching the treasured time on her hands slip between her fingers like grains of sand.

"None of us did at first. Roland Hayes reworked the play and is the director. He retired from the high school English Department in June and is great, a pro. You can't imagine the performances he's getting from everyone. Because of work schedules, it's hard to rehearse all at once, so we're doing it piecemeal; that's why someone who can be there consistently is so important. With the shop and the wedding, I haven't been able to do much."

Making a last-ditch effort, Faith said, "It's been

years since I read any Shakespeare. I think *Romeo and Juliet* was in ninth-grade English."

Jill wasn't buying. "Think of the pool. Think of everyone on the island learning to swim. Come on, Faith. You know the drill. Balcony/tomb: love/death."

There was no escape.

"So nice of you to help out with the play," Ursula commented.

She and Faith were sitting on the porch after supper, watching Tom teach Ben to row while Amy sat in the bow like a miniature figurehead. The Pines had a large lawn that gave way to a rocky beach and pier. Ursula's father had replaced the original dock with this larger one to serve all the houses. The Rowes kept a variety of craft moored offshore, among them the small wooden dory Tom had picked for the lesson.

Faith had not mentioned a word of her capitulation—or Capuletion, she thought punnily to herself—to anyone. Jill had left the supermarket when she had and presumably went straight home to prepare the feast for her fiancé. Ursula seemed to be able to read the ether, and Faith was not at all surprised by the remark. But she did have to know.

"Who told you I was going to do this?"

"Jill was stopped at that blueberry stand near the causeway just as Serena was driving me home. I thought I'd pick up some berries, too."

"And besides, you and Serena had to hear all

about Jill going down to Portland," Faith said, teasing her.

"Of course we would be interested, but she didn't have much to say about it. She was mostly talking about you and how providential it was that you bumped into each other—literally, I take it. You'll have fun."

Faith doubted this. The Miller/Rowe family's ideas of fun and hers differed markedly. When they were home in Aleford and Pix said, "Let's go have some fun today," she meant grab a PB & J, then head for Mount Misery, her favorite walk in nearby Lincoln. Faith, on the other hand, thought more in terms of lunch at Figs and a leisurely troll through the antique shops on Charles Street, finishing up at Savenor's Market for something tasty to cook for dinner. She was especially partial to Ron Savenor's crown roasts, and Ron himself, who had a smile like that of his father, Jack, wasn't bad, either.

Feeling like Scarlett, Faith firmly pushed the thought of the play to the "I'll think about that tomorrow" part of her brain and concentrated instead on the beauty of the scene before her. They'd eaten early—she'd succumbed to beef, too, and had marinated a flank steak, which Tom grilled on the barbecue. She'd bought some imported corn—the sign said FROM RHODE ISLAND, not exactly her notion of the Corn Belt. Since it wasn't fresh, she'd scraped the kernels from the cob and made corn pudding, a rich, delectable southern version, steamed in the oven (see recipe on page 319). Now the sky was still bright with the end-of-day, long, flat light that made everything look like a stage set. It was her favorite time. A time that offers endless possibilities, Janus-like facing day and night. The lighthouse stood in sharp relief, the simple unpainted solid stone column capped by its powerful lens, with only a small catwalk around the outside of the room to interrupt the lines of its square blocks—blocks of the same granite that were scattered helter-skelter at the base, without a single straight edge.

Her family was close to shore and she could see Ben concentrating hard. She never wanted to forget this minute, or the other minutes like them. Minutes when it was possible to block out everything except the people and place in front of one's eyes. Minutes when the world seemed safe.

"He might do better standing up," Ursula observed. "I still row that way sometimes. It might be easier for him."

Pix had tried to teach Faith to row once, but after retrieving an oar for the fourth time, she gave up. Faith had remained seated throughout. Ben seemed Olympic material in comparison.

"Aren't there more boats than usual?" she asked, eager to add anything remotely nautical to the conversation.

"Mackerel are running in the Reach, and a lot of local people leave their skiffs tied to our dock. They know they don't need to ask. Kenny Sanford and Lyle both brought theirs over yesterday."

"I wouldn't have thought they'd have time to fish," Faith remarked, slightly dismayed at the possible incursion into their work schedule.

"There's always time to fish. We should be out there now ourselves. Gert said you can practically scoop them out of the water with your bare hands. Mackerel is one of my favorites."

It was one of Faith's favorites, too—lightly floured, then browned to a crisp in plenty of butter. Or smoked. Or filleted. Or served with scrambled eggs. Or . . . The phone rang, and both women gave a start at the unaccustomed sound.

"It may be Pix. She said she'd call tonight. I'll get it." Ursula went into the living room, where one of the house's two ancient black dial phones resided. The other was by Ursula's bed.

Faith continued to watch the little boat. Ben learning to row. It seemed he had just learned to walk.

Ursula was back almost immediately. It couldn't have been Pix.

She sat down. Looking at Ursula, Faith was alarmed. This was not the woman who had led the Aleford Historical Society contingent in last April's six-mile Patriots' Day Parade with her usual vigorous stride. She was visibly pale and shaken.

"What is it? What's wrong?"

"That was Serena. Seth's doing that big house off the old quarry road. He went back to take some pictures for the owners after he'd had his supper. The window of the little office he put up was smashed in, the door wide open, and someone had poured kerosene all over everything. He saw the flames right away. Fortunately, he had a fire extinguisher in his truck and was able to save most of it."

"Thank goodness for that. What if he hadn't come back!" Faith breathed a sigh of relief. Seth had become a friend during the time he'd worked for them.

Ursula's voice shook. "There was also a dummy hanging from a noose tied to a tree in front of the house. It had a sign around its neck that said DEATH TO THOSE WHO RAPE THE EARTH— and a knife stuck in its chest, stuck right where a heart would be."

Three

"Thou desperate pilot, now at once run on the crashing rocks thy seasick weary bark! Here's to my love! O true apothecary! Thy drugs are quick. Thus with a kiss I die." Romeo, known to friends and family as Ted Hamilton, threw himself on the floor and then sat up expectantly, toppling the empty vial of poison, a Moxie bottle, in the process.

"Excellent, excellent, except it's 'dashing,' not 'crashing.' 'Dashing rocks,'" called a voice from the back of the auditorium.

"Damn, I always get that wrong. 'Crashing' sounds better. Do you suppose Shakespeare meant to write 'crashing' and put down 'dashing' instead? 'Crashing' makes more sense." Ted rubbed his elbow. He'd come down hard, and there wasn't a lot of padding on his lanky frame.

"We cannot know what the Bard had in mind. True, logic was not always his strong point, but we'll stick to the text. Why don't you take a break while I hear Juliet? By then, the Nurse should have arrived and we can go through those scenes."

Faith left the flats she was painting and came out onstage to make sure the props were in place. Props, hearing lines, and painting scenery were her assignments so far. All was well at the moment, but things had been a bit dicey at first. Arriving shortly after 9:00 A.M., she had introduced herself to the first person she saw backstage, an ample lady clad in a voluminous smock. Whether she was younger or older than Faith was hard to tell. And Faith learned that she, the new recruit, was expected to help make costumes and was forced to explain that her needlework skills barely covered sewing on buttons. She wouldn't know a bodice from a bodkin. Most of the costumes were being supplied out of the actors' own wardrobes, since the play was being done in modern dress. Someone, however, had recently had the bright idea of dressing the Chorus as a harbor seal and this called for needle and thread. Eventually, Faith convinced the woman of her total lack of talent, was reassigned to scenery, and introduced to the director, Roland Hayes.

While Faith had been abasing herself, he'd come around from the front of the stage, which was in the new elementary school, site also of Island Day Camp.

"You must be perfectly frank, Mrs. Fairchild. I know how people get hornswoggled into things here. If this is not something you want to do, just say so. I'll understand," he'd said.

Aside from the sentiment expressed and never having heard *hornswoggled* used in everyday speech, Faith was immediately captivated by Roland. He looked too young to have retired, despite a mane of gray hair pulled into a short ponytail at the nape of his neck. Medium height, muscular, he had clear blue eyes that shone when he smiled, as he had been since approaching Faith. But it was his voice that had pushed any thoughts of bailing completely from her mind. It was deep—but not too deep—smooth as velvet, the words flowing without hesitation and wrapping themselves around the hearer like a cloak. He was the one who should be onstage.

"I don't mind at all. It should be fun," she'd heard herself say. "The only problem I have is being free to pick up my kids at day camp, but since it's right here, I can stay until it ends. Oh, and today I have to go to the farmers' market at ten."

He was mesmerizing, but food was food, and Faith was close to the point where she'd kill for fresh produce.

Neither was a problem, Roland had reassured her. She was tempted to come up with more stumbling blocks simply to hear him speak, but she figured she had the rest of the summer. If she didn't get to the market on time, nothing would be left but zucchini.

The market started at ten o'clock to give the off-island farmers and manufacturers of everything from homemade soap to wooden benches time to get there. During July and August, people started lining up at 9:30, but nothing was sold until 10:00. Fair was fair. As she had stood in line, eyeing the containers of jewel-like red and yellow cherry tomatoes nestled next to some arugula, Faith had realized that the only natives present were among the sellers, not the buyers. It gave her an odd feeling, as if she had wandered into a farmers' market far removed from Sanpere—in Chilmark or Southampton. The weather was wrong, too. It was supposed to go over ninety during the day, and the air already felt sweltering, an uncharacteristic temperature for this part of Maine. Global warming, the work of an angry God, freak climatic incident—by the time the market opened, she'd heard all the possibilities.

After the conversation with Ursula, she'd found herself looking at the customers with new eyes. Carrying environmentally friendly tote bags or baskets, they represented a broad age range, but there was a great similarity in their tennis visors, wide-brimmed straw hats, and, most of all, leisure time. They could stand in line. They didn't have to be anywhere, except at a sailing date or a doubles match. In addition to expendable time, they had expendable income. Baskets brimmed with items. Faith herself winced at paying New York prices so many hundreds of miles away from the Big Apple and was choosing carefully. She didn't begrudge the sellers. Like the fishermen, everyone here had to get top dollar during the short season in order to make it through the year. The story was the same up and down the coast as millions of visitors poured into Maine, "Vacationland," "The Way Life Should Be."

Groups. She'd recalled Ursula's categories. Or were they tiers? These were notions she hadn't confronted other summers. Where did she fit? Yes, she was contributing to the Sanpere economy, but why had it made her feel so uneasy to be at the market with her basket and, yes, straw hat? She'd looked around at her fellow shoppers—parasites or catalysts?

And what about the Keep Sanpere Sanpere people. Were there any KSS members here? The island abounded in bumper stickers from the rude to the fuzzy: SUPPORT LOGGING OR TRY USING PLASTIC TOILET PAPER to THINK LOVERLY THOUGHTS. She hadn't seen any KSS ones yet.

She'd greeted her friend Bob from Sunset Acres Farm and bought some of his chicken—admittedly, the best she'd ever had outside of Bresse in France—and an assortment of his goat cheeses. He was as much showman as salesman, and the steady patter he'd kept up with his customers had echoed throughout the parking lot, "Yes, deah, I've got eggs today. They're so fresh, you may have to slap them." Faith could easily picture him in a shiny black suit, string tie, and top hat in another time, selling cures for all that ails you. Buying from him was unambiguous.

She'd gotten into her car, realizing with a start that it was one of the oldest ones there. Lexuses,

Mercedes, BMWs—when had they become part of the scenery? A man got into a Miata next to her. He was loaded down and gave a friendly wave. She waved back. He was outfitted by L.L. Bean, down to his Tevas. If a summer person or year-rounder from away really wanted to blend in and look like the natives, he or she would have to give up Bean's, even the outlet store, and shop at Wal-Mart. They'd have to wear T-shirts that had Harley-Davidson emblems on the front or camp logos from all over the state above one breast. The supplier was located in Granville, and the August sale of overruns and seconds for a dollar a shirt outfitted the entire island. It was not unusual to see a fisherman in oil pants, boots, and a Camp Minnehaha sweatshirt with the pine trees upside down. Or they'd have to don the dark green Dickies work pants and shirts favored by island workmen, softened from hundreds of washings and bearing oil stains even Tide couldn't get out. The pants would have to be belted tightly below a large belly, smartly at the equator, or perilously near the armpits.

As she'd driven to the Pines to put everything away, she'd wondered if the police had any information about last night's fire at Seth's building site, and the gruesome warning in the tree. The new house was being built deep in the woods, the site on a high bluff looking out to sea, with a view of the Camden Hills. No one would have been around the isolated spot to witness any unusual activity. Maybe Ursula had talked to Serena again. In any case, if there was news, Ursula would hear it. There had been a lot of talk at the market, but not about the fire. Weather, comparison shopping, more weather, and general rejoicing over the news that Jill was carrying the daily *Times* at the Blueberry Patch, albeit not until late afternoon—that was the buzz. Not the fire.

But that had all been several hours ago, and Faith's total attention was now on the stage.

"O churl! drunk all, and left no friendly drop to help me after?" Juliet declaimed, perhaps a little too dramatically. She turned the Moxie bottle, which Faith had made sure was close at hand, upside down and dropped it. She paused for effect, recited the rest of her lines, and reached for the happy dagger—a Buck knife, a duplicate of those in pockets, drawers, and sheds all over Sanpere. Plunging it close to her breast, she moaned and expired.

"Nice, nice, Becky, but take it down a notch. Let me see it again without the moan. Remember, Juliet hears people coming and wants to kill herself before they can stop her. There's no time for moaning and groaning."

"But Mr. Hayes, wouldn't it have hurt? I mean, she has to make some kind of noise. You can't tell me someone would stab themselves and not say a word. I know she says, 'let me die,' but she'd say something like 'ouch,' too."

Roland's voice rolled sonorously over the heads of the people scattered in the auditorium waiting to rehearse or just watching.

"I take your point, although 'ouch' is not what leaps to mind. Why don't you try a moan after all, except a little less Casper, a little more Camille—piteous, not pitiful. Try this." He moaned—a sharp cry that trailed softly and quickly to its sorrowful conclusion.

"Okay," Becky said, tidily arranging herself on the top of one of the simple pine boxes that had been lined in a row to represent the Capulets' tomb. She was wearing jeans and a bright pink T-shirt; her pretty blond curls were encircled with a daisy wreath. Like the soda bottle, it was one of the props Faith had to keep track of—the plastic daisies indistinguishable from real ones under the lights. Becky had told Faith she'd be wearing her prom dress for the performances—"a white silk strapless"—and didn't want it to get mussed up in rehearsals, since it cost the earth to get it dry-cleaned. Plus, she had to go to Ellsworth to do it.

"Ready," she called cheerfully, crossing her arms over her chest and closing her eyes.

Many moans later, Roland declared himself satisfied and they broke for lunch, since the Nurse still hadn't arrived. Faith went to call Tom. Things were going well. She could barely hear him over the sound of the hammering and sawing. Then she took the sandwich she'd made that morning and went outside. The auditorium was dark and she needed to see the sun.

The building was surrounded by woods that gave way to grass, sere now due to the lack of rain. Clumps of pine and tall balsam had been left near the school itself, supplemented by more traditional "builder" shrubs. Faith sat on a bench under one of the pines and bit into the tomato sandwich she'd hastily put together after dropping her market purchases at Ursula's. The juice from the tomato had mixed with the mayonnaise, oozing into the bread, sliced thick from one of Gert's whole-wheat loaves. Unashamedly, Faith licked her fingers. Simple food. The best food? A perfectly ripe, juicy tomato, corn picked fresh and rushed into the waiting pot, steamed lobster so succulent, it didn't even need melted butter. But then there were all those complicated, labor-intensive delights: puff pastry for napoleons and beef Wellington, mortal enemies united by common flaky layers; cassoulet with duck confit and truffled sausage; osso buco, a turkey galantine, coulibiac of salmon, fresh peach ice cream, made in a hand-cranked freezer. No need to choose—life had plenty of room for them all. She drank from the thermos of iced tea she'd brought and stretched her legs out. The play might devour her free time, but it was also giving her a delicious sense of freedom. She never *had* done anything like this before, and it had been a fun morning, far removed from her usual tasks. A paintbrush, not a whisk; props, not car pools.

She glanced at her watch. She had a few minutes more, and it felt good to bask in the sun—the very hot sun. When Faith had headed outside, the woman Faith had first met, the one who'd been allotting tasks, said, "They're frying eggs on Main Street." Her name was Linda Forsythe, a local artist and stage manager for the show, she'd explained. She was also responsible for all the scenery. Faith had been impressed. What had been completed was well done, extremely professional. The ball at which Romeo and Juliet meet had been rewritten as a clambake, and Linda had designed an effective backdrop with a vivid sunset splashed across the granite ledges and beach. Today, they were painting the equivalent of the streets of Verona—rows of lobster shacks, hung with nets and neon-colored buoys like the ones dotting Jericho Bay. A few real traps were stacked offstage, to be added to the set later. Faith had been humming "It Was a Real Nice Clambake" to herself as she worked. She wondered if they'd considered a musical. There was "People Will Say We're in Love" and, of course, "Teen Angel" for the end. She was getting up to return to her labors, when something pink caught her eye. It was Juliet herself, streaking out of the woods, the color of her T-shirt matching her flushed cheeks. She was radiant. Faith waited a moment. Sure enough, Romeo followed, sprinting smoothly for the back door, just far enough behind so they wouldn't be seen entering together. He was grinning. So it was like that. Art imitating life, life following suit. Faith smiled to herself. Unlike Juliet, Becky wasn't thirteen. She had graduated from the high school last year and was a freshman at the U of Maine. Ted was sternman for his father and had been out of school the same amount of time as Becky. His younger brother took Ted's place on rehearsal days. Becky was working part-time at the inn.

It was only when Faith walked into the dark, cool auditorium that she remembered something else about the pair. Becky was a Prescott and Ted a Hamilton. Oh life—forget art. These were star-crossed lovers for real, and if their families got wind of what was going on, the play would grind to a halt—or worse.

"I'm here! I'm here! Radiator on the Caddie boiled over, and I'm 'bout ready to do the same."

It was the Nurse. It had to be. She wouldn't need any pillows for the part. Despite the weight, she was an attractive woman with fair skin, large green eyes, and light auburn hair that crackled with an occasional streak of pure red. She was wearing a well-cut white linen pant-suit, and her makeup and nails were salon-perfect. Did she think it was a dress rehearsal? Was the white suit intended to suggest a nurse?

"That's Persis Sanford," whispered Linda. She seemed about to say more, but then clamped her mouth shut.

The real estate agent. Of course. Persis needed to look as well groomed as her clients—better, in fact. And drive a fancy car. She and her son, Kenny, were about the same height, yet the resemblance ended there. His pale face suggested one of those grubs that emerge when a rock is turned over; hers was ivory, with a dusting of Revlon Honey Beige. It was hard to tell the color of Kenny's crew cut, but it was at the other end of the spectrum from his mother's hue, and Persis's girth could easily span two or three of his.

"Tell me when you're cool enough to start. Get a cold drink," Roland said.

"Oh, I'm ready," Persis declared. They'd have no trouble hearing her in the back rows. "Let's get the show on the road."

They began rehearsing the scene with Romeo and Mercutio, where Romeo confides his secret marriage plans to his beloved's nurse, but not until Mercutio makes sport of her—she matching each jest with a bawdy one of her own. Faith stopped painting to listen. The three actors spurred one another on and the scene was marvelous. Jill had been right: Roland was coaxing some truly amazing performances from people whose only prior experience trodding the boards had been walking on a pier. The Nurse's servant, Peter, was being played by one of Nan and Freeman Marshall's grandsons. Nan and Freeman were the Fairchilds' nearest neighbors on the point; they lived on the opposite side, and Freeman fished, except when "that fool of a doctor gets my blood pressure wrong." Faith could picture them on opening night, pleased as punch, sitting in the front row—Freeman in an unaccustomed dress shirt, his hair slicked down, wavy comb marks visible; Nan with her apron off, large Monet pearl earrings and matching necklace,

Christmas gifts from her children. Peter, his name on stage and off, didn't have too many lines, but the way he belted out "Anon" was sure to be remembered.

It was getting close to three o'clock, and there was a sudden increase in activity as new actors arrived to rehearse, while some left for home or work. There were others, too, who, having finished one workday, were volunteering their time to construct the sets or help in other ways, which amounted to another job. It really was a community effort, and Faith marveled anew at Roland's ability to weave all the strands into one whole.

Persis crossed the stage and called out, "Got to run, Roland. See you tomorrow. I can make it at ten. Have to show some Boston people a piece of land at nine, but they aren't going to buy it. Browsers." She wiped her sweating brow with a hankie from her pocket. "Lord, it's hot, and these lights don't help." She walked to the rear of the stage and picked up the Moxie bottle, which was on the floor next to the coffin, where Faith had put it after the earlier scene. She put it to her lips, took a swig, and instantly fell to the floor, clutching at her throat.

Roland ran to her, pushing the buttons on his cell phone, but Faith reached the woman first.

Her eyes were glazed and she was breathing with great difficulty. Faith leaned over. There was a faint smell of violets on Persis's breath. The bottle had been empty earlier. Had someone filled it with perfume? and if so, why?

"I've been poisoned," Persis whispered. "And I know . . ." Her eyes and mouth closed, as if a puppeteer had pulled a single string.

The stage was oddly silent; then Roland called for someone to put a blanket over her. She was still breathing. There was no mistaking the rise and fall of her bosom.

"The ambulance corps will be here soon. It doesn't take them long," he said, pacing back and forth. "Ted, go outside and make sure they know where to come."

Romeo and Juliet had been standing together. He'd put his arm around her, their faces terrified. He jumped from the stage and ran up the aisle. The sound of the door closing startled everyone and the quiet began to be replaced by low, anxious conversation.

Faith continued to crouch at Persis's side. The Moxie bottle had tipped over when Persis dropped it, and Faith knelt to smell the clear liquid that had trickled onto the floor. She had no idea what Moxie was supposed to look like, and the only notion of its taste had come from Tom, who occasionally drank a bottle as a symbol of his New England roots. "Good for you," he always said, which was enough to keep Faith away.

Careful not to get too close—she didn't want to inhale a deadly poison—Faith took a cautious sniff.

Turpentine. She'd been using it all morning and, in any case, had enough artist friends to know the smell well.

"Roland, tell them it's turpentine. I'm virtually positive."

He looked surprised, but he relayed this information to the person on the phone.

"Keep her still. We don't want her to vomit. Somebody get some glasses of water. If the EMT crew decides that's what it is, they're going to want water at hand." He paused, listening. "They want to know if you smelled anything unusual on her breath," he told Faith.

"Yes, a floral smell. Like violets. I thought she'd drunk some perfume."

He repeated her answer into the phone and then shut it off.

"They're pretty sure it's turpentine, then. Apparently, that's what it smells like when ingested."

"Turpentine." Becky Prescott's voice was trembling. "Can it kill you?"

Faith's reputation as a sometime sleuth was not unknown on the small island, and many eyes turned toward her, the closest thing they had to a resident expert at the moment.

"If you swallow enough, yes, but I don't think Persis did. The taste and the burning in her mouth made her spit it out."

The victim's eyes and mouth stayed closed, but Faith was sure it wasn't her imagination that the woman's body visibly relaxed.

"I read something in some art book about never keeping a bowl of ice-cold soup, like gazpacho, near where you're working, in case you accidentally dip a turpentine-soaked brush in it, because then when you eat the soup, the cold will numb your tongue and mouth, so you won't taste or feel the turpentine until it's too late. Sounds like something from a mystery novel." Linda Forsythe was rattling on, obviously in a state of shock herself. Faith wished someone would slap the woman across the face before she further incriminated herself. But why would Linda put turpentine in a Moxie bottle? She knew the props better than anyone, and they were using old coffee cans for soaking their brushes.

The ambulance corps arrived and cleared everyone away. They concurred with Faith's opinion and, after consulting by phone with the emergency room staff at Blue Hill Hospital, got the woman to drink some water, then rushed her off in the ambulance.

"I'm sure Persis will be fine," Roland said firmly to the group. "And I know she would want us to keep on going. That's the type of person she is, as we all know." His words were less mellifluous now, although still powerful. Faith had the distinct feeling of being in a locker room.

She left soon after and collected the kids. Amy was hot and sticky. Ben was hot, sticky, and cross. "Why is it so hot? It's never this hot in Maine. What's wrong? Can we go swimming? We need to go swimming."

"That, Benjamin William Fairchild, is a perfect idea, and if the tide is right, we can go from our very own beach."

Faith couldn't believe she was actually saying this, but the lure of the frigid water was irresistible. She thought of all those Norwegians who jumped into snowbanks right after leaving their saunas. It would be something like that. Think of it as a spa treatment, she told herself, scooting the kids along to the air-conditioned car.

She passed Linda in the parking lot. The woman was so intent on her conversation with a worried-looking man Faith had never seen before that it took a repeat of her greeting before Faith got a response.

"Oh, Faith. Thanks for your help. See you tomorrow. Are these your kids?"

Tempted as she was to reply that they were merely rentals—what did the woman think?—Faith introduced her children. But Linda did not introduce *her* friend—a short, stocky man, his graying curly hair joining an equally wiry, bushy beard. He graced the Fairchilds with a cursory glance and appeared not to find them of enough interest to merit more than a nod before returning to his intense conversation with Linda. Then the two got into a shiny new red pickup, taking off with a slight squeal of tires before Faith had strapped Amy into her car seat. Ben, who had adopted a winsome smile and appeared cool as a cucumber, relapsed into his previous fretfulness. Faith was seized by a panic-stricken thought and blurted out, "You like camp, don't you? Didn't you have fun today?"

Ben gave her a sidelong glance, seeming to

read her mind or the balloon coming out of her mouth: If camp doesn't work out, there's no plan B. She hoped he wasn't going to be precocious, grateful for the lack thereof so far.

"I *do* like camp. It's great. We made mobiles out of shells today. I just *don't* like the weather."

Faith breathed a sigh of relief and headed for home.

Simply putting on a bathing suit made Faith feel ten degrees cooler. She slipped on an oversize T-shirt and emerged from the bathroom. The crew was packing up, and Tom had already taken the kids down to the cove. Things looked pretty much the same as the day before—incomplete— but Faith was heartened by the fact that she could see some cabinets stacked against the wall.

Elwell Hamilton stopped on his way out the door. "Heard about Persis. They called Kenny and he went up to the hospital."

Faith had forgotten about Kenny. She had trouble putting the mother and son together.

"I'm sure she's going to be fine. They'll probably keep her overnight, but fortunately, she didn't actually swallow any of the turpentine."

Lyle came over and shook his head. "Helluva way to start the month. The fire last night, and now this. Too goddamn hot. That's the problem."

Elwell left, but Lyle didn't seem to be in a hurry. Faith could hear squeals of delight or acute pain— she wasn't sure which—coming from the water. In any case, she had cooled down considerably, and plunging into the icy brine was fast losing its appeal. She had a pitcher of iced tea in the fridge and fresh mint in the front garden.

"Would you like a glass of iced tea? I thought I'd sit outside on the deck for a while and think about not swimming."

Lyle laughed. "I'm happy to think about that any day. I've never gone in on purpose my whole life. Iced tea sounds much better."

They took their glasses, and Faith grabbed a hat for herself. Lyle's Snap-On Tools cap was a permanent accessory. She added some mint to the glasses, and left the pitcher conveniently close.

Lyle wasn't just passing the time of day.

"You see the whole thing?"

"With Persis?"

"Yup."

She described what had happened, omitting only Persis's words. Persis could, and would, broadcast that news herself. Faith didn't want to be responsible for repeating such a hot potato, a potato that would be passed quickly from hand to hand. But Lyle was obviously pumping her, and turnabout was fair play.

"You must have a lot of dealings with Persis. She sells houses. You work on them. What's she like?"

Lyle took a long swig of tea. Faith chided herself. She'd been too direct. Lyle did respond, though.

"Not like anybody else. Course, you could say that about anybody. But it especially applies to

Persis. She's one of the sharpest on the island when it comes to business, and that's saying something. Smart enough to realize she couldn't compete with the big agencies that cover more of the coast. So, from the get-go, she came up with her own way of attracting customers."

Faith was skeptical. "I've never seen any signs on lawns with her name; she must not have that many listings." These harbingers of the tourist season sprouted like daffodils each spring, often in the same spots for years in a row.

"That's just it. She doesn't advertise. Doesn't even have an office. Works out of her house. It's all word of mouth. Say you're looking for a place here. What's going to reel you in faster—something widely advertised, or someone telling you that there's a local woman who represents a select few sellers and may or may not show you what she's got?"

It *was* brilliant. Persis had been a femme fatale as a younger woman, and she'd translated playing hard to get into a moneymaking real estate operation.

"It's exactly like New York!" Faith exclaimed.

Lyle looked startled. He'd never heard anyone make this comparison before.

"If you want to sell your apartment, the first person you tell is the doorman—or, if you don't have one, the guy at the nearest newsstand. Everyone wants to believe they're getting in on the ground floor."

"It is the same, I guess." Lyle laughed. "The

other thing Persis has going for her is that she really does get listings no one else would get, because we all know she's going to get top dollar. Besides, she's from here. Most islanders use her when they sell. She takes a smaller percentage than the others, too."

"But she must make up for it if she gets a higher price."

"Yup, and in the end, everybody's as tickled as a cat with two tails. This tea is some good, Faith. You'll have to tell me how you make it."

Lyle poured himself some more. She wasn't about to reveal that without a functioning kitchen, it was Arizona iced tea in the pitcher, to which she'd added ice—ice made from the tea, though, so it wouldn't dilute it. And the mint was her own. The request for a recipe didn't surprise her. Lyle was single—at least at the moment—and had told her he liked to cook. When Faith had asked Tom whether there was a girlfriend in the picture, Tom had said, "Not to my knowledge." Supply and demand was a problem on the island, especially since it was the same of each just slightly older, or too much younger, as time went by. This explained why Lyle wasn't rushing home to his supper.

"I've fixed up a lot of places for Persis, getting them ready for her to sell. Not too finished, but basic stuff."

"I'd have thought she'd use her son. More cost-effective—keeping it all in the family."

"Kenny does fine work, but he's better at woodworking—furniture, cabinetry, not the rough stuff."

Faith filed the thought away. They hadn't found a chest of drawers that would fit under the window in the master bedroom. Maybe Kenny could take on the job.

But back to Persis, she thought.

"Is there anyone who might have a particularly strong grudge against her?"

Lyle choked slightly on his tea and cleared his throat. It wasn't a question he'd been expecting.

"Guess she's stepped on some toes, like most people. Plus, Persis says what's on her mind, even if no one wants to hear it. I've never had a problem with her. Kind of admire her for the way she always pitches in. She's done a lot of good for this island. The KSS people—you know who they are, right?"

Faith nodded.

"They haven't joined the choir when it comes to our Persis. They hate her, of course, but they hate anyone who's destroying the island by daring to sell a foot of land or cut down a branch. Not that there isn't a problem with everything being sold out from under us, so's all we'll be able to afford if we want to stay here is a tent, but Persis isn't a developer. She's not out to make Sanpere into Bar Harbor or Camden."

In Faith's experience, the invocation of those two place names produced much the same impact on islanders that Sodom and Gomorrah must have on the communities on their outskirts.

Lyle elaborated. "Harold Hapswell—he's a Realtor *and* a developer. Now, you *have* to have seen his signs. He's what you might call Persis's archrival. Right now, he's putting all his eggs in a basket called Sanpere Shores, a gated—if you can believe it—community on that big point of land in South Beach, Butler's Point. KSS is mightily pissed at him, too. But I can't see any of these people creeping onstage and putting turpentine in an old Moxie bottle."

The kids and Tom were racing up from the beach. Amy's lips looked blue, or it might be the late-afternoon shadows.

"Neither can I," Faith said, standing up to wave at them. "I'm pretty sure the turpentine was meant for Romeo."

"The first lighthouses were huge bonfires on the shore, set to guide mariners safely into port. Then someone had the idea of building stone towers and burning the fires up high on top."

Ursula had given Ben some paper and colored pencils. He was busy drawing lighthouses while she talked. Amy had conked out early. All that salt air. Tom and Faith were reading, but both had put down their books to listen to Ursula.

"The smoke was sometimes a better guide than the fires." She opened a book at her side. "This is a picture of the Pharos, the lighthouse at the mouth of the harbor in Alexandria, Egypt."

"Two hundred and eighty B.C.," Ben read. "Wow!"

"One of the Seven Wonders of the World," Faith added, then promptly doubted herself. Or was it Ten, the Ten Wonders of the World?

"That's right, dear," Ursula said. Faith breathed a sigh of relief. She wasn't good at these things, so she resolved to keep her mouth shut if any more *Jeopardy!* categories arose.

"The study of lighthouses is called 'pharology,' after the Pharos," Ursula told them.

"I never knew that," Tom said. He, on the other hand, *was* good at this sort of thing, coming from a game-playing family.

Ben was poring over the book, and he soon started copying the picture. "It lasted a thousand years and was forty stories tall. I bet if they sent divers down, they could still find some chunks of it. Why don't they do that?"

"I think they've tried, but the bottom of the Mediterranean has been filled up with layers and layers of sand, silt, and what have you for all those years."

Faith looked at her watch. It was time for Ben Cousteau—she could see the plan forming in his little mind—to climb the stairs to bed.

Once again, a look and a snack—a raisin-laden hermit cookie—from Ursula sent him off without protest. How does one develop this skill? Faith wondered. She resolved to ask Pix if her mother had always been thus. Could Ursula teach "the look" to Faith? Or Tom? She didn't care who had the gift, because it was a gift—no whining. She sighed. She knew in her heart that she could study Ursula's brow, eyes, and the faint turn of her lips forever but would never achieve the same result. She followed Ben up to help him along. He

80

still insisted on their nightly ritual, started when he was a toddler. The bedding was an envelope, he was the letter, and Faith or Tom would write an address on his cheeks with a kiss above the right eye to stamp the missive and send it to sleep. Sometimes it worked; sometimes it didn't. But Ben himself was consistent. They'd always done it, and so far as he was concerned, they always would. Faith pictured herself driving to his dorm at college each night and smiled to herself. The smile changed to a pang when she realized just how soon the tucking-in would stop.

Tom was looking at the book and talking about lighthouses with Ursula when Faith came back downstairs.

"It's fascinating. And I'd like to know more about the ones near here. There's one on Isle au Haut, on Mark, and another on Eagle, right?"

"Yes, and you forgot Butternut. That's why the Coast Guard didn't automate this one, just replaced it with a lighted channel pole. They didn't really need two so close together. I've often wondered if it wasn't some sort of government boondoggle that got this one built."

"No matter what it was, I'm glad. I can't imagine the shore without it," Tom said firmly. He was as enamored of Sanpere as any of the Rowe/Miller family.

Faith smoothed the tousled curls on the top of his head. "There are some blueberry muffins left. (See recipe on page 322.) I'll make tea or coffee if anyone wants it, and we can finish them off." The blueberry harvest had been affected by the drought, yet there were still plenty of berries around for this delicious treat.

"I'd love a cup of tea, but no muffin. I shouldn't have had what I did at dinner, after all I ate yesterday at the Sewing Circle," Ursula said. "Enough calories for the month. Serena outdid herself, and of course Louella always brings a pie, or two or three."

Louella Prescott had a bakery, closed only on Sundays, holidays, and Sewing Circle days. She was renowned for her anadama bread, blueberry muffins, and flaky piecrust. She'd generously given Faith all her recipes, but Faith had never been able to duplicate the flavors exactly. It had to be Louella's ovens, or some essence of Louella herself—a woman who had sampled her own wares over the years, to the point where she looked as if she was made of her own fragrant, soft, yeasty dough.

Faith made tea and returned as quickly as possible. She had been waiting for the kids to go to bed to talk about what had happened at the rehearsal. She was sure the Sewing Circle telephone tree had had plenty to say about it, and also about the attack on Seth Marshall's building site. Placing the tray on the table, she reflected that, as usual, more seemed to going on in tiny Sanpere than when she went back home to the Big Apple. In her experience, vacation time was virtually an oxymoron on the island.

"What have you heard about what happened to Persis?"

Ursula shook her head. "No one can make head nor tails of it. Why would anyone want to do a thing like that? And especially to Persis. She's a pillar of this community."

She stopped and looked at Tom's and Faith's faces.

"Oh, you *are* naughty. You know what I mean. Besides, as I'm sure I told you, Persis was one of the most beautiful young women this island has ever seen. Slender as a reed. Her hair was long—down to her waist just about. And she had the most perfect skin. Still does, in fact. I can see her now. She looked like a Pre-Raphaelite painting, only in a miniskirt. It was the style then."

"And now," Faith said, thinking of the microminis she'd seen on Aleford's teenage girls and women on Fifth Avenue.

"Persis is a rescue squad volunteer, helps out at the nursing home, raises money for whatever the island is trying to get for the medical center or fire department. And she does it all quietly. You'd never know how much she does unless you lived here."

Faith nodded. This was the impression she'd received from Lyle.

"What happened to her husband? Kenny's father. I haven't heard anyone mention him," Faith said.

"I don't think Kenny had a father," Ursula answered, then blushed slightly. "I mean, of course he had a father, but no one has ever mentioned who he was. When she was young, Persis was pretty keen to get off the island. Took off for Port-land the day she was out of high school, and I guess we all assumed some man was involved. Came back pregnant the following year, just in time for her father's funeral, and stayed. Persis and her mother brought the boy up in the house where he and Persis still live. It's on the shore. Off the main road, going toward Granville. It's where Persis grew up, too. Persis's mother was as strong-minded as Persis, and they were both of the 'Spare the rod and spoil the child' school. Kenny was always a quiet boy. Had to be, I sup-pose. I've always felt sorry for him. If he ever did have any spirit, it's long gone. Anyway, if Persis was married, I never heard about it. Sanford is her maiden name."

If Ursula didn't know who had fathered Kenny Sanford, nobody did. The Sewing Circle was San-pere's equivalent of the CIA, possibly better.

"What about last night?" Tom asked. "I wanted to call Seth, but it's gotten late. Did his mother say anything more about it?"

Faith was amused to watch Tom availing him-self of the local underground.

"They're terribly upset." Ursula set her teacup down firmly. "Everyone is pretty sure it's those KSS people. Oh, why did they have to pick such a fool-ish name? Every time I say it, I feel foolish, too!"

Tom also put his cup down. "These ecoterror-ists get carried away, certainly, but I'd have thought cooler heads would have prevailed here. I understand Donald Osborn and his wife, Terri,

84

are involved with the group. I met him last summer, and he seemed very reasonable. We were talking about computers; he telecommutes. It didn't have anything to do with the environment or Sanpere, yet somehow I can't see him creeping around at night, setting fires and hoisting effigies into the trees," Tom remarked.

Her husband never failed to surprise her. He'd never mentioned Donald Osborn. Faith's own clerical father never displayed any interest in the mundane, presumably because his thoughts were on a loftier plane. Tom, thank God, had a keen appetite for gossip, but Faith was normally the supplier.

She felt compelled to reestablish her position.

"You can never tell what someone will do." It was the first thing that popped into her head. She might just as well have said, "You can't judge a book by its cover" and been done with it. Then everyone could have said, "Duh," which is how they were regarding her.

Ursula smiled and patted Faith's hand.

"That's true, dear. Now, why don't I take these things out to the kitchen and you two run along upstairs."

Faith felt about ten years old, but fortunately, Tom took care of that in the privacy of their own room.

While Faith was drifting off to sleep, Persis prone on the stage flashed into her thoughts. Persis whispering, "I've been poisoned. And I know . . ."

But the feud. The lobster war. The turpentine

had to have been meant for Romeo, Ted Hamilton. No one could have known that Persis would drink it. Yet why was the woman so positive she was the target?

When Faith went down to the kitchen to make breakfast the next morning, Ursula was sitting in her nightclothes at the table, sipping a mug of coffee. She looked up at Faith, but there was no good-morning smile.

"Gert called a half an hour ago. Helen Marshall died last night."

"I'm so sorry," Faith said, putting her arms around her friend. "Had she been ill long?" She remembered that Helen, a cousin of Freeman's, lived in a small house right on the shore, outside Granville. She'd dropped Nan there for a visit last summer when their car was in the shop.

"She had a great many things wrong with her," Ursula conceded, "Mostly as a result of diabetes. She wasn't good about her diet, but we all expected her to go on for some years longer. She was only seventy-nine."

Faith was getting used to hearing ages like this described as "only." Apparently in this new millennium, everyone would live well into the hundreds—especially on Sanpere—although anything past fifty or maybe sixty seemed light-years away in her own life.

"I'll bring something over for the family." Faith knew her duty, and Ursula had plenty of casserole dishes.

"There isn't any. Oh, she has nieces and nephews. Then there's Freeman and Nan. But Helen never married. She told me once that she was too particular in the beginning; then she got so she liked it. She worked in the cannery for years, and when it closed, she was happy to stay home and tend to her garden. She'd put enough by to get along. . . . I must get dressed now. Look at the time!"

Faith looked up. It was a little before seven o'clock.

"I'm glad you're here, Faith. Having you, Tom, and the children is nice company for me. I don't know why this is hitting me so hard. At my age, you'd think I'd be used to losing people, but you never do and these last months have been especially bad ones on the island. I can't remember so many going so close together."

Faith mechanically took eggs and butter from the fridge. She started to cut some thick slices of bread. She'd make French toast. Tom had slept in, and it was his favorite.

"So many going so close together," Ursula had said. So many deaths. Older people, yes, but death was death, and Faith hoped there wouldn't be any more for a long, long time.

Four

"It's the dog days." Freeman Marshall was wearing a suit and sweating profusely. He took out a large bandanna handkerchief and mopped his brow. "Well, let's go in and see Helen off."

"Freeman," his wife chided him. "What a way to speak, and why ever did you bring one of your work kerchiefs when you have a drawer full of perfectly good white ones?"

"The Lord is mighty pleased to have such good company as Helen always was, and neither of them is commenting on the color of my pocket handkerchief right now." Freeman stepped aside to let Ursula, Faith, and his wife precede him through the door leading into the small church. With the large turnout, it was hotter inside than it was outside. A ceiling fan was valiantly moving the steamy air around. Ursula reached into her pocketbook and took out three folded paper fans, handing one to Faith and another to Nan. Feeling like Yum-Yum, Faith was once again impressed by the older woman's resourcefulness.

The Italians who had come to work in the quarries so many years before had brought their religion with them, and after much intermarriage, the congregation of St. Erasmus, named for the patron saint of sailors, had more Marshalls, Prescotts, and Hamiltons than it did the original Espositos, Toccis, and Romanos. The quarries had also supplied the material for the building, and for the simple altar, the baptismal font, and the pulpit. Today, two stiff arrangements of gladioli had been carefully placed on either side of the cross. Below, there was a large wreath of white carnations—"From your family" was inscribed in gold script on a deep purple ribbon. More gladioli, an abundant sheaf, lay on top of the casket.

"Funeral flowers," whispered Ursula. "I've told Pix. No gladioli, no mums. You be sure she remembers."

Faith nodded as the priest began to speak. She'd told Tom much the same thing, adding white calla lilies. They were all right for weddings, but too sad for funerals.

It was a sweet service. A few tears were shed when one of Helen's nephews read the Twenty-third Psalm, but whatever other grief was felt was kept hidden. This wasn't the death of a young person or the result of an untimely accident or illness. Helen had lived a good and happy life.

Faith wished they could have gathered whatever was in bloom in Helen's garden and filled the church with the flowers she loved, although, now that Faith thought about it, Helen *had* gone in for glads.

The graveside service was in the same cemetery where Ursula's husband was buried. After they had laid Helen to rest, Faith and Ursula went to Arnold Rowe's grave.

"It doesn't seem long ago at all, yet it's more than twenty years. He would have enjoyed Pix's children so much, and they him. It doesn't seem fair." Ursula smiled ruefully. "How many times has God heard that, do you suppose? Fair or not, it wasn't God's work. To paraphrase William Sloane Coffin, God's was the first heart to break."

Faith felt tears start. She'd heard Coffin's words before, spoken after his son's accidental death. He'd been responding to the inevitable question, "How could God do this?" The answer was that God didn't. But she still choked up at the thought of Ursula's husband, Pix's father, who had suddenly dropped dead one sunny autumn day, a massive stroke, after never having been sick a day in his life. Would it have been better if he had been? Her thoughts rambled. People always said this in sorrow, suggesting a little warning in the form of chronic illness would have helped. Which was, of course, absurd. Death was death, no matter what the prelude.

The cemetery was the oldest on the island, and some of the headstones were indecipherable under the lichens that had grown over names, dates, and the pithy epitaphs so beloved of New Englanders: "As you are now, so once was I" and, even more to the point, "I was drowned, alas! in the deep, deep seases./The blessed Lord does as he pleases." Some stones had been cleaned, and their white marble stood out against the blanket of moss and grass, crooked teeth compared to the upright, newer granite stones. Ursula's grandparents and parents were here, a sister, and many more from the Lyman clan. Ursula would be here, too—and Pix, her husband, her children, and so on. Faith felt a deep longing for this kind of rootedness. She wondered if there were any plots left.

As if in answer to her unspoken thoughts, Ursula pointed down the row and said, "A nice plot has come up. An end one, so you won't feel hemmed in. I've often wished Grandfather had purchased one on the end, although I'm very partial to the stand of birch that has grown up here." She motioned toward the trees at the side of the plot; they had sprung from seedlings dropped by gulls or other birds. Ferns grew in lush abundance beneath their branches, spreading out at the foot of the trees. Despite the dry weather and the heat—the dog days—the shaded cemetery was green and cool.

"You girls coming back to the house?" Freeman called. He was standing in another part of the Marshall plot, away from the mound of fresh earth that covered Helen's grave. Freeman was busy clearing dirt from the incised letters on his mother's headstone with his knife. It was just like Romeo's dagger, and Faith realized a truce had been called for the funeral. There were plenty of representatives from both warring families, Prescotts and Hamiltons kneeling side by side in the church.

"Do you want to go?" Faith asked Ursula. She was worried that the older woman might be tired out from the heat and the emotion of the day, but Ursula had every intention of seeing it through.

"Certainly we'll go. We should pay our respects. See you there," she said, raising her voice so Freeman would hear. He nodded and waited for them, helping Ursula into Faith's car. Faith was skipping a rehearsal to accompany Ursula, who'd asked that she come with her. Ursula so seldom asked for anything that Faith was glad to do it. Besides, she'd liked Helen, though she hadn't known the woman well, and wanted to say good-bye herself.

Family and friends were gathered at Helen's little house. Jackets and ties were shed and the food was set up in the yard to take advantage of the breeze. Helen had an ideal spot overlooking the thoroughfare, and one of her delights had been to watch the activity on the water, often using the brass spyglass that had belonged to her father, a member on two of the all-Sanpere crews that had defended the America's Cup in the late 1800s.

"Got us an offer already. Gorry, I would never have believed it! Aunt Helen was sitting on a gold mine all these years," said a man as he helped himself to punch.

Faith tuned in.

"Persis always does the best. Had a buyer up her sleeve the whole time, I bet," his companion agreed. "Maybe we can all go in on a time-share or something in Florida. I would dearly love to get away from this island in the winter."

"Keep your voice down, Sally. The will hasn't even been read yet."

"We know she left everything to her nieces and nephews! Probably a little to the library and the Garden Club, but Aunt Helen knew what was right."

The man nodded. Faith was pretending to be very interested in the delphinium just beyond their sight. How could Persis have sold the house if the will hadn't been read yet? Persis had been at the funeral; Kenny, too. She'd been discharged from the hospital on Saturday morning and aside from looking a bit paler than usual—Faith suspected no makeup—Persis looked fine. Helen must have been related to them, as well, or perhaps, since Persis was so involved in the community, she went to every funeral, like a mayoress.

"Sad to think we'll never have any more picnics on this pretty beach," Sally said. "I remember coming here when I was just a little kid, and you practically grew up on it, you old cuss." She gave the man, who Faith assumed must be her husband, a pat on the shoulder.

"It'll be off-limits to us, that's for sure. We might break a shell or disturb the seaweed. In a way, I wish we could keep the place. . . ."

Sally looked startled. "Now, Norman, how could we all share it? We'd have to rent it out, which is the same as selling. And what about Florida?"

Persis had reached the table and cut a large slice of devil's food cake. Kenny was behind her, perhaps enjoying the respite from the sun that her large shadow afforded—or perhaps because that's where he always was.

"Florida? You wouldn't want to be there now. Bugs as big as my fist, and so hot, the clothes drip off you. All of them want to be here." She laughed.

"Helen was very grateful for your help, Kenny," Norman said. "She could never have managed the garden without you. I believe you must have been one of the last to see her before she passed—when you came to water it. Sally saw your truck."

Faith was not surprised to see Kenny turn scarlet. Nightclothes, gardens, whatever—it was his first reaction.

"Didn't have anything better to do," his mother boomed. "Why shouldn't he help out? Could do a whole lot more, if you ask me, 'stead of going off in his skiff all the time. Taking up room at the Rowes' dock right now, and do I ever see any of those mackerel he's supposed to be catching?"

Kenny mumbled something that sounded like

"I'll get you some tonight, Mumma." He slunk off toward the driveway, where a group was smoking in silence, taking in the view, and getting rid of a few beers.

Ursula came looking for Faith.

"I think we should go. You'll want to pick up the children on the way home."

"Tom said he would, but I'll call him and tell him not to bother. Do you think it would be all right for me to use the phone?"

"Of course. It's in the kitchen. Just go in through the back door."

Helen's house was as tidy as her garden. Nan was cutting brownies and putting what she called her "Comfort Cookies" (see recipe on page 325) on a large plate.

"I have to call Tom and tell him not to pick up the kids."

"Go right ahead. And take some of this home with you." She gestured toward the goodies.

"Thanks, I'll take a few cookies as a treat. Ben and Amy love them—as do the rest of us." And well they should. Nan had invented them for her grandchildren, to take the hurt out of a skinned knee or bruised feelings. They literally melted in your mouth, walnuts, butterscotch, and chocolate.

Nan looked sad. "I'll miss Helen. She was Freeman's cousin, but we'd been friends since we were girls. I thought she was doing so well. She was sticking to the diet the new doctor gave her and she told me that her last checkup was A-okay.

That's exactly what she said, 'A-okay.' Guess she couldn't help herself. They found an empty box of jelly doughnuts beside her. Helen always had a sweet tooth, and it looks like it killed her."

Nan left, and Faith started to follow, after calling Tom.

"Three hundred thousand. That's what I heard."

"For this tiny place!"

The voices came from the living room.

"Helen Marshall was a rich woman. Too bad she had to die to cash in."

Too bad for Helen, that is, Faith silently amended as she left the woman's little house with its garden by the shore.

Life on Sanpere soon settled into a pleasant routine. No one tampered with any more of the play's props. Opinion was divided between the belief that one of the crew had used the bottle for turpentine and didn't want to own up to the mistake, and a deliberate act by a party unknown. Persis, of course, continued to tell one and all that it was "K-S-S my you-know-what." Ursula's shock over Helen's death was fading, and KSS was quiescent—if it was KSS that was responsible for the wave of ecoterrorism on the island. Even the Fairchilds' remodeling job was showing noticeable progress. Faith found herself relaxing into the rhythm of the summer. She took the kids to camp, then went into the auditorium to work on the play. Reversing the process, all three went to the house to see what had been done, ending the day happily at the Pines. Ben was learning an enormous amount of lighthouse lore and Faith was enjoying Ursula's pleasure at the meals she prepared. Although Gert often left something for her employer's dinner, it was plain fare compared with Faith's offerings.

They had been at Ursula's almost a week and yet it seemed as if they had been there forever. Faith would be glad to get into her own house, but in another corner of her heart, she was grateful to the skunks and the builders. She'd never spent this much time with Pix's mother. Ursula was very different from Faith's own mother. Jane Sibley was quite a bit younger than Ursula and still working more than full-time. Although delighted by Ben and Amy, she dealt with her grandmotherly obligations as efficiently as she handled the rest of her life, taking them to the Central Park Zoo or the Museum of Natural History for a well-planned, educational afternoon when they visited. Tom's mother was more like Ursula. Marian Fairchild would play board games with Ben and read to Amy ad infinitum. She was teaching them to identify birds common to New England. Jane Sibley, like her daughter, could only reliably identify pigeons—enough ornithology to know a nuisance when she saw one.

Mulling over these interesting differences, Faith almost collided with Linda Forsythe backstage. The young woman—Faith had learned Linda was the same age as she was, hence "young"—was bubbling over, as usual.

"My goal is to finish the clambake scenery and Main Street by tomorrow," she said enthusiastically. "Then we only have to do the tomb, inside and out, plus Juliet's bedchamber. I'm thinking a trailer, with her room open to the stage."

"What would you use for a balcony?" Faith asked, wondering also if a trailer might not be an affront to some of the islanders. There were trailers and then there were trailers. Juliet's family would have had the top of the line, but Linda might be picturing something out of *The Beans of Egypt Maine* instead. Faith liked Linda, although the occasional ditziness that resulted from the combination of cheerleader and aging hippie could be annoying. While she talked as if she should have a megaphone in one hand and pom-poms in the other, Linda wore the shapeless Indian-print bedspread shifts and masses of beads so beloved of yore. Faith still didn't know much about her beyond this; they hadn't had much time to talk except about the production. There was so much to do and they were indeed shorthanded.

"Tree house off to one side? No, too contrived. Maybe she could be sleeping on the roof of the trailer?" Linda proposed

Faith was doubtful. "I don't think people do that. What about something like the Pines and the other houses here from that period—sprawling Victorians with sleeping porches on the second floor? We could just paint most of it as a backdrop and construct the porch, then put a ladder against it—like an elopement."

"Perfect!" Linda exclaimed. "The Capulets would live in a big house—you're right. We'll do a simple backdrop and Romeo can climb a ladder instead of a tree. It will be easy to construct the sleeping porch/balcony from the scaffolding we've been using to paint the sets."

Happy to have been of service, and not a little pleased with her growing sense of stagecraft, Faith went to get the containers, brushes, and paint she had left in a storeroom behind the stage the day before. She'd just switched off the light and was about to leave, when she heard voices in the hall. It was Roland and Juliet—Becky. They were arguing heatedly. Surprised, Faith stepped back in and pulled the door almost shut.

"I will not have the entire production sabotaged because of your hormones!"

Roland had raised his voice, and from the tone, Faith expected Becky to fall to pieces. Becky was apparently made of very stern stuff, however.

"My hormones are none of your business, and I don't know what you mean anyway. We happen to live in a free country, Mr. Hayes, and I can be in love with anyone I please. Not that I'm saying I am."

"No, you can't. Not until this play is over. If your family and Ted's find out about you two, we'll be lucky to have ten people in the audience. No Hamilton or Prescott will come, *nor* any of their relations, *nor* anyone who knows them— which takes care of the entire island population except for the summer people, and you never know if they'll turn up for something or not."

"What makes you so sure Ted and I are . . . you know, that hormone thing?"

"I have eyes. And while you're both good actors, you're not that good."

Becky sounded relieved. "Well, you don't have to worry. We *are* just acting. I guess you haven't been giving us enough credit."

"All right," Roland said in a resigned voice. "Make sure it stays that way—acting."

"It's just a play, Mr. Hayes. And Ted Hamilton is just a friend."

Standing in the storeroom, Faith thought it was a good thing Roland Hayes didn't have X-ray vision like so many schoolteachers. Otherwise, he'd have been able to see Miss Becky Prescott's crossed fingers behind her back.

The highlight of the morning was Persis Sanford's triumphant return to the company. Faith had seen her in blooming health at the funeral, but prior to that, Persis had been recuperating at home. She'd probably gotten bored, with no one except Kenny around. So far, the only words Faith had heard issuing from his lips were "Hi" and " 'Scuse me," not exactly scintillating conversation. This lack of communication skills would be understandable if Persis's mother had been anything like her daughter; growing up, Kenny would never have been able to get a word in edgewise. Like Ursula, Faith found herself feeling sorry for the boy—or rather, the man. Except Kenny, even as his name suggested, would always be a boy—Kenny, never Ken.

"I'm back!" Persis called, stretching the word out and plainly enjoying the effect as everyone rushed to greet her. Almost everyone. Linda looked positively terror-stricken and took a giant step toward the rear of the stage, ducking behind the curtain.

"Welcome, welcome," Roland said. "I don't know what we would have done. You are irreplaceable, my dear."

"Thank you," Persis purred. "It takes more than a dollop of turpentine to do me in. Up to the hospital, they said it was pure luck that I spat it right out. Must have been an accident, *they* said. Painting scenery and using any old container to hold the turps. I know they called our stage manager about it."

She pierced the curtain Linda was hiding behind with her eyes. Faith fully expected another Polonius, but Linda neither cried out nor fell forward from the arras.

" 'Cept everybody knows I always take a drink of tonic after my scenes. Whatever's handy."

"Be that as it may, let's get to work." Roland was clearly uncomfortable at the turn the conversation had taken.

Persis wasn't done. "Oh, I know who did it all right. We all know. KSS. Well, Kiss is right. Kiss my you-know-what! And the brakes on my car giving out in July. I know all about that, too!" She flounced off, returning with the sunhat that served as her wimple and holding her script. With all her recent downtime, Faith thought, the woman surely should have learned her lines by now, but apparently not. She had the kiss line down pat, though.

Everyone got back to business and Roland started rehearsing the scene concerning nuptials with Juliet, her mother, and the Nurse. It was a perfect showcase for Persis's talents, and Faith couldn't keep herself from laughing at the broad sallies. Linda had crept from behind the curtain and was busy painting faux mausoleums and other funerary statuary. She wasn't laughing; her grim face was suited to the task. *What is wrong with her?* Faith wondered. *Why has she been afraid to greet Persis?* The hospital probably did caution Linda about the proper storage and labeling of potentially lethal materials, but no one could hold her responsible. *Why would Persis?*

"Wonderful, ladies," Roland enthused. "May I hear the last speech, Lady Capulet? And at the end of it, you come in a little sooner, Nurse. As soon as she says, 'By having him making yourself no less,' jump on the line with your 'No less? Nay, bigger! Women grow by men.' Then leave a pause for a laugh. You might give a slight suggestion of a wink to the audience, too, Persis, or even make a gesture of a swelling belly. But you keep playing it straight, Lady Capulet."

Lady Capulet was wearing a housedress and bib apron—her own wardrobe. Offstage, she was

Sharon McDonald, married to a fisherman who thought his wife—part-time at the bank—had taken leave of her senses and hoped she wouldn't get any fool notions about going to Hollywood from all this playacting.

"Why would Persis be so certain that KSS was trying to poison her?" Faith asked Ursula. "The whole business is getting truly Shakespearean. She kept muttering about previous attempts and having to keep her guard up during the entire rehearsal."

Faith had brought the kids back to the Pines after the level of activity at their own house convinced her they'd be very much in the way—and she certainly didn't want to put them off their stride. Tom was happily shingling and said not to wait dinner for him—that he'd work as long as there was light. The transformation from *This Old Testament* to *This Old House* was somewhat astonishing. Well, whatever the calling, Faith had promised to go whither he went, and she would. She'd already gone to Aleford, and what could be more of a sacrifice than that?

"I don't know about any attempts to poison her or other accidents, but they do hate Persis—and all the other Realtors, developers, builders, and anyone who doesn't agree with them. Still, I wouldn't have supposed they'd try to kill any of them. From what I know, KSS and similar groups want to make their statements by attacking property, not people. Besides, if they killed off people like Persis, they'd have no one to attack. Then what would they do with their time?"

Faith nodded. Her thoughts exactly. Especially the notion of how such people needed targets like that to give life meaning—or, as Ursula had so succinctly put it, to fill up their time.

The two women were sitting on the beach at the foot of the long sloping lawn in front of the house while the kids were exploring the tide pools. Faith kept a sharp eye on Amy. The tide was out, but the rocks were treacherously slippery.

"Why would Linda Forsythe have run away when Persis appeared? The woman looked as if she'd seen a ghost." Again, she noted, this time to herself, it was getting too, too Elizabethan. They weren't doing *Hamlet*—or *Macbeth*.

"That's easy. Linda's a member of KSS, and she certainly would not have wanted to see Persis after Persis has been blaming them all over the island since she got out of the hospital."

"Linda's a member of KSS! But she wouldn't have put turpentine in the props bottle. She's the stage manager and would be the obvious suspect if KSS did turn out to be responsible. They'd have someone else do it, if they did, which you doubt." Faith was aware that she was tying herself up in pronouns. "Who are they, anyway, and how many of them are there? Anybody else I know?"

"Not all the members want to go public, so it's hard to say who's in and who's not. The Osborns, I think you know who they are—Terri and Donald—started the group and roped in their friends. A lot of the members live near them in South Beach. That's where Harold—Harold Hapswell—is putting what he calls Sanpere Shores. The lots are all laid out, and he's put roads in. I don't know how many have been sold, but it's going to be a separate gated community—a world apart—with an indoor pool, tennis courts, and who knows what."

"Lyle told me about it, and it sounds absolutely horrible!" Faith exclaimed, thinking if anyone was going to find turpentine in his Moxie, it should have been this guy. "The island hasn't been able to raise the money for a pool to teach people *here* how to swim, and he's putting one in for these fat cats." She stopped, arrested by her choice of words, and realized she'd automatically modified her speech for Ursula's ears. "And isn't that where the big swimming beach is? The only one around other than the smaller one on our point with fine white sand?"

"Yes, and now yours will be the sole place open to the public." Tom and Faith had given it to the Heritage Trust when the point had more or less fallen into their laps a few years earlier.

"There's no way to stop this Hapswell guy?" Faith asked dismally. KSS was beginning to sound attractive.

"I'm afraid not. He's in compliance. We may not like it—it's a crime—but it's all legal."

"And Persis is probably in on it with him."

"That, I would strongly doubt. The two hate each other like . . . well, like poison. They haven't spoken in years."

"Competitors?" Faith remembered Lyle had said they were "archrivals."

"That—and maybe something else."

Whatever the something else was, it would have to wait. Faith sprinted to the edge of the shore a few seconds short of pulling Amy back from attempting a belly flop into the mud.

After cleaning up her daughter, Faith packed some juice boxes, granola bars, plenty of sunscreen, and the kids into the car. She was curious to see the site of Sanpere Shores for herself. Ursula declined. "It will just make me madder—or sicker."

She drove across the causeway that separated Little Sanpere, where Ursula was, from the rest of the island. The barely two-lane road was lined on either side with large boulders, painted white. Today it was fine, but in bad weather or at night, even with the reflective boulders, the road was rough going and had been the scene of too many accidents. Faith looked at her children. They'd want to drive someday, she supposed. Massachusetts kept upping the age and placing restrictions on junior licenses. With any luck, she could keep them out of the driver's seat until she was too senile to notice.

It was impossible to miss the turn for Sanpere Shores. It was marked by a sign as big as a billboard, on which was sketched out not only the placement of the lots but the pool, courts, and several of the "dream" houses. As Faith had suspected, they were the kind of McMansions currently in vogue: *grande* French provincials with porches, tremendous Tudors with porches, and mammoth Mediterraneans with porches. Porches were the thing now. A nod to a bygone way of life, when everyone sat on the front porch after supper, watched the children catch lightning bugs, and listened to the whir, whir of lawn mowers drift across the summer evening. She doubted if any of the occupants of these houses would ever sit on their porches. Yet front porches they had to have—and decks in the rear. Also windows that didn't match. Round ones, eyebrows, octagonals, two-story plate-glass Palladians, and, of course, bays—large bays to accommodate window seats, where no one would ever sit and read.

She pulled off the road, figuring as long as they were there, they might as well walk on the beach. It might be the last time. She was surprised the way wasn't barred already. No NO TRESPASSING signs and a chain-link fence. She handed each child a pail and shovel and grabbed the provisions. Ursula had been right: Faith felt mad—and sick.

Who was Harold Hapswell? She'd never met him. The name conjured up a silent-movie villain with handlebar mustache gleefully tying peril-stricken Pauline to the railroad tracks. Was Harold, like Persis, from here, or from away?

The beautiful long sandy beach looked straight out to Isle au Haut across an expanse of water presently teeming with activity: lobster boats, sailboats, small motorboats, and one *grande* dame of a windjammer, majestically moving into sight from behind the shorter point of land opposite this one. The opposite point was near enough for Faith to see that it had a number of cottages and a lobster pound with a small pier. The contrast with what would be going up across from it was ludicrous. The lords and the serfs? At any rate, it would be authentic Down East color for the new home owners and far enough away so there wouldn't be any authentic Down East bait smell.

The kids began to dig straight down to China, as children automatically do on a beach. Faith reached for her book and was soon lost in the pages of *Who Killed the Curate?*—British writer Joan Coggin's hilarious 1944 mystery. Where was Lady Lupin, Coggin's improbable sleuth, when the world needed her now?

"Hi, Faith—is that you?" called someone not at all British from the other end of the beach.

Returning to the present with some difficulty, Faith saw it was Linda Forsythe, and she waved. Stage manager Linda. KSS member Linda. What else Linda?

Linda made her way to where they were sitting. As she watched her approach, Faith tried to figure out whether Linda's bulk was due to girth or some odd fashion notion of the appeal of layers.

"It is wicked hot," Linda said, her roundish face shiny with sweat. Maybe it wasn't layers—of fabric, that is. "I thought I'd go for a swim, and this is the best spot. My rocks aren't bad, but the barnacles can cut your feet to ribbons getting in and out. I keep meaning to buy some of those water shoes, only I never seem to get off the island."

Faith started to commiserate, then realized that for Linda not leaving Sanpere was a badge of honor and she'd announced this fact with pride.

"Oh well then, here you are." She sounded like Lady Lupin. It was the type of thing she said. "I mean, don't let me interfere. Go have your swim."

But Linda seemed disinclined to move. Inertia. A body at rest tends to stay at rest, Faith thought, proud of her recall, since physics had been one long nightmare of ohms, joules (the wrong kind), and newtons (again, the wrong kind).

"You've been such a help," Linda said. "I don't know what I would have done if you hadn't turned up. I think everything's going well, don't you? Roland is a marvel."

Faith agreed, "He is, and the whole island will be astonished. Your sets are perfect, too. Have you done much of this sort of thing before?"

"Not really, but I am a painter, and Maine—Sanpere—has been my subject for years. The sets aren't that different, only larger, and with broader brushstrokes."

"I'd like to see your work sometime. Is it in any of the local galleries?"

"Yes. I'm a member of the Granville Artists Co-operative, and we have a gallery on Main Street. I also have work at various places up and down the coast, but why don't you come to the house? I have some pieces there—ones I can't part with and some I did earlier this summer. It's not far. I live about a ten-minute walk from here."

"From here? You mean you live on this point?"

Linda nodded. "I'm the only one at the moment. There were a couple of other people, but everyone else sold out to Harold. He's developing this obscenity called Sanpere Shores. You must have seen the sign."

"I did. I'm sorry. It will be horrible for you—and the island."

An obstinate expression crossed Linda's face.

"Maybe it will and maybe it won't. But do come. I'd love to show you my work, and the view is very special, too."

"Can I take a rain check? I have to get the kids home. And besides, I'm sure my husband, Tom, would like to see your paintings, too."

"Why don't you both come to dinner tomorrow night? Nothing fancy. I get halibut from a fisherman I know, and there are plenty of vegetables in my garden."

Vegetables. Could she possibly mean tomatoes?

Faith's face must have revealed her thoughts, because Linda said, "I have such a deep well that the pipe acts as storage; plus, I collect rainwater, so I've been able to keep things going. I even have tomatoes."

"You said the magic word. We'd love to come. I'll bring dessert."

"Ben and Amy will enjoy meeting Rufus, my cat. He loves kids."

"Ben and Amy will meet him another time. They'll be with a sitter."

Faith firmly believed that children did not belong at dinner parties, no matter how casual and *intime*.

"Fine. See you tomorrow at rehearsal and then later. Say six o'clock?"

"Six will be fine."

Sanpere's dining hours were as quixotic as Aleford's.

Driving back down the narrow dirt road to Route 17, Faith came upon a parked car blocking the way. It was empty.

"Damn," she said to herself. "We could be stuck for ages." The car was a large black recent-model Mercedes, miraculously free of the dust that covered Faith's and everyone else's vehicles. It must be someone inspecting his future house lot, she thought bitterly as she got out of her car, telling the kids not to move a muscle. They were near one of the new side roads—actually, very long driveways. Why couldn't the person have pulled in there?

"Hello," she shouted. "Hello, I need you to move your car."

There was no response. She noticed the car had Maine plates, which was odd. It was out-of-staters who were buying properties like this.

"Hello," she called again, then resigned herself to a search, kids in tow.

"We have to go see if we can find out who belongs to this car," she told them, unstrapping Amy, who was beginning to drowse off.

"I'd like to belong to it," Ben piped up. "It's so cool. I want to have a car like this when I grow up."

Not sure whether to quash his materialism or encourage his ambition, Faith settled for saying, "That's nice, dear. Now let's see if we can find the owner and get it moved."

Ben and Amy joined her, shouting more hellos as they walked down the new drive, heading in the direction of the water.

Their quarry was sunbathing on a flat rock, her position suggestive of an offering to the gods. Her already-bronzed body was glistening with oil. They could see a lot of it. Three small triangles inadequately covered the appropriate areas. Faith doubted she could qualify as a vestal virgin.

"Wow," Ben gasped, then, catching his mother's eye, had the sense to be quiet.

The woman stood up.

"Yes?" She was what Freeman would call "a long drink of water." She was also what he would call "a real looker."

"Is that your car in the road, a black Mercedes?" Faith asked. She'd been about to apologize for disturbing the woman, but the arrogant tone of voice and thoughtlessness in blocking the road kept Faith from saying more.

"Is there a problem?" She reached down and took a swig of Evian from a bottle that was leaning against a rock in the shade.

"You're blocking the road and we can't get out."

The woman shoved her feet into a pair of espadrilles and sauntered off. No "I'm sorry," no nothing.

Faith was fuming.

"Is she mad at us, Mommy?" Amy asked. Ben chimed in: "She sure seems mad. She didn't even say hello."

"Maybe she's had a hard day. Don't worry. Now, let's scoot." Faith put her arm around her son. She was already carrying Amy, who now seemed on the verge of howling.

A hard day. Deciding bikini or monokini, coconut oil or Bain de Soleil, Evian or Perrier—tough choices. Then there was the question of where to park. Where to place her car in order to cause the greatest possible inconvenience to others.

Faith caught up with her.

"You may not know it, but someone lives farther out on this point. The road goes there." Faith didn't want to mention the beach. They'd probably been trespassing.

The blonde—she had to be a blonde—unlocked the car and got behind the wheel. Just before she pulled the door shut in their faces, she said, "Oh yes, I know someone lives out there."

Faith awoke, startled, and reached for the light. A hand was grabbing her shoulder. Completely alert before the bulb went on, she realized it was a small hand. A flash of lightning outside the window explained everything. Ben. It was Ben, instantly transformed from seven-year-old world conqueror and ogler of babes to a very little boy. He was terrified of thunderstorms. Had been from infancy. Amy—and her father—slept through anything.

She pulled him into bed and he snuggled down under the covers.

"You know there's nothing to be afraid of, but it does sound loud." She could feel his body relax. "I'm going to turn out the light now."

"Okay," he answered tremulously.

In the dark, the lightning crept around the corners of the shades, turning the rocker where Tom had flung his clothes into an eerie shape. But in the light, Faith could see that Ben had already closed his eyes. Roller-skating in heaven hadn't satisfied him when he was younger, and scientific explanations didn't work in this case. He'd have to outgrow it.

"Think how wonderful it will be for all the flowers and vegetables to get this rain," Faith murmured. She was falling back to sleep herself. The claps were getting fainter; the storm was moving away, but the rain continued. There was nothing so cozy as sleeping in an old house with the sound of rain falling on the roof. She waited to make sure Ben was in a deep sleep before carrying him to his own bed. Otherwise, by morning, she and Tom would be squeezed to one side, with Ben sprawled out, taking up all the space.

Back in her room, Faith went to the window to look at the downpour. Slow and steady—a good drenching. She'd heard Sanpere had had only an inch and a half of rain during all of July. What they needed now were days and days of precipitation like this. She thought about how the lighthouse must have looked during past storms, when its beacon meant safety. Whoever had slept in this room would have become accustomed to the long sweep of light filtered through a curtain or around the edge of a shade. Constant, it would have become virtually unseen in time, like the train whistle, unheard now, in Aleford, which had kept her awake at first every night. On the rare occasions when it did waken her, it had become as comforting as a heartbeat. But there was no steady beam outside this window anymore, although the distant red light of the channel pole, its replacement, was clearly visible. Aesthetically, it was no substitute. She was about to let the shade fall, when she realized that there was a car parked by the lighthouse. She hadn't seen one after dinner, when they were sitting on the porch. The sunset had been spectacular, and it was not unusual for a car or two to be there. The spot was well known for the view. Tonight, though, the only cars visible had been the Fairchilds' own in Ursula's driveway. As Faith watched, this car's headlights went on and it drove off. Probably teens looking for a place to neck. Romeo and Juliet? Getting back under the quilt—there was a small hollow, still warm, where Ben had crawled in—she glanced at the clock—3:00 A.M. Late for anyone to be canoodling on the island, and about an hour before the fishermen and others were abroad. But if it hadn't been lovers in the car, who else could it have been?

Five

"We have a major problem!" Jill Merriwether's panic traveled straight through the telephone lines, hitting Faith's ear with such a wallop that she switched sides.

It was impossible that the groom was getting cold feet after all these years of trying to get one in the door. Jill herself, once her mind was made up, seemed blissfully happy—and totally committed. Surely the state hadn't suddenly canceled Earl's time off? The wedding *was* Labor Day weekend, after all, and he'd told the Fairchilds he'd practically had to "get a grant from God," but he would only miss a day and a half of work.

"Shellfish. She's allergic to shellfish, and Earl's mother just thought to tell me. Also told me it would be a shame to make her feel bad by serving something different just to her!" Jill wailed.

"Earl's mother is allergic to shellfish? I thought I saw her eating clam fritters at the Fish 'n' Fritter Fry last summer."

"No, she's fine. It's his great-aunt Wilma from Presque Isle! What are we going to serve as a first course *now*?"

Jill had been adamant that Faith would attend the wedding as a guest and not as the caterer. Therefore, the reception was being catered by the inn. They would handle the entire thing, but Jill had not been shy about asking Faith for advice, and Faith had been happy to give it. Guests would begin with hot and cold hors d'oeuvres and champagne outside, weather permitting, then move in for the meal, starting with the first course—lobster bisque.

"Do I have to change the mini crab cakes, too, and the Thai scallops and veggie skewers?" Jill asked.

"I'm afraid so. You don't want to have your wedding ruined when Wilma is rushed to Blue Hill Hospital after nibbling one by mistake." She didn't add what she was thinking: And have everyone remember your nuptials for writhing Wilma, rather than jubilant Jill.

"But don't worry," she told her friend. "Call the inn and tell them right away. You have plenty of time to make this kind of change. They'll have some suggestions. If you like, I can come up with more; then we can sit down and decide. Probably the sooner the better. It's been so hot, I was thinking a cold soup might be better anyway."

"Faith, you're an angel. Could you come this morning? No, wait, the play. Could you come for lunch? I'll get sandwiches from Lily's."

Even without the enticement of Kyra Alex's sandwiches, Faith would have agreed, but the prospect of a Russell's Special—melted Havarti, salami, artichoke hearts, lettuce, and a mustardy vinaigrette on crusty homemade French bread— or maybe Ethel's Barbecued Pork—pork loin simmered in a raspberry barbecue sauce and served on their sourdough bread—was definitely an added incentive.

Salivating slightly, she said, "I'll be at the store at noon."

All morning while she was working on the play, Faith went through her mental recipe Rolodex and came up with a number of alternatives. She agreed with Earl's mother, although it was an inconvenience. Knowing about a food allergy ahead of time, it was so much more gracious to work the menu around it, rather than call attention to it.

When Faith arrived at the store, Jill hung a CLOSED sign on the door of the Blueberry Patch and they went upstairs to her tiny apartment. They sat at a table overlooking the one and only street in Sanpere Village, the harbor beyond stretching toward the islands dotting Penobscot Bay. The sea was flat today. There wasn't a ripple of a breeze.

"I like the idea of a cold soup," Jill said, blowing at her bangs, which were clinging damply to her forehead. "It would be too much to hope that the temperature will drop before then. What do you suggest?"

"There's always vichyssoise or a fruit soup, but I'd go with avocado bisque. (See recipe in *The Body in the Bookcase*.) It's a beautiful pale green color, and I spike it with a little white rum. We can serve it with a rosette of sour cream and sprinkle a little caviar on top of that. Very elegant. Perfect for a wedding."

"Great! And the little girls' dresses have pale green flowers against a creamy white background, so they'll match—or is that too Martha Stewart?" Jill's brow crinkled.

"It's not too anyone, except you," Faith reassured her. The only attendants were going to be Earl's small nieces, dropping rose petals, and Earl's small nephew, clutching a pillow with the rings.

"Now for the hors d'oeuvres."

"Dean said it would be easy to replace the scallops with chicken, and we don't have any others with chicken. We'd wanted to avoid it, but now maybe we shouldn't," Jill said. Dean Barth, the innkeeper, was an island favorite and from the beginning had treated Jill's wedding as if it were his own daughter's.

"People like eating things on sticks. It seems exotic, and I'm sure the inn has done these often, so make your life simple and substitute the chicken."

Faith was unabashedly licking barbecue sauce from her fingers—she'd gone for the pork loin—while Jill wrote the change down.

"Now that just leaves the crab cakes," Faith said. "You could do mini Bries *en croûte*, mushroom tartlets, or *gougères*, very yummy cheese puffs. I also like the idea of smoked trout on a small spear of endive. You're not having any fish at all now, so maybe we can do something fishy for one of the starters. It's only shellfish she's allergic to, right?"

"Right. I double-checked. Too bad about the crab cakes. I love crab cakes." Jill was not a cook, and she sounded wistful.

"I'll make crab cakes for you and Earl as soon as we move back to our own house. That's a promise. Of course, you could simply have mini fish cakes. The remoulade would work with them, too."

"Why don't I mention all these to the inn and see what will be best for them—and we don't want to add to the cost at this point."

"Eliminating the lobster bisque will help, but I think that's the best idea. Ask Earl, too. He seems to have pretty definite ideas about all this."

"Don't I know it!" Jill said.

Earl had insisted on prime rib for the main course—and a chocolate wedding cake. The icing could be white or any variation thereof, so long as what was underneath was dark and rich.

"I want people to go away from this wedding fat and happy," he'd told Jill and Faith at an early planning meeting. "No three little dabs of something on the plate, connected by a coulis."

Unlike Jill, Earl loved to cook and had read his way from Child to Waters.

The food settled, Faith reached for one of the blondies Jill had also bought for their lunch. She'd be fat and happy herself if she didn't watch it. Happy was good, but fat . . .

"Has Earl said anything about the fire at Seth's, and the horrible dummy?" she asked Jill. Now that the wedding crisis had been averted, Faith's mind went back to Sanpere's recent disturbing events.

"He doesn't tell me about anything to do with work until the whole island knows, and by then, I've heard it. But he did show me something pretty upsetting, which makes me think he believes KSS really *is* behind all the attacks. With this dry weather, I know he—and everyone else— is worried to death about more fires. Come here and I'll show you."

Jill wiped her hands on a napkin and walked over to her desk, where there was a laptop set up. After connecting to the Net, she entered an address.

"Just wait," she told Faith, who was peering over her shoulder.

It took a while to load and then, to Faith's horror, a burning building filled the screen. Above the image appeared a message: "Every Night Is Earth Night!"

"Earl says it's Vail. They planted some sort of incendiary device and caused twelve million dollars' worth of damage in 1998. The irony is that what they burn down is merely replaced by something bigger and more invasive. All these places are heavily insured. Now more than ever."

She clicked some more, and up came an ad for a guide on how to set fires with electrical timers: "The Policies and Practicalities of Arson. Down-to-Earth Advice."

Faith gasped. "First amendment, yes—I may not agree with what you say, but I'll defend to the death your right to say it—although this is pretty heavy stuff."

Jill nodded, then clicked some more. By the time she shut down, Faith had learned enough about the ecoterrorists to believe KSS was with them in spirit, if not in fact.

"Earl says these people are organized like other terrorist organizations, in cells, so nobody knows anybody else. Anyone can act in their name and claim responsibility. There are no leaders, dues, membership cards. After something happens, the media gets an anonymous communication claiming responsibility."

"But they haven't harmed individuals, right? Just property?"

"So far, and in statements made after various attacks, they're quick to point that out. But what if someone had been in an office when they burned Agriculture Hall at Michigan State as a protest against research on genetically modified crops?"

In the news articles Faith had just read, the movement's lack of belief in political means, combined with their own brand of spiritual ethics—that any action was justified to prevent human beings from bringing the Earth to mass extinction—spelled anarchy. The difficult part of it all was that she agreed with much of what they said about their targets. She and Tom worried constantly about the kind of world Ben and Amy would be living in—global warming, the destruction of rain forests and forests in the United States, and, very close to home at the moment, sprawling luxury homes, with no thought given to long-term implications. A recent letter to the *Island Crier* had laid it on the line, describing a massive 250-foot complex on the Sellers Point high head—"an inconceivable monument to excessiveness that now sits prominently for all to see as it blights the landscape for miles."

"KSS has identified itself as a group, so Earl thinks it's unlikely that it aligns itself as such with ELF, but individuals in KSS may."

"And the other members wouldn't know."

"Exactly."

The rain from the night before had continued all morning, bringing joy to one and all, then stopped as abruptly as if some unseen hand had turned off a spigot. Now the temperature had climbed back into the eighties. During the late afternoon, it was so hazy and humid that Faith regretted having accepted Linda's invitation. A cold shower, a minimal dinner, and a gin and tonic were all she wanted for the evening. She took the shower and by 5:30 felt better. It had cooled off, as it almost always did in the evenings on Sanpere. Tom was home and eager to see not only Linda's work but also her house and a part of the island he didn't know as well. Gert Prescott had numerous nieces and nephews glad for the extra cash baby-sitting brought in, which was why Faith had felt so secure in immediately accepting Linda's invitation. Tonight, the sitter was Lisa Prescott. She'd come before and was a favorite. Lisa moved into the kitchen with the kids to get dinner on the table, displaying a maturity beyond her tender years. She shooed the elder Fairchilds out the door. At thirteen, she was the oldest of five, and it showed.

Tom and Faith turned off Route 17 at the Sanpere Shores sign.

"A pustulous pockmark on the face of Sanpere," Tom said dramatically as they passed the new drives extending from the existing dirt road. Faith raised an eyebrow. Perhaps her husband should hang up his hammer for a part in the play—boards for boards.

"I don't see any power lines, unless they're underground, and they're only doing that with new construction," Tom observed. "Linda's lived here for some years, hasn't she?"

"She must have power. How can she live?" Faith was appalled. No electricity, no phone. Suddenly, a vision of what dinner might be crossed her mind, and she was glad Gert had left a meat loaf large enough for leftovers. Gert made very good meat loaf—just the right bread-crumb-to-meat ratio, and with a slight mustard tang.

Soon they saw an artfully carved sign pointing

the way—FORSYTHE—and followed the grassy track.

"Whatever does she do in the winter?" Faith wondered. "No town plow would come this far, and it must cost a fortune to hire someone." Used to city services, erratic as they were, Faith had been amazed to discover that people in New England had to dig themselves out, except for the main roads.

"Paints a lot, I'd say," answered Tom, and stopped the car.

The house was a small log cabin, surrounded by pines, except for the large garden. It all looked like something from a fairy tale—one of the cheerful ones. Linda's scarlet runner beans were gaily climbing up the wooden tepees she'd constructed. Vines were laden with tomatoes of all sizes; mounds of squash and melons were scattered in between, as well as other varieties of beans, lettuce, and other vegetables. Faith felt as if she'd entered a Burpee ad as she walked past the produce to the front door, which was framed in cascading morning glories. Linda rushed out, drying her hands on a dish towel, her usual bumptious manner raised up a notch. Maybe she didn't have guests often.

"I'm so glad you could come. I hope you like ratatouille. It's really just a mishmash of all sorts of things from the garden. You must be Tom."

"I am, and thank you for inviting us. Now, is the house from a kit, or was it built without one?"

Having summarily dispensed with the amenities, he was obviously eager to get to the important subject—construction—Faith noted with amusement.

"Not a kit, although that probably would have been simpler. Or at least we should have had plans. I built it with Seth Marshall. Maybe you know him. He's a fine carpenter and has done a lot of houses on the island, but he did this with me about ten years ago, when he was first starting out. I paid for the materials and he exchanged his labor for artwork, a lot of meals, and a lot of vegetables."

"Seth built our cottage, the one we're remodeling. Lyle Ames is doing that, since Seth is so busy—and taking on larger projects."

"Well, here it is." Linda led them in.

The cabin was basically one large room. Brightly colored braided rugs covered the floor, and there was a good-size Vermont Castings woodstove at one end, surrounded by a comfortable-looking couch and some uncomfortable-looking twig furniture. The kitchen area consisted of a small refrigerator, gas stove, white porcelain sink, and counters covered with bright blue tiles. The cabinet doors had been fashioned from old windows, and Linda's unmatched collection of china, canisters of staples, and other foodstuffs were clearly visible. A wide ship's ladder led to her sleeping loft. The most arresting thing about the whole house was not what was inside, however, but what was outside. There were no windows on one side wall and only small ones on two, but the fourth wall was almost all glass, opening onto a deck. Linda had been modest when she'd said the view was "special"; it was spectacular. If this is what Harold Hapswell is marketing, Faith thought sadly, his houses will go like proverbial hotcakes.

Linda had a prime spot on the point—far enough out so she just missed the shore on the other side of the inlet and had an unobstructed view out to Isle au Haut and the other islands. The sun wouldn't set completely for another hour and a half, but the sky had already taken on a rosy glow. Thin clouds near the horizon streamed out in long lavender ribbons. Linda was on deep water, and, in any case, the tide was still high. Sea, earth, sky—it was all one glorious whole. Linda didn't need to search for subjects.

Faith turned from the view reluctantly. "It's incredible. But we came to see your work. . . ." The walls were covered with paintings, but none reflected the style in which Linda had painted the stage scenery.

Linda opened one of the two doors on the wall without windows, explaining the arrangement to Tom as she did so. "We had to think about insulation, especially because I wanted a wall of windows on the front. I board up all but the one over the sink in the winter, and you'd be amazed at how warm the house stays with the woodstove. I do go through a lot of wood, though. And wear my woollies."

The door she opened revealed an oversize

closet, which was fitted on one side with racks to store canvases and had shelving for materials on the other. Several easels were pushed to the rear.

"I haven't had much time to paint this summer, but I've been doing a lot of watercolor sketches, which will keep me going this fall and winter. I like to paint outdoors, so I do these as studies for my oils."

She began pulling paintings out, handing them to the Fairchilds, who took them over to the couch. While Tom and Faith lined the pictures up, Linda went back for a few more.

She was good, very good, as Faith had suspected. All the canvases were large, and she had a very bright palette. Some were too garish for Faith's taste, but they were still compelling. Others were quite wonderful. Linda had captured the constantly changing Maine light in innumerable ways from sunrise to sunset.

They were quick to voice their enthusiasm, and Faith could see Linda was pleased.

"I like to look at them myself, but on an everyday basis, I want to see my friends' work, or work I've collected. The exception is this piece." She pointed to a small landscape by the door. It looked like a Gauguin, except the trees were pines, not palms. It was exquisite, and Faith instantly coveted it, but she also knew instantly that Linda would never part with it.

Tom was taking his time going from one painting to the next. The Fairchilds had some good pieces in Aleford, mostly contemporary. Since coming to Sanpere, they'd bought some work by such local Maine artists as Siri Beckman, Francis Merritt, Jill Hoy, Penny Plumb, Mary Howe, and Ethel Clifford, the basket maker.

This part of the coast had been drawing artists for many, many years: John Marin, John Heliker, William Keinbusch, the Wyeths, Eliot and Fairfield Porter. It wasn't hard to see why. Faith looked outdoors again. The rose tones had deepened and the sinking sun was turning the islands into an endless series of dark silhouettes.

"But enough of all this. 'Art is not meat nor drink,' remember, no matter how all in all it is." Faith and Tom had brought a bottle of cold Sancerre, a Blondeau 2000, and soon they were sitting on the deck, sipping it and eagerly devouring the tiny pear-shaped tomatoes Linda had put out and the zucchini blossoms she'd dipped in flour and egg and fried to a delicate crisp.

First they talked about the house. She had propane tanks for her stove, refrigerator, hot-water heater, and pump; oil lamps for reading. No phone, just a CB radio for emergencies.

"In all this time, there was only once when I was worried. It was during an unusually severe ice storm, and the trees were falling like pick-up sticks. I knew the road out wasn't passable, and getting into the car wouldn't have been any safer than the house. I didn't have a shed for it then. Seth made me put one up the following spring."

"Seth is big on sheds," Tom commented. "Thank goodness."

"I stayed inside and hoped nothing would fall my way. A huge tamarack came down parallel to the house. When I ventured out the next morning, I saw it was so close, the branches were smack up against one of the shuttered windows."

"You were lucky."

"I guess. It was beautiful, though. I did a whole series based on that ice storm. It was as if a magician had touched everything with his wand, encasing the world in shimmering ice. By the following day, it was gone. Spring thaw."

Well, there was no ice now, but a magician was definitely in order. One who could rid the world of insects. The mosquitoes were not fierce, merely peevish—one at a time whining close to Faith's cheek. She lifted her hand to slap one, stopping when she saw the horrified look on her hostess's face.

"Mosquitoes?" Faith protested. "Reverence for life, but surely not for mosquitoes!"

"I know." Linda sighed. "Everyone thinks I'm nuts, but yes, even mosquitoes. And mice, which I hate, yet I can't bring myself to set traps. Rufus takes care of them, and I try not to think about the whole thing. I mean, he *is* a cat."

Tom smiled, "I'm a fan of Albert Schweitzer myself."

Faith kicked her husband's ankle—well out of Linda's line of vision. He was the first to start cursing—and smacking—when a mosquito invaded his territory.

"I have plenty of citronella candles, which

work very well, but it's a little hard to see what you're eating," Linda said.

Reluctantly, they went inside for dinner.

The meal was delicious and Faith was glad to be able to see what it was. Linda had baked the halibut with fennel and white wine. The ratatouille was delicious, flavored with several varieties of thyme instead of the more traditional basil or oregano.

"Baguettes from Lily's?" Faith asked, taking another crusty piece to soak up the sauce on her plate.

"Yes, I make my own bread in the winter, but it's been so crazy lately, I haven't done any baking this summer. And between Lily's and Louella's, I don't know why I bother. To make the place smell good, I guess."

Gradually, over coffee and the blueberry tart (see recipe in *The Body in the Basement*) Faith had brought, Linda told her story—or some of it. No mention was made of KSS.

She'd come to the island from her home state of New Jersey twelve years before as an au pair for summer people who'd rented a house for July and August. When they left, she stayed.

"I was in love—with the island and also, I thought, the fisherman who sold the family lobsters. I was right about the island and wrong about him, but it didn't matter. I would have stayed in any case."

Faith was about to make a New Jersey remark, but then, remembering the stinging rebuttal her aunt, who lived there, had delivered the last time Faith had deprecated the Garden State (where were all those gardens anyway?), she closed her mouth. Linda was a Jersey girl, after all, and Jersey girls were tough.

By nine o'clock, the evening was over. They were pleasantly full and the soft light of the glowing oil lamps made Faith feel ready for bed.

They thanked Linda for a lovely evening and invited her to come see what they were doing at their house. As they drove off, Faith could see lights twinkling on the opposite point of land. Those people hadn't turned the clock back the way Linda had. Probably had bug zappers, too.

"She must get lonely, especially in the winter," Faith remarked. Nothing would ever induce her to spend that season on Sanpere. It was bad enough in Aleford. Pix once told her about a friend of theirs who had decided to live on Sanpere year-round and got such a desperate case of cabin fever that she went to every meeting on the island, even the preschooler's Story Hour, for company.

"People choose this kind of life because it suits them," Tom said. "Don't worry, I'm not entertaining any fantasies of moving here permanently. Aside from the bleak fact that I know I'd be doing it sans wife, I wouldn't like it any better than you would. An occasional trip in the winter, though, to see how pretty the snow looks . . ."

"The thin end of the wedge, Tom. You can take the kids and I'll go someplace warm."

"She was wrong about art not being meat nor drink."

"What do you mean? She was just being poetical, silly. It was a very good meal, too. You never know with artists. They get carried away with presentation sometimes and forget taste," Faith said.

"It's love, not art. Edna St. Vincent Millay. A Mainer, except she couldn't wait to get away. 'Love is not all: it is not meat nor drink.' "

Ministers were good at quotations, Faith had learned early. Her father and grandfather both usually had one handy for any given situation.

"Maybe for Linda, art is love," she retorted.

"Mebbe; mebbe not," Tom replied, testing his local accent, to Faith's great chagrin. He was turning into a codger before her very eyes.

They reached Ursula's and got out of the car. Tom still had to drive the sitter home. He yawned. "I hadn't realized how late it was," he said.

"Yes, almost nine-thirty," teased Faith.

"You forget, my sweet, that we need all the rest we can get. We have to be sharp as tacks. Tomorrow night, we go before the Planning Board, remember?"

Lyle had discovered that the Fairchilds could extend their existing deck by five feet without violating any ordinances, but since it hadn't been in the original proposal approved by the Planning Board, they had to go back.

"It's unlikely anybody would make you rip it out, but it's best to tell them before you do it," Lyle advised, and the Fairchilds agreed.

The meeting room of Sanpere's Town Hall was packed. The Town Hall was a square white clapboard building on Main Street in Granville. It housed the town office, the state police, which Earl used when he was on the island, and an old jail cell, now occupied by file cabinets. Town Meeting was held in the school auditorium, although the room they were gathered in had been the site for years before that.

Faith looked around. Aside from Lyle, Seth, and Tom, she didn't recognize a soul. Wait, she thought craning her neck. There was the man with whom Linda had driven off after work last week, the man with the curly hair and beard. She nudged Lyle. "Who's that guy sitting up front next to the woman with the long braid and purple dress?"

"That's Donald Osborn." He grinned. "And that's his wife, Terri, and a whole lot of KSS members. Guess we're going to have some fireworks tonight." He seemed to relish the prospect.

Faith whispered the news to Tom, who wasn't pleased at all.

"If they disrupt the meeting, it will hold things up. Maybe Lyle knows where we are on the agenda. Since KSS has been making such a fuss, the Planning Board doesn't post it anymore. Just announce in the paper what's being proposed. According to the law, they don't have to do any more than that, and when KSS started making all those accusations, the board decided they'd go by the letter of the law. Now everyone is inconvenienced, because they shot their mouths off." Tom sounded bitter. He was definitely weighing in on the side of the native-born islanders.

He leaned over Faith and asked Lyle if he knew when they'd be up.

"Don't worry, Tom. You'll get your deck approved," Lyle said, and winked.

The board consisted of three members, one of whom was the Code Enforcement Officer, who had held the post for as long as anyone could remember. So long as Willard was around, they didn't need to consult the files for precedents or the thick books of regulations. Willard's memory was infallible.

Things started well. The first item on the agenda was a simple request for change of use, and it was approved rapidly. Two more items were dealt with, and then it was the Fairchilds' turn. Lyle had been keeping Faith amused by his running commentary on what was happening and the participants. She made a mental note not to tell him anything she didn't want made public—very public.

Lyle made the presentation and then, after consulting Willard and recalculating the spring high-tide mark just to be sure, the Planning Board approved the expanded deck. Faith reached for her purse.

Tom appeared scandalized. "Honey, we can't

leave before the meeting is over. People will think we only came to get what we wanted." He stopped as soon as he realized how ridiculous he sounded. "I mean, it would be rude."

"How late do these things go?" The wooden folding chairs were almost as uncomfortable as pews.

"I don't know, but it's interesting."

To you maybe, Faith thought, then immediately sat up straighter. One of only two men wearing a suit and tie got up and went to the front of the room. The other man followed with a large portfolio and easel stand. He unzipped the case and began arranging the contents—very sleek architectural renderings of very large houses—for all to see. The next item, a board member announced, was a request from Harold Hapswell for the construction of three additional houses on land in South Harborside, presently known as Butler's Point, called Sanpere Shores by the petitioner.

A third man got up. He looked to be in his early fifties and was dressed like Lyle, Seth, and the other builders, who'd exchanged dirty jeans for clean ones and their T-shirts for blue denim work shirts. He was tall, very thin, and had probably been attractive in a boyish way when younger. Now he was a plain man, and a man who looked tired, as well.

"Looks like this project is getting to old Harold," Lyle whispered. "He looks plumb wore out."

Harold Hapswell himself. He didn't look like a

real estate mogul. "Where is he from?" Faith asked. The suits were conferring with Harold and passing out fancy-looking folders to the members of the board.

"Comes from Connecticut or someplace like that, but he's been here thirty years or more. Didn't get into this business until about ten years ago. Before that, he did a little of everything—mostly fishing, though he tried selling his photographs to the tourists for a while, but this was before the whole art thing caught on big."

Hapswell smiled at something Willard said, and his whole face changed. It was as if an unseen hand had erased one chalk drawing from the blackboard and then drawn another, handsomer, happier, more energetic one in its place. He was talking about his project. That was clear. And Sanpere Shores was what made him happy.

"I was with him once when he was trying to sell some land to some summer people. He wanted a builder to come along, and I was the only one desperate enough for the work at that time. You'd think his cradle had been a lobster trap, the way he talked. Straight out of 'Bert and I.' The customers were lapping it up. They agreed to buy the property, and the moment they left in their car, Harold was back to being the hard-nosed, son of a bitch businessman he is, voice and all. He was going to take his cut for bringing me aboard, and it was going to bleed something wicked. I told him to find another pigeon."

Faith laughed, then stopped. Lyle's words had

been lightheartedly spoken, yet his eyes reflected a deep and bitter hatred. It shocked her. Hapswell was apparently as horrible as everyone had been saying. Could he have been behind the attack on Seth Marshall's job? To drive away the competition? Except his own projects had been under fire, literally, too.

"Oh shit, here comes Persis!" Lyle said. The look was gone. Now he was just plain annoyed.

"What's the matter?" Tom asked.

"She and Hapswell are like oil and water. She'll start asking questions; he'll get riled, raise a ruction, and we'll be here until dawn. She's just pissed she didn't think of Sanpere Shores first. That land has been sitting there for years. Just ask the people Harold gypped out of it."

Persis did look like someone who had failed to get in on a major deal. Again, Faith was struck by how similar the cutthroat real estate action on Sanpere was to Manhattan's. Substitute "Deep Water, Shore Frontage, South Beach" for "Prewar, Parking, Upper East Side" and there you had it.

Persis took a seat in the front row. Everyone was facing forward and things looked like they were getting under way. Then a few heads turned toward the rear, although there hadn't been any noise. Curious to see what people were looking at, Faith turned around, too. It was the lady in the Mercedes. She had more clothing on this time, but it clung to her body so tightly, she might as well have dispensed with it altogether. For some reason, she was wearing dark glasses.

"Who *is* that?" Faith quizzed Lyle. "I saw her on one of the Sanpere Shores lots on Tuesday."

"I have no idea," he said, drooling along with virtually every other male in the room. Faith cast a hasty glance at her own husband, who had suddenly found the floor extremely interesting. "And," he added, "I'd keep that fact to yourself, or you'll have every male with a breath in his body out on Harold's land, hoping to get a glimpse of her."

"She must have some connection to Harold if she was out there. Maybe she's buying one of the lots," Faith speculated.

"We can only pray." Lyle put his hands together. "But you were there, and you're not buying. She may just have turned off the road. Anyway, we'll know who she is soon enough."

Faith nodded. One of the virtues of living on a small island.

"Ahem." Heads swung forward and the younger of the two suited men shone a laser pointer on the first visual, an overview of the entire Sanpere Shores subdivision.

"Now, here we have the existing lots, for which plans have already been approved by this board. And here." He moved the red beam farther along. It looked like a gash from where Faith was sitting.

Donald Osborn stood up and began speaking, interrupting the proceedings. He seemed completely unperturbed by the angry looks directed his way from the presenters and Harold, and some of the audience.

"On behalf of the citizens of Sanpere Island," he intoned, "I would like the following statement entered into the minutes: 'We the undersigned do fully and forcibly object—' "

The chairman rapped the gavel.

"Mr. Osborn, you are not on the agenda. We are hearing a proposal from Mr. Hapswell at the moment. If you wish to present a proposal to the board, you know the procedure. You must file it a week in advance, so it can be duly noted in the newspaper. Our next meeting will be in three weeks."

Donald ignored the chairman and began reading again. "The so-called Sanpere Shores development threatens the habitats of endangered wildlife and violates the State's wetlands code."

"Sit down," someone shouted from the rear.

"Better still," called another voice, "go home."

There was a lot of laughter, but Faith could see that Donald and those around him, who were standing in solidarity, weren't amused. He raised his voice and continued. The chairman raised her voice, too.

"I must ask you to stop, Mr. Osborn. You are disrupting this meeting. Please!"

Harold walked over and stood in front of Osborn.

"Shut up and sit down," he bellowed.

"We're in for it now," Lyle said. "Be ready to make a run."

"What!" Faith exclaimed.

It was hard to tell whose face was more purple

with rage—Donald Osborn's or Harold Hapswell's. They were both about the same age. Harold had the advantage in height, Donald in weight. The two men in suits, an architect and a lawyer from Blue Hill, were looking disdainful. Faith felt an immediate need to wipe those smug "Look at this rabble" expressions from their faces, no matter what she thought of the positions each side held.

The KSS members started to chant, "Take back the land! Take back the land! Keep Sanpere Sanpere!"

Harold shoved Donald, or Donald shoved Harold, and suddenly the room exploded. Chairs were being overturned and voices were raised in furious shouts.

"What is this? The 1968 Democratic National Convention?" Faith cried as Tom pulled her to the side of the room and made for the door Lyle had opened. In a moment, they were on the sidewalk with others who had streamed out of the building. Sounds of the scuffle still going on inside were plainly audible.

Laughing, Lyle left them to join a group across the street. Faith heard someone greet him, "Put the whole lot of them in a leaky bucket! Gorry, did you see old Harry's face? Thought he would bust a gut!"

There was no sign of the woman in the Mercedes.

Six

Faith found Harold Hapswell's dead body wedged between two granite ledges at the base of the old lighthouse at 7:38 P.M. on Friday just as the sun was setting. She noted the exact time, because she had an idea it might be important. The tide was going out.

Harold was wearing jeans and a dark T-shirt. It could have been black or navy. It was wet, so it was hard to tell. In the waning light, the yellow rockweed sparkled like gold. It was wet, too. Wet and slippery. Harold's long, thin body was lying on its side, as if he'd been filed between the two large rocks. His hair was wet and his eyes were closed. He'd been there at high tide and he hadn't gone anywhere. It was a tight fit.

She thought of his angry, mottled face at the meeting the night before. It was drained of color now and expressionless. She stood looking down at him. It had been such a lovely evening and she had wanted to be out in the night air—cool, clear. It was still clear, but the cool had turned to cold. The seaweed made a faint popping noise. A crab scuttled out from beneath the thick strands, strands hiding all kinds of activity, large and small.

Her children were asleep. Her husband was nodding over an ancient *National Geographic*. Ursula was knitting and listening to a broadcast of the Boston Symphony Orchestra's concert at Tanglewood.

I need to call Earl. I need to tell someone, Faith almost spoke aloud. Yet still she didn't move, her eyes locked on the corpse below. Was this what the summer had been leading toward? This odd, out-of-kilter summer on Sanpere? What would happen now? She didn't know whether Hapswell was married or had any children. KSS would be pleased. The thought was not so much unbidden as unwelcome. She thought of it immediately, although she didn't want to. Those kinds of groups don't kill people. Ursula had said so. But they'd been talking about Persis, about the turpentine. The raucous cry of a gull startled Faith from her thoughts. She turned and ran as fast as she could to the Pines.

"A glooming peace this morning with it brings. The sun for sorrow will not show his head. Go hence, to have more talk of these sad things; some shall be pardoned, and more punishèd—"

"It's 'some punished,' not 'more,' Prince, and remember who you are. A statesman, a leader. Look straight out at the audience." Roland's correction was made gently. Death was on every mind—not Romeo's, Juliet's, or that of the others who perished in the play, but the real death of Harold Hapswell. There had been no official mention of it at the rehearsal. He was not connected to the production, unlike Persis—that one-woman Sanpere chamber of commerce, involved in every project no matter the size. Harold might have come to the play, or not. No official mention, but much conversation in lowered voices offstage.

After repeated assurances that Faith was fine, Tom had gone to work on the house; then Ursula had pushed Faith out the door for the Saturday-afternoon rehearsal. It was one of Gert Prescott's days. "If the two of us can't manage two small children, we'll have to resign from the grandmother club," Ursula declared.

Faith was actually happy to leave the scene. It was filled with too many images—images that hadn't faded yet. Last night, the quiet landscape had exploded into noise and movement. The area around the lighthouse had teemed with police cars, an ambulance, and other vehicles. Lights had whirled, voices had shouted, and tires had squealed. A crime scene. It didn't seem like their lighthouse anymore, but something menacing, a dark pinnacle piercing the night sky. Faith had watched from the window. "But it's too late," she'd kept repeating to herself. "Why are you hurrying? The man is dead." Mercifully, the children had not awakened. Their rooms were at the rear of the house, away from it all. Ursula had made Faith drink a large mug of very sweet peppermint tea. The mint had taken over a corner of the back garden and was thriving despite the drought. She'd found herself talking about the mint to Ursula. The way mint would grow anywhere, spreading its runners underground, invasive, impossible to kill. Ursula had listened and brought more tea while Tom draped a blanket over Faith's shoulders. She hadn't been aware that she needed it—she had felt as if she was burning up after drinking the hot tea. Then, feeling the warmth of the wool, she'd clutched it tightly, chilled to the bone. Soon after, Earl and another officer had come in and she had told them how she'd found the body. It was a short story. "I went for a walk and there he was." For the life of her, she hadn't been able to think of anything to add.

Earl had snapped his little notebook shut and put his pen in his pocket.

"No marks on him to suggest anything other than an accident. Those rocks have a slick coat of mud, plus the seaweed, and he was wearing sandals. Feet must have gone out from under him. He fell, was knocked out, and then the tide got him. Anybody around wouldn't have seen him until it was low again."

Faith hadn't noticed the sandals. Harold didn't seem like a sandals kind of guy, but it had been a hot day. Too hot for work boots.

"What do you think he was doing here? And why would he have been climbing on the rocks like that?" she'd asked. She hadn't wanted Earl to go. He was so steady, so sane. He'd make a good husband for Jill. He'd make a good husband for anybody. If she kept asking questions, he'd have to stay.

Earl had shaken his head. He never pretended to have all the answers. "No idea yet. But his truck is parked by the lighthouse, and someone mentioned that Harold owned the place."

At that, Ursula had appeared surprised. "I thought it belonged to one of the Prescotts. They bought it from the Sanfords, who got it when the government auctioned it off. My father had first refusal—he'd missed the auction—and I guess I thought I did, too." Her voice was filled with regret.

"Probably did belong to the Prescotts, but just now I heard that Harold bought it last spring. Was going to make it into apartments or one of those bed-and-breakfast places. What we think happened is that he came out here to make some plans, take some pictures. There was a camera hanging from his shoulder, wedged under the body, and enough keys in his pockets to fit every house on the island. We're checking to see if any are for the lighthouse door."

"Good Lord!" Ursula had exclaimed. She obviously wasn't responding to the comment about Harold's keys. It was as close as she got to real profanity, and a sign of extreme agitation. Faith concurred, choosing a silent, more pithy epithet.

Hapswell had been planning to turn Ursula's—and by extension, their—own personal lighthouse into a kind of motel, complete with brochure!

". . . and *some* punishèd; for never was a story of more woe than this of Juliet and her Romeo.' How was that, Mr. Hayes?" The Prince of Verona, who would be dressed in his high school graduation suit, but wore cutoffs today, turned as he finished to grin at his friend Romeo, who was lying on the stage.

"That was perfect, except for the smirk you have on your face now. *Always, always* stay in character until you're actually off the stage. No, make that out of the auditorium. No matter what." Roland was walking toward them, a smile on his face. "I'm the only one allowed to do whatever I please."

Romeo got up and pulled Juliet to her feet. Clearly, Roland's injunction was good news to them. Stay in character. No problem.

Faith had been keeping a close eye on Linda Forsythe. Yes, Earl had said it was an accident, "a tragic accident," he'd repeated this morning when he brought a typed statement of Faith's account for her to sign. It was too soon for an official report from the medical examiner, but he'd initially concurred with the conclusion the police and EMTs had reached the night before. Unless an autopsy turned up something in Harold's system. Earl had stopped at this point, and Faith had filled in the blank—poison. Not hard to come by on an island where people saved not only string too short to be saved but everything else as well, including all those tonics, pills for what ails you, weed and pest killers Grandma bought, which contained hefty doses of arsenic, strychnine, nicotine, and cyanide. Of course, it would have had to be something that didn't produce death throes, no ghastly final grimace. Harold's expression had been blank. Totally blank. Totally dead. An accident.

But it was a happy accident for Linda—and the other KSS members. Faith's conversation with Linda on the beach about the existence of Sanpere Shores kept getting mixed up with the lines onstage as she filled in Linda's sketch for the balcony scene with bright paint. "Maybe it will and maybe it won't" Linda had said firmly, determinedly, stubbornly—in sum, like someone who was extremely sure that Sanpere Shores wouldn't be built. Today, Ms. Forsythe, the stage manager, was strictly business, instructing Faith and a visiting friend of Roland's about how to paint the new flats. If Linda was pleased—or worried—she wasn't letting on. Until she got a phone call.

Roland had been explicit about calls. There was an extension backstage, but they had all been told it was for emergency use only. There was a pay phone in the school lobby if you needed to tell someone you were going to be late. Faith had discovered that her cell phone didn't work on Sanpere. Some sort of warp. Roland had one, but no one else did. When the backstage phone rang, three people ran for it at once and everything on stage stopped.

"It's for Linda," Becky called out. She'd sprinted to the front of the pack.

Linda put her brush down deliberately and walked off.

"Come on," Roland shouted from the rear of the auditorium. "We don't have much time, and there's no rehearsal tomorrow, remember."

Fishermen didn't go out on Sundays—couldn't. It was against the law in Maine. Some went to church; some didn't. But Sunday was a day off, a day of rest for people who didn't get much. A day when everyone in the cast was free to rehearse. But this Sunday was the Fish 'n' Fritter Fry, which was held yearly to raise money for the swimming pool project, and if you weren't helping out, you were going. Roland had canceled the rehearsal, since no one would show up anyway. He was signed up for the Wacky Rowboat races himself, he'd told them. The entire Fairchild family had been looking forward to the event all summer. The kids still were. Faith wasn't sure what forward was anymore.

She followed Linda. "Maybe it will and maybe it won't" was all the justification she needed to linger in the hall, listening to Linda's side of the conversation.

"Oh, it's you. You shouldn't call here. You know what Roland's like." There was a long pause.

"If they came to you, they'll come to me. We'd better get our stories straight." Another longer pause.

"Okay. Same place. At nine."

She hung up, and Faith ducked into the girls' lavatory. For a moment, she was startled, feeling like Alice in the "Drink Me" scene, then reminded herself that it was the K–3 section of the elementary school and the fixtures were conveniently smaller-scaled.

Linda had said, "get our stories straight." She had obviously been talking to a fellow KSS member, a fellow KSSer, KSSite? Faith wrenched her mind from inanities. Whether Linda was involved in Hapswell's death or not, there was no question that there was something she didn't want the police to know. Clearly, "If they came to you, they'll come to me" was not a reference to the Jehovah's Witnesses.

Back at work, Faith went over to where Linda was sketching out the new sets.

"Linda," she said, and the woman snapped her head around, obviously startled.

"Linda, I just wanted to know what I should do next," Faith said.

"Oh, why don't you . . . I mean . . ." She was stuttering, then stopped. "Ask Roland if anyone needs you to hear lines," she said finally.

"Sure. Good idea," Faith said, leaving. It was impossible not to notice that Linda Forsythe's hands were shaking like the leaves on the aspen trees that grew in a grove beside her cabin and that her face was as white as the sand on the beach Harold Hapswell had owned until yesterday.

Sunday dawned, gray and hazy. They arrived at church early to get Ben settled into his Sunday school class and Amy in child care. As usual, there were small knots of people congregated outside talking, some smoking, until the first bell rang. Today the groups seemed more subdued than usual. Ursula went to join her Sewing Circle friends and Faith hurried the kids off. Tom was assisting with the service. Upon her return, she joined the stitchers.

"More spray painting," Ursula told Faith straight out. "On the Sanpere Shores billboard."

"Pretty sick," Louella Prescott said. "Man isn't even in the ground yet. I wouldn't have believed it, even of those people."

Faith's heart sank. She wouldn't have believed it, either—at least not of Linda. Whom had she met at nine o'clock, and what had they done besides getting their stories straight? The woman's cabin was conveniently close to the large sign.

The bell rang and the obedient flock moved quietly into the church. "Did they mention what it said?" Faith whispered to Ursula as they sat in a pew near the front and handed the hymnals around.

"Something about 'Good riddance' and 'Power to the people of Sanpere.' Poor Harold."

"I didn't know you'd known him," Faith said,

thinking what a stupid assumption that had been. Ursula knew everybody.

"Hush, dear, we'll talk later," Ursula said as the strains of "Lead Kindly Light" filled the church.

But later would have to wait until still later. As soon as she got home, Faith rushed to change and took her car down to Granville to help with the food for the Fish 'n' Fritter Fry scheduled to start at one o'clock. Life, especially Faith's life at the moment, went on.

Huge vats of fish chowder were already simmering on the burners under the tent that had been erected on Granville's fish pier. The weather had stayed iffy. Rain wasn't predicted, but the sky was overcast, although the sun was making a valiant effort to burst through the clouds.

Sonny Prescott, owner of a local seafood business and a friend from her first summer on the island, immediately put Faith to work shaping clam fritters. "Not too big, deah, but not skimpy, neither."

Faith discovered she was starving for the first time since Friday night. The fritters were being deep-fried to a golden brown and she took time out to devour one. In addition to the chowder and fritters there was deep-fried haddock, as well as hot dogs and hamburgers for the kids and uninitiated adults—plus onion rings and piles of crisp fries. Mainers ate their fries doused in vinegar, and Faith grabbed a handful before going back to work. They were almost as good as Thelma the Fry Queen's at the Blue Hill Fair, the standard against which Faith measured all fries anywhere, from Paris brasseries to North Carolina barbecue joints. For dessert, the island women had been baking pies all week, and Louella had contributed what looked like a pickup truck load of whoopie pies.

"I hope we have enough," one of the organizers said, fretting. "There are two windjammers in the harbor, and I've never seen so many tourists on Main Street in my life. Last year, the chowder ran out at six o'clock and we had to go up to the School Street Rest"—no room over the door for the full name—"and throw together some more."

"And this year, we'll have it left over," a coworker commented dryly. "You never know with people."

Which, Faith thought, was definitely an understatement. But she couldn't imagine that there wouldn't be plenty to go around. As Sonny had handed her a hair net and plastic gloves, he'd proudly listed the grand total: 300 pounds of potatoes, 50 pounds of onions, 160 pounds of fish, and 15 gallons of clams. "Give or take," he'd added.

There were a lot of children's games first—old-fashioned ones like three-legged and egg-relay races, blueberry pie–eating contests, water-balloon tosses. In between watching and participating, people ate—and then ate some more. Faith was kept busy making and frying fritters.

"Why don't you take a break," said one of the women, who hadn't stopped for a minute herself.

"You look tired. Here, take a can of tonic and go sit down."

Faith gratefully accepted the soda and went to find her family. The pier was jammed with people and it was hard to make much progress. Plus, every group on the island had something they were raffling, all trying to make money at this optimal time of the year, and their tables further encroached on the space. Before she'd gone more than a few yards, Faith had purchased tickets for a quilt (the library), a hooked rug (the Grange), ten pounds of lobsters, courtesy of Sonny Prescott (the Boy Scouts), and *Islands at Sunset* by Linda Forsythe. The latter wasn't for KSS; it was for the play, and Becky was selling tickets to the production, as well. Faith was sure she wouldn't have bought any tickets if the proceeds were for KSS, even though this was one of Linda's paintings she liked. No sign of green spray paint. No, Faith was not lending support to KSS in any way, and she regretted that she shared some of their opinions. What a bind this was—disliking the means, methods, and many members, but agreeing with many of their objections to change. If the island didn't do something to regulate itself, it *could* turn into another Bar Harbor or Camden—there were those names again—and nobody wanted that. Well, maybe Harold had. She sighed. She didn't want to think about Harold.

"How'd you like to go home with me, sweetheart?" a seductively smooth voice called out. "I mean with us?" Tom was carrying Amy on his shoulders. She had the remains of what was probably a Klondike bar smeared around her mouth (all proceeds to the Fish Hawks, an island softball team). Equipped with Grandmother's sunshade *and* a broad-brimmed hat, Ursula was polishing off a crab roll (the Eastern Star). Ben was ahead of them, oblivious to his father's admonition not to get lost in the crowd. Faith scooped her son up, stopping him in his tracks.

"I want to see the lobster-boat races, Mom. We can stay till then, right? Sonny's going to let me go with him when I turn nine. That's not long. But I can enter the rowboat races next year. Dad said he'd do it with me. He says I'm a natural."

Considering that a lot of the activity in the Wacky Rowboat races degenerated into rowing in circles, Tom was right.

"Of course you can stay to see the races. They should be starting them soon. Are you guys having fun?"

Amy had immediately reached for her mother, delighted to find a face she recognized in the crowd.

Tom grabbed a kiss. "Eau de Fritter, very sexy," he murmured in her ear, then announced proudly, "Ursula and Ben came in third in the three-legged race."

Faith had wondered why Ursula and Ben each had a bright green ribbon with a fish stamped on it safety-pinned to their shirts.

Ursula smiled. "We've been practicing, and we'll keep on. We're hoping for second next year."

Or Carnegie Hall, Faith thought.

"I've got to get back to my post," she said. "Come and get some food before the races start."

The Wacky Rowboat races attracted a big crowd. Faith had a clear view from the food concession and found herself cheering madly along with everyone else. Whoever dreamed up this idea? she wondered. They'd been doing it forever, of course. The originator—and he or she must have been intoxicated at the time—had long since disappeared into the mists, or fog, of time. The object was simple: row out and around a distant buoy; fastest time wins. But the catch was that you had to do it blindfolded. This was where the wackiness came in. The only guidance you had were instructions from your partner in the stern. These instructions—"Now left!"; "Straighter!"; "No, go right!"—were complicated by loudly voiced comments from the onlookers. It was hard to tell who was saying what—or who was laughing the hardest. One contestant, overcome with mirth, ripped the cloth from his eyes and threw it into the water, declaring he'd wet his pants if he continued. His brother, in the stern, promptly took care of that for him by throwing him overboard, much to the crowd's approval. Roland and his guest had dressed up as old salts, complete with pipes and beards, painting their dinghy with rainbow stripes like the *Tidely Idley* in Robert McCloskey's *Bert Dow, Deep-Water Man*. They won the prize for best costume but lost the first-place trophy to a ten-year-old and her mother, who calmly rowed out, never saying a word, but relying on prearranged taps on the rower's knees to steer. It wasn't hard to figure out the system. A tap on the left meant "go left"; a tap on the right, "Go right"; taps on both knees, "Go straight." Faith was impressed.

The sky had cleared to a mottled blue by the time the lobster-boat races were due to begin. As the various classes—their winners and losers—came and went, tension on the pier mounted. Everyone was waiting for the showdown between the Prescotts and the Hamiltons, who had gathered in two very large, very distinct groups, with a uniformed Earl planted smack between the two factions. Raffle sales and the food concessions were abandoned and a wave of onlookers swelled behind them. Tom whistled a tune from *West Side Story* softly, and Faith wished she could smile. It was the last race. Sonny Prescott, all thoughts of fritters far from his mind, was revving his souped-up boat, his pride and joy, the *Misteak,* complete with 500-hp Cummings engine. He'd won last year *and* the year before, but Junior Hamilton, popularly known as "June," had a new boat, *Down East Girl.* He'd sworn she could take anything on the water, including Sonny's sorry excuse for a vessel. Testosterone and gas fumes filled the air. Faith mused for a moment on the incongruity of two men who would never see forty again, each weighing as much as the entire Fairchild family altogether, still being referred to by their little-boy names. Then the starter's gun ripped her from her thoughts and the crowd roared, certain that their decibels would influence the outcome.

Faith couldn't get a line from the song Tom had been whistling out of her mind: "We're gonna rumble tonight . . ." Amy was on Tom's shoulders again, clapping her hands. Ben had wiggled up to the front of the crowd, standing precipitously close to the water. Faith called out to him, but it was hopeless. She started to snake through the solid mass of people in front of her, her repeated "Excuse me" so inaudible that she soon stopped. She reached Ben just as the Hamilton boat crossed the finish line a hair ahead of Sonny's.

"Hot damn!" the man next to her said, while the man on her other side seemed ready to throw a punch. She looked wildly around for Tom, Earl, anybody. With a firm grip on Ben, she eyed the water. If worse came to worst, they'd jump in. But it didn't. Someone had the foresight to start the music and the "Beer Barrel Polka" began to blare from the loudspeakers—the familiar cadences of the Melodic Mariners, one of the island's musical mainstays. Hamiltons and Prescotts retreated— some grumbling, some elated. "Get you next year!" "In your dreams!" And then it was over. With a sigh of relief and legs like rubber, Faith delivered Ben to Tom and returned to her fritters.

After what seemed like a short time, Faith looked at her watch and was amazed to find that it was almost five o'clock. Her family had reappeared. Tom and Ben were consuming one last fritter and one last hot dog, respectively. Amy was talking to a little boy she'd met, who was now her new best friend, announcing firmly to her mother, "I want to play with Bobby."

"That sounds like a good plan, but it's time to go home soon." Faith prided herself on her parenting skills. "Soon," not "now," even if "now" was what was going to happen.

"Ursula's meeting us at the car, so we have to be going. Do you want to duck out, honey?" Tom asked. "You look tired."

Faith wasn't tired, not really, yet she figured she must be, since people kept telling her she was. Sure, she wasn't feeling as perky as she might have, but it had been pleasant to turn her mind off and concentrate on the fryer, all the while listening to the banter back and forth between the customers and the cooks. "Sure you can handle two of our fritters?" Sonny had asked, teasing a skinny brunette. "Don't want to be responsible if you can't budge an inch afterward."

"No, I want to stay," Faith said. "Besides, the dancing starts at seven."

Tom loved to dance. She'd learned early on not to laugh at his Ichabod Crane–like motions and the fact that he was apparently dancing to a different drummer. Marriage was nothing if not tact.

"Okay, then I'll get these guys settled and come back."

She gave them all hasty kisses and pushed them along before her offspring could object to leaving. Another paradox, like the whole KSS thing: You wanted your kids to be independent and strong-minded, but absolutely not with you.

The crowd was thinning as parents took weary children home. The teenagers had not arrived yet, considering it much too early to be cool. She left the stand and wandered toward the end of the pier. Granville was *not* Bar Harbor. It was still very much a working fishing village. On this summer Sunday night, the harbor was packed with fishing boats of all sizes and shapes, waiting for dawn and another day's hard labor. Sanpere Island had never been a resort. Off to the right, past the Sanpere Thoroughfare, she could see the skeletal derricks on Crandall Island, whose granite quarries had supplied the stone for New York skyscapers, museums, memorials, and jobs for several generations of island men. Shut down in the 1960s, it caused a major exodus, and attempts to start the business again in other, smaller quarries on the island had failed, too.

"My father worked there all his life. He'd never have believed that all that would be left was some rusty pieces of metal and big holes in the ground." It was Ken Layton, the island's historian. He sometimes wrote a column in the paper and had written a short history of Sanpere. He planned a longer one when he got too old to fish, which he hoped would be never.

She wondered what he thought about Sanpere's recent history. Most specifically Friday. Besides total recall of the past, Ken didn't miss much of what was going on in the present.

"What do you think about Harold Hapswell's death?" she asked him, realizing as she spoke that all day it had never been far from her mind, despite the fritters, the races, the roar of the crowd. She blurted the question out directly. As with Lyle and all the other locals she knew, it was pointless—and rude—to beat around the bush. They could always tell. They might not answer, but at least they wouldn't be offended.

"I think it was an accident. A terrible accident. Man was only in his fifties. Had another fifty left," Ken said firmly. "You found him, so you know there wasn't any sign of foul play."

"That's true. It just seems too much of a coincidence that he should die the day after a major blowup at the Planning Board meeting."

"What would be odd woulda been if it'd happened after a Planning Board meeting when there wasn't a major blowup. Those are as rare as hen's teeth. You think about it, now. How could it have happened? You'd have had to get Harold out to the lighthouse to start with, and he was nobody's fool. Then you'd have had to push him just so and get him to conk out in the exact spot for the tide—which would run ten, maybe eleven feet or so high—to cover him and hope nobody decided to have a picnic there before it did. Nope, it was an accident."

"Did you know him?"

"Course I knew him. We all knew him. He's been here more than thirty years. Liked him better when he fished and took pictures, but I had no grudge against him. He made some money and wanted to make a whole bunch more. Lot of people around here feel the same way."

As if on cue, Persis Sanford moved into view, her mountainous frame clad in a bright pantsuit the color of ripe eggplant.

"Used to be quite an item, those two. Although you could say that about Persis and a lot of folks. Before she got so beamy. Still, there's plenty of men on the island who wouldn't mind Persis keeping them warm at night. Didn't bother with us near and dear, though. Went for the summer boys. She knew us all too well, she said." Ken laughed. "You know, as Aesop said, 'Familiarity breeds contempt.' Well, that was the problem." He laughed some more. "Course, it was Mark Twain who added 'and children' to the line."

Ken had a degree from the University of Maine, Faith knew, but she was still startled when he sprinkled references like these in the midst of his decidedly Down East parlance. It reminded her of what Lyle had said about Harold—the way Hapswell adopted the local speech patterns to lure customers, returning to his native Constitution State cadences once the deal was done.

The mention of children reminded Faith of something that had been nagging at her. She hadn't heard any mention of wife or family. Ursula had said that as far as she knew, Hapswell wasn't married. Maybe Ken knew more.

"Was he ever married? Have any kids?"

"Not that I know of. Always had a woman

around, but they generally moved on and Harold stayed put."

Faith wasn't surprised. She remembered the way the man's smile had transformed his face. He wasn't bad-looking, and in the last few years, anyway, he'd have had money, although the vehicle he'd left by the lighthouse was an old Ford pickup.

"What about other family?"

Ken smiled. "Why don't you just ask who's going to get his pile, Faith? And I'll tell you I haven't a clue. Had a few dogs. Mebbe he left it to them, because I never heard of anybody else, but relatives have a surprising way of crawling out from the woodwork when there's money around."

Faith laughed and slipped in another question. "Why did he come to Sanpere?"

"I suppose it was like a lot of people who aren't local. Came for the summer when he was young—his folks had a place. Then, too, there used to be a couple of camps on the island for kids. Maybe he was hitching up the coast with nothing better to do when he was older, came back again, and stayed. People did that in the sixties. It was a very safe choice."

Realizing his blunder, he amended it.

"I mean, for most people. The ones who know enough to stay off slippery rocks when they want to snap a picture. Nobody bothers you here, unless you bother them. Until recently, you could scrape by on not much. Now with all these out-of-staters buying up everything, housing's a problem. But not when Harold came. Also a good place to be if you don't want to be found."

At that, Ken apparently decided he'd said enough on the subject. "Did I ever tell you that in my dad's time lobster was two cents a pound? You could hardly give it away, and we'd complain when Mother served it twice in a week." Faith took the hint and went back to work. Ken was going to stick to neutral topics. Besides, a new crowd was arriving, a hungry crowd.

Sanpere was a very musical island, and the Melodic Mariners had been followed by a variety of offerings, ranging from a man who looked to be in his nineties delighting the audience with old tunes picked out on a flat-back mandolin to one of a number of local garage bands, good enough to have played Camden. Now a sixteen-piece all-island swing band was setting up in the dusk. The swimming pool fund-raisers had strung Christmas lights between the poles with floodlights, which normally illuminated the pier at night. By the time Tom came to claim his wife, all the lights were on and the place looked dreamlike.

"Believe it or not, the only food left are hot dogs, hamburgers, and whoopie pies. Plenty of soda—sorry, make that tonic—and coffee. But not a single fritter, no chowder, nothing with scales of any kind."

"Except for that," Tom quipped as the band tuned up.

"If you make another pun, I won't dance with you."

"Just try and stop me."

Working on an all-male crew, pounding nails, and staining his T-shirts with the sweat of his brow were definitely having an effect on her husband. Much more of it and he'd be out banging drums in the woods.

"Come on, you. Let's dance," she said, stripping off her hair net and gloves, enjoying the light breeze once she was out from under the tent. Her talk with Ken had left her feeling the way she was supposed to feel on Sanpere—relaxed and on vacation. Harold had gone to the beach to take pictures of the lighthouse for a brochure for a bed-and-breakfast or even for Sanpere Shores, the lighthouse being notable local color. He'd slipped and drowned in the incoming tide. The spray painting, arson, and ghoulish dummy were the work of KSS, whose over-the-top actions would be bound to get its members caught soon and then they'd be forced to disband. There was nothing mysterious about any of it. At least not tonight, she told herself, settling into her husband's arms. It was a simple waltz, and that was something Tom could do.

The band was good. Better than good. Great. Faith and Tom whirled about, passing the other dancers. Their plumber passed them with his little girl. She was standing on his shoes, clutching his hands, her head thrown back in delight as he danced her close to the band. Couples who'd obviously been dancing for years matched their steps as perfectly as Arthur and Katherine, if not Fred and Ginger. The Fairchilds kept dancing as the band played on, number after number. Nan and Freeman Marshall passed them. Freeman winked as if to say, Didn't know the old geezer could cut a rug, did you? Faith heard his voice inside her head, and other voices, too. Their friends Elliot and Louise Frazier—Elliot, the retired postmaster; Louise still with a trace of the southern accent she'd brought to the island as a bride. And Jill and Earl—Earl still in uniform, Jill in a gauzy white linen sundress, looking like a bride already. She blew the Fairchilds a kiss and happily called out something they couldn't hear. The music kept playing. Terri and Donald Osborn swept by, their steps unrecognizable. A tango? A samba? Or perhaps the two combined? Their Birkenstocks hit the asphalt pier with a steady *splat, splat*. Like Linda, Terri favored the flower-child look, and some of her beads had become entangled with her long earrings. Then there was Linda herself, dancing with Kenny Sanford. And why not? He'd probably worked on her cabin, too. They rocked from side to side, just barely in time to the music. Kenny seemed to be counting. His mother careened by, scattering couples in her wake. She was dancing with Roland, who was red-faced from the exertion of keeping up. And they kept coming—Seth Marshall, his mother, Sonny, Becky, and yet more Prescotts, as well as Hamiltons and Sanfords, and John Eggleston, the wood sculptor, and the Durgen brothers from the funeral home and so many more people that it seemed the pier would collapse from the weight. Tom spun Faith around faster and faster. The tempo increased. Above her head, the lights streamed against the darkness like a string of comets. The music got louder and louder. The saxophone player was playing into her left ear. People were laughing. Tom was laughing, too. He was kissing her neck, then her mouth. Faith realized she was going to scream, and she broke from his arms, running to the side, where onlookers sat on the beach chairs they'd brought or perched on the stone blocks that lined the sides of the pier. Panting, she dropped onto the nearest one and closed her eyes. The music grew fainter and the whirling in her head stopped.

"Faith, what is it? Are you all right?" Tom took her hand in both of his.

She opened her eyes to the man who had seemed to be a stranger a few seconds ago.

"It's all right, darling. I just got a little dizzy."

"Do you want to go home?" he asked. The concern in his voice surrounded her like the fog that was starting to roll in.

She nodded, realized that away from the lights, it was too dark for him to see her, and said, "Yes. I want to go home."

There weren't many streetlights on Granville's Main Street. An overflow from the crowd on the pier had gathered in smaller groups—some in the light, some in the shadows, and a whole lot in cars and trucks. Brown paper bags were being passed around, and as Faith walked to where Tom had left the car, she heard the sounds of laughter, love-making, and an occasional argument.

Persis's Cadillac, directly under one of the lights, was as conspicuous as the woman herself, and she made no attempt to hide the bottle of Wild Turkey she and her friends were passing around. Their conversation was no secret, either.

"See my Kenny with that witch from KSS—you know she tried to kill me—doing something that mighta been dancin'?"

"Come on, Persis. Maybe Kenny's just trying to get some for himself."

"Even that Miss Mouse is too much woman for him. If I hadn't been in labor for God knows how many days, I'd swear he wasn't mine!"

There was loud laughter, and someone said something Faith didn't catch. Then Persis said, "Can't pretend to be sorry when I'm not. Good riddance to bad rubbish."

"Ssssh," someone said. "Here comes that minister and his wife."

"They're okay. She's working on the play," Persis replied, and hailed Faith from the open car window.

"We appreciate all you're doing to help us get the pool. You must have fried five hundred fritters today. You have a good night, now. See you at the next rehearsal." She rolled the window back up on the smoke-filled, whisky-fumed interior before Faith could answer.

"Didn't know you and Persis were such buddies," Tom commented, tightening the arm he had around her waist.

"I don't think we are, but you never know." They were almost at their car. "I hope Kenny didn't hear any of that. He was in front of us."

"I hope not, too, but I don't see him now," Tom said, and then abruptly they both stopped walking, hesitating in the darkness.

Behind them, they had heard a sharp slap, the unmistakable sound of flesh connecting with flesh. But it wasn't Kenny and Persis or anything to do with that family's dynamics. It was another family's.

"If I ever catch you doing anything like that again, you will go straight to your grandma's until school starts! Do you hear me, young lady!" shouted an angry male voice.

"I was only being polite. Someone asks you to dance, you don't want to hurt their feelings."

Faith knew that voice. It was female; it was Juliet's.

"Hamiltons don't have no feelings, and don't you forget it. I see that boy around you again anywhere 'cept where he's supposed to be for this play, he's dead, you hear me. He's dead."

Seven

"It's the loneliest of all the lighthouse stations in the United States. Twenty miles from the mainland, and I don't know if you could even call it an island. More like a big ledge or rock. That's what it's called, Mount Desert Rock. The force of the winter seas there can move seventy-five-ton boulders as if they were some of your LEGO bricks." Ursula was continuing her lighthouse tales before a rapt audience of Ben and both his parents.

"But it goes to show you what people will do even in the worst of circumstances. Mount Desert Rock—a half acre, if that—is the site of God's Rock Garden. After the lighthouse was built, lobstermen and other mariners would bring bags of soil of all sorts and sizes every spring. Sometimes they just had the dirt in their pockets. Yet it was worth all the money in the world to the people on the rock. The keepers and their families would pat it into the cracks, then plant seeds. I heard one of the keeper's wives on the radio once, reminiscing about what she grew: nasturtiums, zinnias, bachelor's buttons, carrots, lettuce, peas, and beans. It must have been a sight—all those colors. During the winter, every speck of soil would be washed off, but they'd just start again the next spring."

Faith didn't know whether to feel uplifted or depressed. The story was inspirational—an example of the indomitable human spirit—but she also imagined herself as the keeper's wife: Here we go again. The damn water's washing all our hard work away and how did I end up on this godforsaken rock in the first place? God should have arranged it so his rock garden was a whole lot farther above sea level.

Clearly, none of these cynical thoughts were crossing the minds of those around her. Ben was quite obviously picturing himself funneling the precious earth into the crevices and planting, say, corn or watermelons or even pumpkins. Big stuff.

"That's an amazing story, Ursula," Tom said. "I'd like to work it into a sermon. Think of the mustard seed."

Faith sighed. She *had* married a minister, after all, and conversations like this were par for the course. Not that she wasn't proud, but when she thought of mustard seeds, she thought of Dijon or dill pickles.

"Tell us some more," Ben begged.

"Well, let me see." Ursula paused to drink some of the rich, chocolately hot cocoa Faith had made.

The weather on the island had cooled down, and they had even had a few showers in the morning.

"There was one group that wasn't happy when so many lighthouses began to be built. These were the mooncussers."

"Mooncussers! What does that mean?" Ben asked, darting a look at his mother. Oh joy, was Mrs. Rowe *swearing*?

"Exactly what it sounds like—people who cursed the moon, the full moon in particular, because it shed too much light, and light was the enemy of the mooncusser."

Tom smiled. "I know about mooncussers."

"Me, too," said Faith, who had read Daphne du Maurier's *Jamaica Inn* at least twice. "They were horrible, though, and caused a great deal of harm. Were there many on Sanpere?"

"They were everywhere. You see, Ben, the law says that if you find something on the beach that the tide's brought in, it's yours. The mooncussers would deliberately cause shipwrecks, then claim the cargo that floated ashore for themselves."

"How could they wreck a ship from the shore?"

"They'd swing a lantern to lure the ships into an unsafe harbor. The captain would think the signal meant it was all right. If the moon was bright, the captain would see what lay ahead and avoid it."

"So the mooncussers cussed the moon!"

"And, later, the lighthouses."

"Mooncussers were really pirates, and there was nothing romantic about them," Tom added.

"They didn't always wait for the cargo to come ashore, but would board the wrecked ship. Laws were passed, making a deliberate shipwreck punishable by death, but the practice continued until the Civil War."

"More," said Ben, reaching for a peanut butter cookie as large as his hand and settling himself comfortably against the cushions of the sofa.

"Tomorrow," Ursula said, and gave him a kiss. "You run along with your cookie."

And he did.

Faith and Tom went up together to tuck him in, returning to sit with Ursula a bit longer.

"It must have been terrifying," Ursula said. "To think you were coming into a good harbor, only to have your boat dashed upon the rocks."

"The precursors of hijackings," Tom commented.

"But pure avarice, no politics," Faith interjected.

"Greed has always been easier to understand." Ursula sighed.

Tom stretched. "Got to get a good night's sleep. I want to be in Ellsworth by ten, and with our luck, we'll get behind someone from Minnesota or some other place who's traveling at twenty miles an hour, and it will add an hour to our trip."

Tom really was going native. Lyle had been complaining the other day about how much longer it took him to get anywhere in the summer; then Faith had heard the same thing from Ted Hamilton at rehearsal. Islanders automatically added at least thirty minutes to their driving time after the Fourth of July.

"You'll have fun, dear," Ursula said, patting Faith on the shoulder as she went toward the stairs. "Choosing paint colors always makes it seem like the work is near completion."

Lyle had announced on Friday that they'd start painting on Wednesday. Pleased that it was so soon and alarmed at having to make such momentous decisions so fast, Faith was about to make her very first trip to a Home Depot.

"Why didn't you tell me about this place before!" Faith exclaimed. "Forget Gracious Home!"

Tom had been spending many, many hours at the Home Depot closest to their home in Aleford, Massachusetts, bringing back countertop samples and cabinet brochures for Faith's consideration. She had had neither the time nor the inclination to go to the store in person. She'd seen it from Route 128. Hangarlike spaces filled with lumber, tools, and plumbing fixtures were not her idea of fun shopping destinations. Now, she had completely changed her mind.

They'd gotten there late. After dropping the kids off at camp at nine, they had indeed ended up behind a slow driver—this one from Maryland: Tom had continued fuming until he ripped past just before Blue Hill. It was after 10:30 when they pulled into Ellsworth. This was lunchtime for contractors, builders, and other early risers who needed nails in a hurry. Like Lyle, they wore serious-looking tape measures clipped to their belts. Tom had taken to wearing one, too, and in his worn jeans, work boots, and Barton's Lumber cap, he blended right in. Even his T-shirt with the slogan DOG IS GOD SPELLED BACKWARD, which one of the only members of the vestry with a sense of humor had given him, didn't raise an eye.

The store smelled wonderful. Like new wood and fresh paint. Then there were all these extremely helpful people. Salespeople. Actually around when you needed them. They had their names on their aprons and wore various sorts of pins for selling a thousand faucets or whatever. It was all very intriguing. Tom wanted to check out a light fixture for the deck while Faith selected the paint colors.

"You're way better than I am at this sort of thing. Knock yourself out."

When he got to the paint aisle a good forty-five minutes later—he'd gotten sidetracked by the solar garden lighting—Faith was deep in conversation with Ted.

"Better stick to the formula, deah. Those fellas generally know what they're doing," he was advising.

"Oh, Tom, I was just explaining to Ted—Ted, Tom, Tom, Ted—that this would be the perfect color for our bedroom, but more tomato bisque, not cream of tomato."

"The names are pretty funny, aren't they?" Tom chuckled.

"They are, but these are my names."

"Mebbe you two want to discuss it a little longer." Ted diplomatically removed himself from the discussion. He'd seen an old movie once where a lady acted the same way—wanted the walls of her "dream house" to match the A&P's best butter and apple blossoms, but just before they fell, not after.

Tom was looking at the chips Faith had laid out on the counter. "Gentle Clarity, Peaceful Time, Nostalgic Tale—I think I may have found my true calling. Forget having to write a whole sermon; I can name paint."

"You missed Angel's Gaze and Hope Floats," Faith added.

"Okay, so what *have* you picked?"

"I feel silly saying them, but here goes—Cozy Melon for our room; Alpine Lace for the big room; Bubbling Brook for Ben's; Touch of Nectar for Amy's and the upstairs bath; Water's Edge—couldn't resist—for the guest room and downstairs bath."

"What about the trim? If we have the same color throughout, it will make life a lot simpler—and the job will go faster."

"Already thought of that," Faith said. Although, the perfect color—crème fraîche with a touch of chèvre—had a name she just couldn't overlook: Lighthouse. She'd think of it every time she dusted, every time she walked by. And at the moment, the word *lighthouse* was something she wanted to keep far from her thoughts.

"How about Oslo? You've always been partial to Scandinavians." Tom had dated a Norwegian exchange student his senior year in high school, and they continued to send each other cards at Christmas. Inge had four children, and Faith was happy to see the effects of that and a little too much lutefisk in this year's picture. Still had that damn long blond hair, though.

"Oslo it is. Now, let's get this all ordered and then I'll take you to lunch."

They wandered around while Ted mixed the paint. Faith found herself unaccountably picking up brochures about refinishing your own furniture and laying tile. She began to think she should have sponge-painted some of the walls. Projects beckoned—and objects, thousands and thousands of objects.

"Look at that tubing, Tom. It would make a wonderful outdoor sculpture," she enthused.

She was heading for the plants and shrubs when he grabbed her. "Faith, get a grip. We can come back. You're like a kid in a candy store!"

He was laughing. This was the last reaction he'd expected from his high-fashion, label-conscious wife. Faith Sibley Fairchild was fast becoming a Home Depot junkie.

He managed to get her out with only the addition of a large round mirror, etched at the edge with leaves. As they pushed the large flatbed cart toward the car, Faith felt her head clear and she came somewhat back to her senses. She realized she had two Formica chips in her hand, with no memory of having taken them.

"Do you think it's the lighting? Do they spray

something in the air or what? And Ted. No one can be that nice after working a long shift. He's got to be an alien."

They transferred their purchases to the trunk.

"Why don't we discuss the matter over two very large lobster rolls?" Tom suggested. "And if you're very good, you can have pie for dessert."

Happily filled with the food and the pleasure of being alone with Tom, Faith went to the school to put in a little time on *Romeo and Juliet*. The lobster roll had been perfect—plenty of lobster meat, Hellman's mayonnaise, and a little salt and pepper piled on a hot dog roll that had been toasted in butter. No frou-frou ingredients like capers, not even lettuce. It wasn't on the Atkins diet—or any diet—but it was sublime.

She went backstage to get the old shirt she wore to cover her clothes. No one was rehearsing at the moment. Roland was sitting by himself, bent over a notebook. He looked up and smiled.

"I haven't had a chance to thank you for all your help."

"I'm having fun," Faith said, meaning it. "The play will be wonderful. I'm amazed at some of the performances you've been able to get from the actors."

"There's a lot of talent on the island," he said. "People underestimate themselves—and of course everybody underestimates everybody else. When I first proposed this idea as a fundraiser, people thought I was crazy. But then, they're used to that. From me, I mean. I got it when I started the Latin program. Now the kids have a Roman banquet, complete with togas, every year and sweep the state in the Latin competitions."

Faith had heard about this. It took just one person. Like the teacher who got all the kids fired up about chess years ago. Since then, Sanpere routinely went on to the national competitions.

"I thought you taught English."

"I did, but Latin is a kind of hobby of mine, and I taught it to the kids who were interested. When I was a kid, my idea of heaven was to go to the Museum of Fine Arts in Boston to look at the Roman antiquities. Yeah, and I learned a lot from the Greek vases, too, although they didn't have the really sexy ones on exhibit then."

"You're from Boston?"

"Home of the bean and the cod. I came here summers and took a temporary teaching job at the high school after college. After a while, temporary became permanent."

"Sanpere does have a way of growing on you," Faith admitted. Her first summer on the island was supposed to have been the only one.

Ted Hamilton walked in, smelling strongly of bait.

"Sorry, Mr. Hayes. I changed, but I didn't want to take time for a shower. Besides, Ma's screaming about the electric bills."

"You want to go over some lines?" Faith offered. They could always sit outside. Downwind.

"Sure," Ted said, and looked at Roland, who nodded.

"Again, our thanks," he said to Faith, who told him once more that she was glad to help.

What was Roland Hayes's story? All these years on the island. Didn't he ever miss the city? Admittedly, Boston was a pale imitation of the real thing, the Big Apple, yet it still offered a wide range of activities—and food. She almost laughed out loud. At lunch, Tom and she had figured out the sure way to make their fortune—a Chinese restaurant on Sanpere. A take-out place with pu-pu platters, sweet-and-sour everything, egg foo yung, chop suey—all the things the islanders were crazy about, driving as far as Ellsworth for a fix.

She told Ted about it as they went outside.

"I wish you would. The chicken wings and egg rolls at China Hill are some good. I can demolish a bagful."

"Well, let's think Italian now."

"Do you think Romeo ate pizza? I mean, did they have it back then? Sure, they must have had spaghetti and meatballs, but what about pizza? Think he had a slice in his hand when he climbed up to the balcony?"

"Why not?" Faith answered. "The Romans ate lasagna, and supposedly the Etruscans, who came before them, had macaroni. This was all long before Shakespeare was around. I doubt if he was familiar with the cuisine, though. The English have always been a little slow to adopt food that isn't cooked for several hours, like their veg-

183

etables. As for pizza . . . well, something like it—toppings spread on dough—has existed virtually since early man started cooking with fire."

"I'll have a thick-crust mastodon, double cheese, to go," Ted quipped. He really was very cute, and Faith had no trouble seeing why Becky was so attracted to him. And he to her. What a mess it all was, and how stupid their families were being. The surest way the Prescotts could drive Becky into Ted's arms was to object. Forbidden fruit.

Juliet herself arrived after her stint at the inn and flopped down on the grass. Faith rehearsed them both, feeling very much like a third wheel, but, in this case, essential. Much as she would like to give them some time alone together, she agreed with Roland's warning to Becky. It wouldn't even have to be a family member driving by. That the two were alone on the lawn of the elementary school would reach Prescott and Hamilton ears like wildfire and the whole production could go up in smoke. Reflecting that a little more supervision of those long-ago Verona teens would have prevented a lot of unhappiness, Faith, the duenna, stood her ground.

Another house site was torched Tuesday night. And this time, no one appeared on the scene to save the construction. Fire departments from up and down the coast fought to keep the flames from spreading to the acres of woods surrounding the lot, which had been cleared for extensive landscaping. Roland and others in the cast were members of Sanpere's volunteer fire company. After dropping the kids off at camp Wednesday morning, Faith found a note postponing the rehearsal until the afternoon.

"They're exhausted," said Becky, who came up behind Faith. "They worked all night. I didn't think we'd have a rehearsal until later, but I thought I'd check."

"It's horrible. Who can be doing this?" Ursula and the Fairchilds had gotten the news before they went to bed, and Tom had left grim-faced this morning.

"Those jerks. The KSS people." Becky was very definite. "Earl will get them."

Linda. Linda was a KSS member. How could she be involved in arson? She didn't even kill mosquitoes. Maybe in her mind, property was different.

"You know the funny thing?" Becky continued.

Faith always wanted to know the funny thing, because used in this manner, it didn't mean ha-ha.

"What?"

"The guy who's building the place took down every tree for I don't know how many acres. Had all the rocks dug out, made a long wall with a big iron gate. We've all been joking about 'the palace.' He wanted to be able to pick apples, so he had an orchard of full-grown trees ordered. Ready to go in this week. If he hadn't done all that, the fire would have spread and burned every bit of forest on that whole point. It stopped at the dirt."

It *was* ironic. His destruction of the environment had saved it.

"Can you believe that, though?" Becky shook her head. "I mean, planting full-grown apple trees, so you can pick the fruit right away? I think God meant for people to have to wait and watch them grow, but that's just my opinion. I wouldn't mind having the money those trees cost. Well, I have to get to work. See you." She jumped in her car, an ancient Valiant. When it came to cars, the island was a veritable *Kelley Blue Book* Who's Who.

With a morning suddenly free, Faith decided to go make sure the paint on the walls looked the same as the color on the chips. Ted or no Ted, she was sure they could always add white—or Oslo.

On the way, she thought about those apple trees. She felt sorry—more than sorry—for the person who had just lost a summer's worth of work on a new house. She had heard about "the palace," but not about the apple trees. The whole notion gave her a slightly sick, "Let them eat cake" feeling—Marie Antoinette and her buddies dressing up as milkmaids to mimic the peasantry, cavorting in an immaculate barn, cows beribboned, sterling-silver milk pails. Becky was right: In nature, you were supposed to wait for the harvest, even if that meant you didn't always get to see it. You planted trees for tomorrow, not today. She had a vision of a couple in knife-creased khaki shorts and Lauren Polo shirts, skipping through their full-blown orchard, an apple basket woven to their specifications in hand.

It was a relief to pull into her own cottage's dusty drive, which was rutted from the various workmen's trucks going in and out. No apple trees.

"Faith! Glad you're here," said Tom. "I thought they'd cancel rehearsal. Roland was out there all night. Lyle, too. It's just Kenny and me. He went home at four, but he says he's not tired."

"Do you want me to paint?" Having done scenery, and with vestiges of her Home Depot mind-set still in place, Faith was ready to tackle a wall or two or three.

Tom looked slightly shocked. Faith? Working on the house? His project . . . He made a quick recovery. "Honey, that would be great. Maybe later. But when I got here this morning, UPS had left a package for Freeman and Nan mixed in with our delivery. Could you take it over to them? It may be important."

Kenny appeared. He still smelled like smoke. She hoped it wasn't getting into the paint.

"Hi, Kenny," she said. "Are you sure you're not too tired to work?"

"Hi. Nope. I'm okay," and, blushing, he went back into the house with the can of paint he'd come to get.

"I'll bring lunch back for you both," Faith promised.

Tom gave her a kiss. "That would be terrific, sweetheart. Take your time."

"Don't worry," Faith looked him in the eye. "I'm not going to invade your turf. Paint away."

He had the grace to look sheepish.

"Well, Mother will be darned pleased. It's her new Crock-Pot. She's been lost since her old one gave out on her and the Sears folks said they couldn't fix it," Freeman said, taking the package from Faith. "Thanks for bringing it round."

Faith wasn't surprised. Although Nan Marshall fried her fish in her great-grandmother's iron skillets, made her beans in her grandmother's bean pot, and mixed her batter in her mother's Pyrex mixing bowls—ranging from the big yellow one to the little blue one—the Crock-Pot was her own addition to the family *batterie de cuisine*. She'd often extolled its virtues to Faith: "I plug it in, turn it on, go fishing with Freeman, and when we come back, there's beef stew—finest kind." "Finest kind" was the highest compliment possible in Maine, used to describe the very best in everything from fried clams to a gas station. Faith had been impressed with Nan's description, yet not enough to trade in her own stew pot, a *marmite*, lugged back from Dehellerin, the Paris restaurant-supply house.

"It was no bother. I'm glad I could drop it off," she told Freeman. Faith was always happy to pay a call on the Marshalls. "Besides, Tom doesn't really want me at the house until it's all done. I guess then he'll break a bottle of champagne against a door, carry me over the threshold, and cry his eyes out."

Freeman nodded. "Nothing like building your own home. We had to live in a tent, then with Nan's mother—and believe me, I'd have stayed in the tent, 'cept the snow kept piling up and collapsing it—but it was worth it." He looked back over his shoulder at their snug little house—the house where they had raised four children and now regularly entertained their grandchildren for overnights and longer.

"Is Nan around?" Faith asked. If she was inside canning, Faith could give her a hand. Everybody seemed to have a purpose, except for Faith herself at the moment. Freeman had been mending traps when she'd arrived.

"Gone to help her sister put up zucchini relish. Told her not to bring even one pot back, unless she intended to eat it herself. Nasty stuff. You give me some bread and butter pickles—or watermelon ones, if you want to get fancy—any day."

"The zucchini seems to be the only thing growing in this drought. I guess they're trying to use them any way they can."

"Shouldn't plant any in the first place," Freeman said decisively. "Never could understand the point of planting stuff that grows well but you don't want to eat. Nan says I'm foolish. If not wanting zucchini every day, disguised on my plate to look like something tasty, is foolish, then so be it."

Sharing his opinion that a little zucchini goes a long way, Faith said good-bye and turned to go.

"Well, aren't you going to tell me about it?" Freeman asked.

"About what?"

"About what's making your face look like it can't decide whether it's going to be mad or sad. Come on, now." He patted the spot next to him on the bench and she sat down.

But where to begin? Looking out over Penobscot Bay—the sky stretched over the sea in an enormous canopy—gave her a moment to search for the words. It was sunny and clear all the way to Swans Island, which lay far in the distance. Freeman's boat, named for his wife, was bobbing contentedly on the outgoing tide. All should have been right with the world.

Finally, she said, "It's that everything is so different this summer on Sanpere. Not just finding the body."

"True, that's not all that out of the ordinary for you," Freeman commented dryly. "But still pretty unsettling, don't you think?"

"Yes, but I was feeling this way before that. The lobster war. The attacks on the construction sites. All these different groups on the island going at one another's throats."

"Aside from the attacks, business as usual, I'd say." Freeman looked up from his work. "I don't mean that all this isn't very serious, but a lot of it is stuff that goes on all the time. Summer people—and I'm using the label in the nicest way where you're concerned—think that Sanpere is some kind of Eden. No one looks cross-eyed at anyone else, there isn't a soul on the island who would ever cheat you, and everyone who lives here, from the babes at their mothers' titties to the old coots like me, is as happy as a clam at high water. Right?"

Faith nodded. It was true that a lot of summer people tended to view the island in Technicolor, music and lyrics by Rodgers and Hammerstein.

"So when you go to"—he grinned—"say, a Planning Board meeting, and see some things that aren't very pretty—course I heard about it—or you come to know that two families are quarreling over what seems like a pretty small piece of this great big ocean, you're bound to think all kinds of snakes have made their way into the garden."

"You're right," Faith admitted. "But why *are* the Hamiltons and Prescotts feuding? I know it has to do with territory, but surely there's room for everyone's pots? Can't one of them move theirs?" The water in front of them looked infinite.

Freeman put the trap down.

"Mother left a plate of molasses cookies and coffee. Let's get some and I'll try to explain. It ain't easy."

"How do you know where you can put your traps anyway?" Faith asked once they were inside at the kitchen table, which was set in front of a bay window Freeman had installed as a gift for Nan last year. Her prize African violets marched along the broad sill. A similar platoon, but this one of photographs, was lined up on a shelf to one side of the woodstove. Babies, brides, and graduates.

Faith reached for a cookie and settled back.

"Where your traps are set," Freeman told her,

"is based on where your family's traps have always been set, going back for several generations,
mostly. My son and I fish the eastern side off Isle
au Haut, because that's where my father and
grandfather had their traps. The whole ocean is
carved up that way. Problem comes two ways.
You have people who are just plain greedy and
don't care about the kingdom of heaven. They'll
move in on your territory and cut maybe thirty
traps so's they can take over."

"You mean cut the rope from the lobster pot to
the trap? Then when you pull a trap, there would
be nothing attached?" Faith was shocked. She
knew the kind of financial loss thirty traps meant.
The metal traps—not so picturesque for the
tourists as the wooden ones—were a boon to the
fishermen. They didn't move around on the bottom the way the old ones did, were easier to main-
tain, and lighter. But they were expensive. Each
one cost about fifty dollars, not counting the lines,
doughnut, and pot buoy. There was also the catch
in each trap—which would be left to rot—to figure in when calculating a loss of this magnitude.

"Yup. They might leave you alone for a week or
so after that, then do it again. Most folks move
right away, rather than risk losing any more
gear."

"But what about the laws? Isn't there a warden
or something?"

"Sure, but how are you going to prove it? Only
way would be for the warden to close down the
whole area to everyone, and that hasn't happened."

"But it's a small island. Doesn't it get around who's doing it?" Faith had visions of enlisting the Sewing Circle and ridding the seas of these pirates, latter-day mooncussers.

"Everybody knows, but we're not talking about the boys who won prizes for perfect attendance at Sunday school. People are too afraid of them to band together. There aren't a whole lot of ways to make a living here, Faith, and you've got to protect and provide for your family in the best way you can. Sometimes that means not doing anything."

Faith felt even more depressed.

"But what about the Hamiltons and the Prescotts? Is this how it started? Traplines cut?"

Freeman shook his head. "No, they fall into the second category." He refilled their mugs.

"Now, this kind of thing between two families gets pretty complicated, because you have Hamiltons with Prescott grandfathers and vice versa. You can be married a bunch of times on Sanpere and never change your in-laws. Who's entitled to fish where has always been a little hard to figure out in these cases, but mostly it's settled in a friendly fashion. Problem started when one of the Hamiltons set his son up with a new boat. The boy was able to get a license and set his traps. The Prescotts claimed that it was their territory; the Hamiltons said it was theirs. Traps were emptied and a few lines cut."

"I heard shots were fired."

Freeman shook his head. "Firecrackers on the

Fourth, but by now, it's the Saint Valentine's Day Massacre."

Like the old telephone game, Faith thought, where you whisper "My dog has fleas" to the first person and by the time the message goes full circle, it's "Head for the high seas."

"How's it going to end?" she asked.

"It will peter out. Or someone will decide to put a stop to it. It's not like the other business. Gorry, I don't know how some of them can look the co-op manager in the eye when they go to sell their catch. Told my son years ago, when he was starting out with me as sternman, that we may not haul as many lobsters as some, but we know each one is honestly ours."

Faith knew how hard it was to make a living on Sanpere, although lobstering had been good enough for the last few seasons to give rise to a whole flock of new 4×4's in driveways and trips to Orlando in the winter. Still, with the necessity for restrictions to ensure that there would be future catches, fishing was, at best, a chancy occupation. Plus, before you even hauled a trap come the end of May, you were looking at an investment each year of over $35,000 for fuel, maintaining your boat, bait, equipment, insurance, a license, tags, a mooring fee, registration, and wages for a sternman. Then for many fishermen, there was what was owed on the boat.

"Did you ever think of doing anything other than fishing?" she asked Freeman.

He shook his head. "It's not just alst I know; it's

what I love. Sounds corny, right? But no one tells me what to do or when to do it. Then, too, I'd go crazy with an indoor job. A job away from the water. Figure it must have been my ancestors who were the ones first started lobsterin' three hundred years ago. Ken Layton tells me lobsters were five or six feet long and the shore rocks were crawling with them when the first off-islanders came—and those people were really from away, Europe." He laughed.

Faith had never heard this, but if Ken said so, she believed it. The crustaceans must have looked like prehistoric creatures—and the meat must have been pretty tough. Her thought reminded her that it was August 15, Assumption Day for some Christians and the day when plants and animals were supposed to shed any noxious traits, producing food that was pure and wholesome—fresh for a long time. To celebrate, Faith reached for another cookie and took a big bite, enjoying the crunch of the granulated sugar Nan had dusted on top. She wondered if the shedding of poisonous attributes applied to humans, as well.

"So has this old windbag helped? Can we see one of your pretty smiles?" Freeman, cajoled. He was a wicked flirt.

"I guess, although it doesn't explain all the fires and the attacks on the construction sites. Do you think the KSS people are doing it?"

"I don't know what to think. It's never happened before—but then, we never had houses like this here before. I'm no tree-hugger, but I'm as upset as the next man about what's happening on this island. These people from out of state who are building these big houses are bringing money to the island. I can't deny that, but they're changing the landscape forever as far as I'm concerned. My grandchildren can't go to the places me and my children grew up loving here. There are chains and wired fences to keep us locals out. The beach where the elementary school had its end-of-school picnic for as long as anyone can remember and then some is off-limits. Private. Clammers and wormers are shut out of the flats that they depend on to make a living. Besides keeping us out, these people do whatever they want to the land. Take down every pine, birch, and tamarack to put in fancy shrubs."

"And orchards," Faith added.

He nodded and looked at her appraisingly. "Got your ear to the ground, haven't you? Full-grown trees, not just fruit trees. I never heard the like. But no matter how much you disagree, you don't go around setting fires, destroying property. It's the same thing as cutting a trapline. And if it is the KSS people, then they're worse than I thought. Obnoxious group of know-it-alls was what they seemed at the beginning. I don't know what they are now. *They* make out that they're the real Sanpere Islanders these days, but just because you pull a cat out of the oven, doesn't make it a biscuit."

Pausing first to relish Freeman's metaphor, Faith asked, "And how about Harold Hapswell's death? Do you think it was an accident?" She drained her coffee mug. Freeman set his down with a thunk.

"Faith Fairchild! Do you mean to sit here in my own kitchen and tell me you're looking to make this into another murder! Harold Hapswell slipped on the rocks. That's it. Case closed."

There hadn't been much to say after Freeman's declaration. Nan's arrival—she tried to hide the bag she was carrying—turned the conversation to safer subjects, like Crock-Pots, grandchildren, and, inevitably, zucchini. Faith left with two jars of relish. After taking Tom and Kenny two large Italians—the Down East equivalent of other regions' grinders, subs, and hoagies—she went back to rehearsal. Throughout the afternoon, as she painted Linda's sketch of the Capulets' Victorian summer "cottage," Faith kept wondering why Freeman had been so adamant about the cause of Harold's death. His words weren't uttered as opinion, but fact. Then fact and opinion joined hands in a very clear message for Faith: Keep your nose out of it.

The Hapswell case was closed. The medical examiner had found nothing inconsistent with a verdict of accidental death. He'd suffered some external injuries, particularly on the right side and back of his head, but he'd fallen long and hard against the granite ledges. Plus, the tide would have banged him about some. She'd heard it all from Tom, who'd heard it directly from Earl.

With her mind filled with thoughts of territory,

tradition, and an unsavory lobster mafia, Faith found it hard to listen to Ben's and Amy's tales of another exciting day at camp—birch-bark boats, a woodland walk, Duck, Duck, Goose. She took the kids back to the Pines and put them to work helping her make dinner. She'd bought fresh crab. Crab cakes were a family favorite (see recipe on page 320). Faith's version included cracker crumbs, and Ben was put in charge of rolling a rolling pin over saltines that had been placed between two pieces of waxed paper. Faith had measured out some Old Bay seasoning, and Amy was stirring it into some mayonnaise for the sauce. All three of them shaped the cakes; then Faith put them in the refrigerator to rest. Later, when Faith served these straight from the skillet, Tom declared they were the best he'd ever eaten.

Her family fed and her progeny in bed, Faith cleaned up and, at last, sank gratefully into one of the chairs on the porch. *Sank* was perhaps not the best term when referring to the Rowes' porch furniture—ancient wicker that left an intricate crosshatching on the back of one's thighs. Faith had had the presence of mind to change into jeans from the shorts she'd been wearing.

"I wonder if I could ask you to do me a favor,' " Ursula said.

"Anything in the world," Faith replied.

"Hmm, maybe I should think a few minutes more," Ursula said, teasing. "No, I don't need them. Could you help me host the Sewing Circle? We're running out of time before the fair, and we all work so much better when we're together than when we're alone. In our own homes, there's always something else that pops up, or maybe we're more competitive than we think. Having someone sitting next to you, needle flying, spurs you on. Anyway, they're coming the day after tomorrow. I hoped you could help Gert with the food and pass things around."

"I would love to," Faith answered readily. She'd heard about Sewing Circle duty from Pix. "I don't actually have a puffed-sleeve smocked dress and Mary Janes on, but they make me feel as if I do," she'd told Faith the last time.

"Nothing fancy. Tea things," Ursula said.

"Tea things it is. Cucumber sandwiches—some with chicken salad or crab, if you like—shortbread, and jam tarts." She'd also do some ribbon and pinwheel sandwiches à la Fannie Farmer.

"Lovely, dear," said Ursula, who was sitting in a Boston rocker. "I knew you'd come through."

Serena Marshall was regaling the group with the story of a camera-laden tourist. She'd looked up from her paper and seen him aiming a lens through her kitchen window.

"Mashing down my petunias, and when I came out to chase him away, he said I'd spoiled his shot!"

"I don't even notice anymore," Louella said. "There are so many pictures of 'Maine Woman in Her Bakery' floating around this country that if I had a nickel for each one, I could retire."

"You should put up a sign and charge them extra for the photos," Serena said. "That's what I told the man who was trying to snap me. Said I had a sitting fee. Well, that's what they call it when you go to a real photographer. When my Donna got married, she had the nicest pictures taken in Bangor, and there it was on the bill, 'sitting fee.' I had no idea you could get charged for sitting down, but she said that was for the curtains and whatnot behind her. So I told this man, 'Hand over a twenty-dollar sitting fee and four dollars and fifty cents for the petunias you've destroyed and we've got a deal.'"

"What did he do?" Ursula asked.

"Oh, he skedaddled. Gave me a dirty look, too."

"No need for him to get all spleeny. He's the one who was trespassing!" one of the women exclaimed indignantly.

Faith knew what *spleeny* meant by now, and it entered the Fairchilds' vocabulary whenever there were disorders associated with said organ, most particularly excessive whining. She wasn't surprised to hear about the insensitive tourist caught up in his Kodak moment. Freeman had told her he felt like he was in a zoo sometimes when he was unloading his catch.

Faith had returned to the kitchen to replenish the plate of tea sandwiches. As she'd predicted, the chive and cheese pinwheels and the chicken salad/Roquefort and walnut ribbons were going fast. She was back just in time to see Mabel Hazard, the town clerk, burst through the front door, pink with excitement. There had been considerable speculation as to Mabel's whereabouts, since everybody knew the office closed at noon and here it was getting on to one o'clock.

"You will never guess what just happened!" she told the group, hushed at her dramatic entrance. Mabel, small and round, with pearly gray hair—ringlets from the perm her sister-in-law had given her at the beginning of the summer, ringlets quivering at the moment—was not a person normally given to dramatic entrances. In fact, Faith thought as she stepped back to become a fly on the wall, this is probably the most dramatic entrance Mabel has ever made, judging from her friends' shocked silence.

She repeated her words, just in case, with a slight alteration. "You will never guess in a million years what just happened!"

"Guess you better spill it out, then," Louella said, and moved over on the couch.

Mabel didn't sit.

"I was getting ready to leave, as usual, when this young woman comes in and asks for Earl. Not by name, but she wants to know where the police department is."

"We don't have a police department," Louise Frazier said, endeavoring to turn the heel of a rainbow-colored sock.

"That's what I told her. I told her that the state police patrol and an officer checks in when he's on the island. 'The room is down the hall,' I said, 'but he isn't there now.' She looked kinda put out and said I would have to do. 'Do what?' I asked her. 'I want to file a missing-persons report,' she said."

Mabel waited for the collective gasp that went up to die down. Faith unconsciously moved farther into the room, forgetting her non–Sewing Circle status.

"Well, I never had anybody ask me that before. You know what I do."

Heads nodded. Mabel collected tax money, issued any number of licenses, collected those fees, registered people to vote, and dealt with all sorts of other things connected to the workings of government.

"I told her she had to contact the state police, and I asked how long the person had been missing."

Relief flooded the room. Mabel had not let whoever it was get away without finding out the salient details. It was this sort of thing that made her such a crackerjack at her job.

" 'Since last week sometime,' she said. That didn't sound like very long to me, but maybe she was supposed to meet someone here for vacation. Except she didn't sound like she was from out of state. I noticed the time and wanted to be on my way, so I told her the office was closed. I suggested she could call Ellsworth and said there was a pay phone outside the Mobil station."

"What did she do then?"

" 'He would have told me if he was going away,' she said, not paying a bit of attention to what I'd said, and I faced the fact that I was going to be late. 'Does the person live here on the island?' I asked. 'Or are they visiting?' She says, 'He lives here. Has for years. His name is Harold Hapswell.' "

"No!" exclaimed several voices, and Faith set the plate of sandwiches down on the nearest table before she dropped it.

"You can imagine my surprise." Everyone nodded. They could.

" 'Oh dear,' I said. 'I'm sorry to tell you that Harold isn't missing. He passed on last week. Are you family?' She just stood there for a moment. I was going to offer her a cup of water from the cooler, but she started to walk out, then stopped and said, 'Damn straight I'm family! I'm his wife!' "

Eight

"Passed on? You mean dead? That's impossible! There wasn't a thing wrong with him. He was supposed to meet me at my house on Monday. I've been calling and leaving messages; then I decided I'd better come on down here. Now, where is Harold?' she said, and meanwhile I'm wondering what more I could tell her. She seemed to think I had him hid in the closet."

The room was hushed. You could have heard a whole paper of pins drop. Mabel had the women in the palm of her hand.

The Sewing Circle, and the entire island, knew where Harold was. In a cardboard box on a shelf in the office window of Durgen's Funeral Home, a great inconvenience to Donald and Marvin Durgen. Space at their establishment was at a premium, and this particular spot had afforded their last clear view down Granville's Main Street. The two brothers were accustomed to keeping their fingers on the pulse of the community. Gazing down at the comings and goings of the local citizenry was not only a favorite pastime but also an occupational necessity. Harold Hapswell wasn't in an urn, because the Durgens were waiting for a relative to step forward and make an appropriate choice—and appropriate payment. The box, not as bulky as their most popular urn—brushed bronze with a perpetual guarantee—was just large enough to get in the way.

As she listened, every woman in the room put herself in Mabel's place—face-to-face with a strange woman, who was obviously in shock, unwilling to admit that Harold's trip to the pearly gates was a fact. How to convey his present whereabouts, as well as the sad circumstances of his demise?

It was Faith who broke the silence. Faith who stepped forward and asked a question—a question already answered in her own mind.

"What did she look like?"

Mabel flushed. "Well, she's tall, pretty, lots of blond hair like Farrah Fawcett has"—time stood still for icons like this on Sanpere—"and she . . . Well, you know the styles today. She had on one of those little shirts, a white one, which stopped before her belly button, and white pants that started pretty far below."

"Was she tan?" Faith asked.

"Just like she'd spent the whole winter in Florida, or maybe owns a tanning booth."

It was the woman in the Mercedes. And she had been on the island at least twice before. Sunning herself on Harold's beach, or, since she was his wife, maybe it was her beach, too. Then at the Planning Board meeting. The Planning Board meeting the night before Harold died.

"Why do you ask, Faith dear?" Ursula said. Nobody minded Faith, or Pix, around when Sewing Circle was at the Pines. Daughters, granddaughters, and nieces filled the same shoes when it was someone else's turn. But aside from a few polite phrases called for by the job, they weren't supposed to speak unless spoken to. Obviously, a lot of things were topsy-turvy on Sanpere lately.

"I saw her first on—let me see. Yes, it was a week ago Tuesday. I had taken the children to the big beach on the point, where Sanpere Shores is going in. When it was time to leave, a black Mercedes was blocking our way. I went to look for the owner. It belonged to that woman. I found her on one of the smaller beaches."

Louella snorted. "I remember when it was a sight to see a clean car in the summer, let alone all these fancy ones. Four or five families could survive for a year on what that must have cost. But who is she? I'd have thought Harold would have said something if he'd gotten hitched. Came to the bakery every morning same time until the day he died, to get a doughnut or scone to go with the coffee he picked up at Sam's place. Guess this wife of his wasn't up to making him breakfast."

Sam Marshall sold gas, coffee, beer, cigarettes, *Uncle Henry's Weekly Swap Guide*, and the other necessities of life in a small store at the top of the hill going from Sanpere Village toward Granville. Louella's bakery was a half mile beyond.

"Then," Faith continued, "she was in the back of the room at the Planning Board meeting last Thursday night."

"Oh *that* woman. I should have put two and two together." Mabel sounded annoyed with herself. "Heard all about her, but nobody seems to know why she was there."

"To give Harold some moral support, and you know he needed it, not to speak ill of the dead," Louella said. "The loonies weren't the only ones with a few questions about that Disneyland he was going to put up."

"How do we know she's telling the truth? About being married to Harold? She must have known him, or else what was she doing at the meeting? But she could have read about Harold's death and decided to try to get her hands on his money," Gert speculated. "Was she wearing a ring, Mabel?"

"Uh-huh. Would have been hard to miss. A rock so big, you'd think she'd have trouble lifting her hand. And there was a thick gold band to match."

Faith was puzzled. The woman hadn't been wearing any rings when Faith had seen her on the beach. She'd noticed her hands, envious of the French manicure the woman managed to main-

208

tain. Perhaps she'd taken the rings off before going to sunbathe. But there hadn't been any tan marks. When Faith took her own rings off to slather the kids and herself with sunblock, she had two bright white lines on her ring fingers. There was another explanation. If married—and there was no reason, Gert notwithstanding, to doubt the woman's assertion—the marriage was a recent event.

Mabel took the floor again. "I told her that he'd slipped on some rocks and hadn't suffered at all, and that Durgen's Funeral Home down the street had taken care of the arrangements. I asked her if she wanted me to call someone, a friend or relative. Said I was sorry for her loss, but she still kept saying it was impossible. Finally, I called the state police myself, and while I was talking to some ten-year-old there who wasn't getting a thing I said, Earl walked in. I've never been so glad to see him in my life, and she was, too. Kind of raced over to him, grabbed his arm, and said, 'What's all this about my husband being dead?' Well, Earl never lets on much, calm as a clock, though he must have been surprised. He took her to his office and told me I could lock up. So I did, and here I am."

Mabel sat down and poured herself a cup of tea. Everybody started talking at once, stopped, and then started again. Faith picked up the plate and passed the sandwiches, which were eagerly consumed. Nothing like a juicy piece of gossip to whet an appetite. As she moved about the room, she heard snatches of conversation.

"Always was a sly one, that Harold. Probably has wives all over the state!"

"What do you think she'll do with Sanpere Shores? Maybe she'll give it to the Island Trust," Louise Frazier said. The Fraziers were active members of that group.

"Hope springs eternal, Louise, but from the sound of the car and the ring, this is someone who's out to cash in, not out."

"No doubt about it. She'll be rich as Croesus."

Mabel had taken out the Sunbonnet Sue baby quilt she was working on, somewhat spent after her time in the limelight. Faith took the last of the sandwiches over and offered to get some of the jam tarts and shortbread from the kitchen.

"These will do just fine, dear. Maybe later."

Questions were nagging at Faith, and she slipped one in before retreating from view, "You said she didn't believe that Harold was dead, but did she seem upset, like she was going to cry?"

"No, I wouldn't say that exactly. Maybe she broke down when Earl talked to her. She just kept on insisting I was wrong. Like I was to blame for him being missing. You know, the way some people think we don't speak English here and say things real slow, so we'll get it."

Faith nodded. She'd witnessed a tourist asking Freeman for directions, using a combination of sign language and carefully enunciated simple phrases. Freeman told her after he'd set the woman on the right course that in situations like that he was tempted to give the wrong directions or fall back on the old "You can't get there from here" line. Either one would reinforce the stereotype nicely.

Loading the cake plate in the kitchen, Faith looked at the clock. The ladies would be here another hour at least; then she'd have to pick up the kids. It would be quite a while before she could get to Earl.

"She's done very well for people. I don't know what you're suggesting, Louella!" Vera Hamilton exclaimed.

"Just think it's an interesting coincidence that she seems to have been so close to the deceased in every case just before they pass on," Louella defended herself. "That's all I said."

"She certainly does seem to make a quick sale," Mabel added. "Sold Helen's house before we even waked her."

"That's because she has all these customers lined up. She gets everyone a good price. And she visits a lot of people. So don't we all, and nobody's accusing us of anything." Vera increased her knitting speed, until the needles were a blur.

"I'm not accusing Persis. She's my own cousin once removed. Just pointing out the coincidences, that's all." Louella, in contrast, was taking her time with the mittens she was making, her needles slow and steady—*click click . . . click click.*

Faith entered with a fresh pot of tea, and the talk instantly turned to Serena Marshall's sister-in-law's hip replacement.

Persis. They'd been talking about Persis. Faith

felt a deep chill, although the afternoon shadows had not yet lengthened. Ursula had been worried about the recent increase in deaths, the deaths of her friends, older friends. Persis Sanford was certainly one hell of a real estate agent, but was she also the real estate agent from hell? Title Mary, as opposed to Typhoid Mary? In some twisted way, might she be justifying her actions—leaving a box of sugary jelly doughnuts on diabetic Helen Marshall's kitchen table, say—by assuring herself she was helping the needy families of these relatives, who would be on their way out in the not so distant future anyway?

Looking at the food arranged on the big round table, Faith felt sick herself. Harold Hapswell, *Mrs.* Hapswell, the fires, the slogans, the dummy, the feuds, now this. Ursula had been right, not Freeman. Something was very wrong on Sanpere this summer.

Faith had just finished washing the last of Ursula's teacups—old Spode, the Buttercup pattern. Ursula's grandmother had brought it to the "cottage" to use for occasions that called for finer china than their everyday white ironstone. Despite many calls for its use, the Spode had survived intact. Nervously, Faith put the last saucer away, thinking about what it would cost to replace it. Tom had turned up as the ladies were leaving, his jeans covered with splashes of Cozy Melon, Alpine Lace, and Oslo. The first coat had to dry, he'd explained, so they'd quit early. The color choices were approved—what they could see of them—and the Sewing Circle departed. It had been quite an afternoon. Amy went down for a nap. Faith had hoped Ben would continue this practice until middle school at least, but he'd drawn the line at kindergarten. Admonished not to tell his sister about this—or the Easter Bunny, although Santa was still real for Ben—Ben had complied, and Amy continued to fall asleep reliably every afternoon. The two male Fairchilds set out in the dinghy for more rowing practice and parts unknown. Tom took a fishing line and told Faith to get ready for a school of mackerel for dinner. With the knowledge that she had a seafood lasagna in the fridge, Faith told him that would be some good, for sure. Then she suggested Ursula lie down, too, and after a mild protest, she had gone to her room, saying, "I don't know why I should be tired. I didn't do a thing. Thank you for everything, Faith."

Faith was a little tired herself. It hadn't been much work, but the constant chatter of the women and the sound of their knitting needles still seemed to fill her ears. The volume and tempo had been increased by Mabel's startling revelation—Harold Hapswell, recently deceased, a married man.

The phone rang and Faith grabbed it, hoping it hadn't awakened Ursula.

"I thought you might like to have someone talk to you woman-to-woman, so to speak, after an afternoon of the Sanpere Stitchers. Was it totally infantilizing?" It was Pix. Faith had been in

Ellsworth, under the spell of Home Depot, when Pix had called earlier in the week. Ursula had informed her about Faith's discovery of Harold's body, and Pix had immediately dashed out and told the family not to strike camp—they were in Glacier National Park, about to head even deeper into the wilderness—until she'd had a chance to talk to Faith directly. That talk had been brief but very comforting, and here was Pix on the line again, the rest of the Millers scaling some glacier, no doubt. Faith was extremely happy to hear her friend's voice so soon after their last conversation. Even before finding Harold's body, Faith had been wishing Pix were here on Sanpere.

"Only partially, because there was big news, and everyone's attention was on that. They even let me ask a question."

Faith related Mabel's account of Harold's mystery wife.

"I'd always wondered why he wasn't married. He was very good-looking when he was younger—and not too bad even now," Pix commented.

Faith thought of Harold as she had last seen him. He hadn't been even remotely good-looking.

Pix was continuing in the same vein. "Really, he was quite the hunk when he was young. Of course, he was older than I am, but I remember all the girls were after him. And after Don Osborn, too. They were quite a pair. Their families used to spend summers here, and I'm sure they had no idea how their sons were carrying on."

"Donald Osborn?"

"He was thinner then—a whole lot thinner—and the two of them were part of a group that partied hearty with the island kids."

Pix had teenagers, Faith reminded herself, and her friend picked up a phrase now and then that sounded totally out of character.

"It's interesting that they both ended up here. And, in the end, on opposite sides of the fence," Faith said.

"I think that happened long before Sanpere Shores, but this certainly would have made it worse. They went their separate ways early on. Don has always made good money doing financial consulting, first traveling all over and now by computer. That's why he can afford to be as green as he wants. Harold struggled for a long time—fished, tried to sell his photographs to the tourists, did odd jobs. He's only been in the money for the last ten years or so. Made a pile on a big piece of land and kept reinvesting in more. Anyway, their lives were very different. Don married a girl he met in college, moved to Sanpere, had kids, became part of the island home-schooling, no-white-sugar group. Harold's been pretty much a loner, especially once he stopped fishing and started the real estate business."

"Does his wife sound like anyone you know?"

"Absolutely not. Besides, if I knew her, the Sewing Circle would, and nobody there recognized her from Mabel's description, right?"

"Yes. But Mabel did say the woman sounded like she came from Maine. She also got the distinct impression that they'd gotten hitched—her word—recently."

"It won't be a secret for long. The Durgen brothers know by now, I'll bet, and you know how they are—that is, if they're in the mood to talk. Earl knows, too, but that won't help us any."

True, Faith thought, remembering Jill's complaint that the whole island knew things Earl repeatedly told her he wasn't at liberty to divulge.

"Well, I'm sure I'll have her name and other vital statistics the next time you call."

There was a pause, and Faith thought the connection had been broken, but then Pix spoke, hesitating between words.

"Faith, you don't think . . . I mean, are you thinking that Harold's death wasn't . . ."

"Wasn't an accident?"

"Yes."

Having to answer Pix—Pix Miller, to whom it was as impossible to tell a lie as it was to Ursula—brought a truce to the warring thoughts that had filled Faith's mind so painfully since she'd found the body at the lighthouse.

"I didn't think it was an accident when I found him, and I've been feeling surer every day. I don't know how it was done, but somebody killed him." Somebody who wanted to stop Sanpere Shores—or now, Faith thought with a start, maybe somebody who wanted to inherit it.

Fortunately, Sanpere did not have to wait long to hear all about Harold Hapswell's attractive widow. She'd wasted no time after she left Earl, stopping first at Durgen's, then at the one remaining granite works for a headstone, and finally at the *Island Crier* to place an obituary. The ensuing stream of information flowed over the island, seeping into the porches of every waiting ear before nightfall.

"Her name is Victoria Viceroy. I mean her maiden name," Ursula said.

"Sounds like a stripper—or a cigarette," Tom commented.

"Sounds made-up," Faith said.

Ursula nodded in agreement with both. The phone had been ringing steadily since dinner—the seafood lasagna—and Ursula had taken all the pieces the Sanpere Stitchers had provided, fitting them into the whole she was presently sharing with the Fairchilds. Faith had been jealous of Ursula's insider status and at one point had actually been tempted to listen in on the extension in Ursula's bedroom. Looking longingly from the doorway at the now highly collectible square black phone, it was not the fires of hell that had deterred her, but the photo of Ursula and Daniel, silver-haired, silver-framed, poised on one side of Mr. Bell's instrument. They peered out at the world, eyes brimming with total and complete trust, calm smiles on their lips.

Besides, Faith had been sure Ursula would catch her.

"She's from Aroostook County but lives in Trenton now. Until her recent marriage, she worked as a hostess at the Jade Island—you know, that Chinese restaurant outside Bar Harbor."

"I told you, Tom! A Chinese take-out place would be a gold mine on this island. There was Harold, driving all the way up to Bar Harbor for moo shu pork or whatever!" Faith exclaimed.

"From the sound of her, I think it might have been the 'whatever,' but we have interrupted you, Ursula," Tom said.

"There isn't too much more. Nobody seems to know how recent the marriage was. The obit she dictated just says 'recent.' She's the only survivor listed, and Harold's described as 'a prominent real estate developer with strong ties to the island he loved.' Well, that's true, but when Aggie—you know, Gert's sister's niece, who works at the *Crier*—asked her where she'd like memorial contributions to be sent, she said she didn't know. They hadn't ever talked about anything like this. Aggie suggested the Medical Center, and so they stuck that in."

"Harold may have had 'strong ties,' but it doesn't sound like she's formed any yet," Faith said.

"Apparently, she would have—and may still. She told Marvin Durgen that Harold had been planning to build their dream house on one of the Sanpere Shores lots. Seven bedrooms, eight baths—counting a powder room—indoor gym, entertainment room—and no remarks about what that might be, Tom." Ursula shook her head. "We've talked about it and talked about it, but it's

218

just plain wrong, houses like that. There are people in Maine still living in tar-paper shacks."

Tom looked serious. "It's not only Maine, of course. I never thought I'd see the gap between rich and poor become so pronounced in this country—between rich and everybody else. And there isn't a single place, rural or urban, that can claim it has affordable housing."

"Sanpere was always a backwater," Ursula said. "We don't have a big golf course or fancy spots to eat. No movies, casinos. Nothing to attract big spenders. Except now. Now we have shoreland. These new buyers are people who would have bought on Mount Desert in the past, but that's priced out of reach even for multimillionaires these days." Faith had never heard Ursula sound so bitter. "Suddenly, Sanpere looks like a bargain."

Turning toward Tom, who was steadily consuming the Sewing Circle leftovers as a bedtime snack, Faith said, "Louise Frazier was hoping Harold's widow would turn Sanpere Shores over to the Island Trust." She laughed hollowly.

Tom raised an eyebrow and swallowed. "I wish I had even one-tenth of her optimism. I'll bet the Widow Hapswell is on the phone with the highest bidder right now, selling each and every pine needle Harold owned—except maybe the lot for their dream house."

In bed, both Tom and Faith had trouble dropping off to sleep.

"What has Lyle had to say about Harold? He must have known him pretty well," Faith said.

"Lyle's a lot younger. You know about the time Harold wanted Lyle to work with him—Harold would sell the land, reel in the big fish, and Lyle would put up the houses, giving Harold a kickback on that action, too."

"I remember, and Lyle wouldn't have any part of it. So they probably didn't have much to do with each other." Faith gave voice to an idea that had been lurking in her mind since the Planning Board meeting, when she'd become aware of Lyle's obvious antipathy toward Hapswell and all of his projects. "Lyle seems pretty passionate about Sanpere, but I don't see him sabotaging the work of another builder. Especially Seth. Seth gave him his start."

"That's true. But Lyle *is* passionate, although you have to look hard to catch it. He hates what's happening here."

Faith had another thought. "If Harold was struggling to make a living here, where did he get the money to buy the first property? Prices were already starting to go up even ten or fifteen years ago."

"Maybe it was a steal." Tom yawned. He was getting sleepy at last. He kissed his wife. "Good night, sweetheart."

"Good night," Faith replied absently. She was remembering something from a few years back, from the time when she'd learned about some of Sanpere's less savory past. The eighties, and earlier, had been a boom time for drug smugglers. Maine, with over three thousand miles of coastline, was made to order for them. It was impossible to patrol. Inevitably, Maine fishermen became involved in the drug trafficking. Some because they were strapped and had no other way to make it, no other way to support their families. Others took to it for the sheer adventure—people with a healthy distrust of government delighting in outsmarting the DEA, much as their fathers and grandfathers had hoodwinked the feds during Prohibition. And some were just greedy and didn't care how they made their money. Who was involved and who wasn't became a tightly guarded secret in these closed communities, still was. The only way anyone from outside might suspect was if a fisherman had a brand-new boat or bought a new, fancier truck. To this day, the island remained conflicted about those days; it had torn apart a lot of lives—especially when someone did get caught. Was this how Harold had amassed his nest egg? And if so, had he made some enemies along the way?

Enemies. Lyle had said some of the people who sold Harold their property on Butler's Point, now Sanpere Shores, had been "gypped." How hard would it have been to whack someone on the back of the head and push him onto the rocks below? People here were well acquainted with the tides—and it could have been an acquaintance who went out to the lighthouse with

Harold. Acquaintances, enemies—sometimes there wasn't any difference.

She closed her eyes and fell into a skim coat of sleep.

It didn't last. Unable to shape her pillow into anything but an anvil, Faith decided to go down to the kitchen and make some cocoa. When she was a little girl and had occasional bouts of sleeplessness, her father had made the cocoa. It had always worked. The novelty of seeing her father turn on a burner—the Reverend Lawrence Sibley couldn't even perk coffee—and the taste of the warm chocolaty liquid drove the nightmares and worries away. Making a cup for herself still sometimes worked, even as she wished for those all-important crises of old: "Margaret has a new best friend"; "I spelled *bowl* with an *e* before the *l* in front of my whole class"; "Why doesn't Hope ever get detention?"

She pulled a sweatshirt of Tom's on over her nightgown, slipped her feet into her sandals, and went softly down the hall.

The landing window was filled with stars as the fourth-quarter moon disappeared into the new one. She went down the stairs. At the bottom, instead of walking toward the back of the house and into the kitchen, Faith took a flashlight from the battalion arrayed on a shelf next to the front door and turned the knob, drawn irresistibly out into the night air as a moth to a flame. She sat on the front steps, taking off her sandals and tucking her feet under her nightgown. This was what she had been missing—the peace, the take-a-step-back perspective that was Sanpere, that was Maine. The tide had been high at ten o'clock, when she and Tom had been trying to get to sleep. It still looked high now, though it was almost one o'clock. The tides—they governed life on an island, and the constancy of their change filled her with a deep sense of contentment. The tide always came in; it always went out. It always would, no matter what was happening onshore. Putting the flashlight down, she grasped her knees and arched her head back to look up into the sky. Pix, Ursula, and the rest of that family knew everything about the stars. They were on a first-name basis with the constellations: "Oh, Orion's not so bright tonight. Too bad." Ursula had told Ben that it would cool off now, because the dog days were over—the dog days, named for the Dog Star, Sirius, so bright at this time of year that people used to believe it was adding its heat to the sun, producing hot, sultry days down below on Earth.

It smelled good. A combination of pine, sea-weed, and something else, something from the ocean—something clean and wet. She released her legs and stretched, feeling happier than she had since she'd arrived on the island—what?— less than three weeks ago. It seemed both longer and shorter, as time does whenever you stop to consider it. She put her sandals back on, picked up the flashlight, and walked toward the shore.

There was no breeze; no sound at all except the soft lapping of the sea. The stars gave as much light as a full moon, so she didn't need her own light. She couldn't recall ever having seen the stars so bright. One fell. Good luck or bad? You could make a wish—that was good. Or it meant someone had died and was on the way to heaven—a mixed blessing. Heaven, all right. Death, not just yet, thank you. She knew she was tired. Her thoughts were all jumbled together—belief, superstition, jokes with herself. On herself? But she wasn't ready to go back inside. It was too nice out.

Up ahead, the lighthouse looked so dependable—and so beautiful. She hoped Victoria Viceroy wouldn't convert it into a motel. Victoria Viceroy—what a name! She was Victoria Hapswell now—maybe that was why she'd gotten married, although Hapswell as a cognomen wasn't much better. No, it was the money. Or Harold, Harold, who was obviously much older, yet still attractive. Or both—money and Harold. Faith pushed a strand of hair behind her ear and walked closer to the lighthouse. The grass, left unmown here, brushed her feet. Orache and vetch knotted their tendrils around the stalks and caught at her ankles. Someone, probably Harold, had cleared the growth from the front of the lighthouse door. It was locked, of course. Earl would have seen to that. Good old dependable Earl. "Calm as a clock," Mabel had said. This was a new one to Faith, and she liked the phrase. Described Earl to a tee. Without thinking, she grasped the handle of the lighthouse door, feeling the cold brass, and pushed down with her thumb—and pulled.

The door swung open, creaking loudly on un-oiled hinges. In a moment, she was in. She clicked on the flashlight and found herself in a large room. The beam of light picked out an assortment of objects—broken chairs, wooden traps, a derelict mattress, an oar. The walls had been whitewashed, but the paint had peeled, leaving rough scars. The stairs to the top of the light were on the right side, winding their way up, following the curve of the wall.

Instantly, Faith began to climb. She wanted to go to the very top, go where the massive light had once streamed out across the water. Maybe she could get out on the catwalk and stand high up over the sea, a part of the night sky herself. She felt giddy with the spontaneity of it all and almost went to get Tom, but she could bring him tomorrow. She'd been silly to avoid the lighthouse and anything connected to it, even selecting another paint name. The lighthouse was like the tide—neutral, an eternal bystander. The door had opened to her touch. It was like a fairy tale. It was meant to be.

They must have been in good shape, those lighthouse keepers, she thought, pausing to catch her breath. And had good heads. She judged that she had gone only a third of the way up, if that. With no windows, it was hard to tell how high she'd climbed—and already she was experiencing some mild vertigo.

The stairs went round and round. She put her hand on the wall to steady herself. It felt damp. Around and around. Amy's current favorite song sprang into her thoughts, "The wheels on the bus go round and round, all around the town-o." But Faith wasn't on a bus. Her sandals made a soft rhythmic sound on the cast-iron stairs. Around and around.

There had been the large room on the ground floor, and she could see another floor above her. The stairs disappeared into the room. How tall was the lighthouse? How many feet high? Ursula knew. After all his conversations with her, Ben probably did, too, by now. It was a beach lighthouse, so it had to be tall. Sandbars and beaches had this kind of beacon. One hundred and fifty feet? Something like that. No windows until the top. She switched the flashlight to her other hand and clutched the railing.

The first time she heard the sound, she thought it must be coming from outside. What could be inside the lighthouse? There was nothing for an animal to eat. Although it could be a mouse. Mice existed everywhere. That mattress would have made a nice nest. Or cockroaches. Cockroaches could live on paint, but she didn't think Sanpere had cockroaches. Manhattan did; even Jane Sibley's Upper East Side kitchen had been invaded. The little man who took care of these things would come and then they'd be all right for a while.

The noise came again. Only it didn't sound like a mouse—tiny claws skittering across a surface. Mice didn't bother her, except when they got into her pantry. But there were no pantries here. There would have been in the keeper's house. But that had burned down. Like the new houses on Sanpere. The fires. Too many fires.

She heard it once more. It was below her—or was it above her? Climbing round and round had disoriented her. She trained the beam of her flashlight up and then down—nothing. Then it was quiet. The inside of the lighthouse smelled musty and faintly metallic. She was very, very tired. This hadn't been such a good idea after all. The exhilaration she'd felt left her in a rush, allowing all the troubled thoughts so recently on the surface to return, bobbing like corks in the water. It was time to go back. She reversed her steps, felt her body pitch forward with the downward momentum, and straightened up. Ramrod-straight. As she descended, the noise began again, growing louder. She quickly turned the flashlight off.

Click.

Instantly, darkness engulfed her, so palpable it seemed to shape itself around her body like another layer of skin.

There was no mistaking what the sound was now. It was footsteps.

Someone was in the lighthouse. Someone was coming up the stairs. Slowly, steadily, purposefully.

She felt a scream gather in the back of her

throat, choking her. She tried to let it out, producing instead a small, strained squeal. Up, she had to go back up!

But what was above her? She was trapped no matter what she did. She could stop and wait, climb and try to hide. Jump? How high was she? Her mind was muddled by fatigue and fear. A thought crashed through and she was able to make a sound.

"Tom, oh Tom, is that you?" she called. "I know you said to wait, that it wouldn't take you a minute to get some wine, but it was so lovely out. Do you have the wine? You're so romantic. It won't take us long to climb to the top."

There was no reply. She hadn't expected one. But now there was silence. Welcome silence. The footsteps had stopped. As long as they stayed that way, she was safe.

Who could it be? She remembered the light she'd seen after Ursula had told them about Abbie Burgess, the lighthouse keeper's daughter on Matinicus. It hadn't been a ghost light. She knew that. It wasn't a ghost now. Was someone sleeping here at night? A squatter? The thought was reassuring. That was what the mattress was for. Someone who needed a place to stay. But how did they get in? The door was always locked. Ben tried it repeatedly whenever they went past. Tonight, it had been open. Why? *Oh, why had it been open!*

Ben. Amy. Tom. She repeated the names as a litany. Ben. Amy. Tom.

She sat on the stair. It was freezing cold now

that she'd stopped her ascent. She didn't care. She would sit and wait and be safe in the silence until the sun rose and morning came.

She jerked her head up. How long had she been asleep? She'd left her watch on the table beside the bed. Had it been hours, or merely minutes? Was it dawn or dark? Her legs were cramped and her feet were all pins and needles. She stood up unsteadily, reached for the railing, and dropped the flashlight. It hit the step below with a crack and fell over the side. She heard another crack, a faint one when it hit the bottom. Faith felt her eyes fill with tears. Even if she had dared to turn it on, she couldn't now. She took a step down, then back up. It was absolutely quiet. Whoever was or had been in the lighthouse was or had been no more eager to encounter her than she him—or her. Was/had been. The person had to be long gone, having left while she slept. Had to be.

She couldn't bear to stay entombed in the lighthouse for a minute longer. She placed her foot firmly down on the next step and kept going this time. She wouldn't let herself think about what she might encounter on the step below. Or the next. Or the next. Around and around, clinging to the wall in the darkness. She reached for the thin railing, but it seemed suspended in the air, insubstantial, liable to give way and send her plummeting after the flashlight. The wall was better. Solid. Around and around. The only noises she heard were her own footsteps and, even louder, the blood pounding in her ears. She was so dizzy by the time she reached the bottom that she fell when her foot failed to hit another step, connecting with the floor instead. She didn't get up, but crawled in what she hoped was the direction of the door, groping for the flashlight at the same time, although it would certainly have been shattered. She put her hand up from time to time and soon felt the rough wood of the door frame. She stood and grabbed the handle. Then she was out.

It was still night and the light from the stars was blinding. She opened and closed her eyes, adjusting to the glare. There was the Pines, their car in the drive, her family asleep. All was as she'd left it. She'd wake Tom and he'd hold her tight. It was over. Tom, who slept so soundly that nothing wakened him except for a child's cry in the night, or a child's cough, didn't know that she had been gone. She'd wake him up and he would hold her tight.

Stepping away from the door, Faith pushed it closed behind her and walked past the boulders that lay tumbled against the lighthouse, dark shapes. These random piles left so long ago that to try to get a sense of the amount of time that had passed was incomprehensible for her. Just as it was to try to think about the time ahead, the expanding universe, the cooling sun aeons into the future. The rocks were heaped on either side of the lighthouse and heaped below where Harold had died. Her steps quickened. The grass was wet.

Then one of the rocks moved. A rounded one,

dark as the water behind it. The rock moved—stood up, ran, and threw her to the ground. She kicked and tried to free her arms, pinned to her sides immediately by other arms. Black, the figure was completely black. No face, nothing but black. A gloved hand was over her mouth. She tried to bite through it and felt soft flesh beneath the rough fabric. A startled cry, the hand moved. The blow to her head was sharp and quick. She didn't feel any pain, just terror. Numb fear. Before she lost consciousness, she was aware of only one sensation: smell.

The smell of turpentine.

Nine

Faith had no idea where she was. She'd opened her eyes and the bright sun had forced them closed again. Her head ached. It was the worst hangover she'd ever had in her life. Only she hadn't been drinking. She opened her eyes again. She wasn't in bed. She was swinging. The sun was like a flashbulb; she saw bright, hot dots in front of her eyes. She closed them. She wondered whether she was going to throw up. It felt as if she might. She tried to sit, but she was tangled in a blanket and the struggle caused more swinging.

Last night. She had no trouble remembering that. The lighthouse. The footsteps. The rock that moved. The longest night of her life. She had to get up. She had to find Tom.

Freeing herself from her cover, Faith was able to turn and see where she was. She hadn't gone far. Her assailant had thoughtfully brought her back to the porch. The porch where she'd sat so contentedly hours earlier. The porch she should never have left. Now she was in the hammock that was suspended in a frame at one end. The blanket was a throw that Ursula kept on the wicker settee in case anyone felt chilled.

Faith felt very chilled.

She managed to extricate herself and stood on the porch. Her sandals were gone, but she was otherwise in one piece. It must still be very early, she thought. There was no sound from inside the house. Slightly unsteady, she turned to go indoors—and stopped. The sun shone down on the lighthouse, picking out the silver shimmer of the mica in its granite blocks, and picking out the shiny green spray paint on those same blocks. The lower portion of the light was now covered with familiar slogans. No mystery here. No doubt as to her attacker. Faith had interrupted the KSS version of paint ball.

Tom was angry. Earl was angry. Jill was angry. Ursula was the angriest of all. Her lips were so tightly pursed that they all but disappeared. Returning from Blue Hill Hospital with strong injunctions regarding rest and notifying them in case of further symptoms, Faith was tucked up on the couch in the living room of the Pines. She had been hit hard enough to knock her out, but it had been her fatigue and shock that had produced her deep sleep, not a concussion. Outside, volunteers were already busy scrubbing the paint from the stones, having been given the go-ahead by Earl after the state police had taken their photographs. The lighthouse was fast becoming a familiar law-enforcement destination. Ben was with the group, assiduously attacking the graffiti, indignant at the assault on his lighthouse; he didn't know about the one on his mother. Amy was at new friend Bobby's.

"They've gone way too far this time," Earl said. "KSS, ELF, whoever. What we do know is that the person who attacked you must be someone you know or have met, Faith, worried you'd recognize him. You're sure it was a him?"

"I'm not sure of anything," Faith admitted, although she had told Earl earlier she thought it was a man. Something about the hand on her mouth. She knew the kind of gloves that had covered that hand. Sold at Barton's, Wal-Mart, Home Depot, you name it. Everyone on the island had a pair—thick dark cotton work gloves. Everyone also had a pair of the tawny orange leather kind, the thickly padded striped ones, and the long waterproof type fishermen wore. The average Mainer might not have an extensive wardrobe, but he did have gloves.

She wasn't afraid. Someone who intended to do you harm didn't pick you up, put you in a hammock, and cover you with a warm blanket. Someone intending harm would have finished her off by the lighthouse—or at least left her there.

Returning from the hospital, they'd discovered

that the Sanpere casserole and comfort-food brigade had been out in full force. The kitchen table was covered with everything from Nan's Comfort Cookies to Louise Frazier's southern fried chicken. Even Persis had left an offering, her standard Tuna Wiggle, and a note telling Faith to get better soon; they needed her for the play. Nibbling on a cookie and watching Tom tuck into one of the pies—Gert's black walnut—Faith wanted to talk.

"I can't tell you for sure whether the person was a man or a woman, short or tall, fat or thin. I know it sounds dumb, but one second I was looking at the rocks; then one of them moved and I was out like a light. I bit the glove and I think I bit through it. Maybe you should go around and see if anyone has a fresh wound on the palm of his or her hand." Stigmata, but maybe not all that useful. The hands of working people on Sanpere were always cut up—and the tourists' were, too, after climbing on rocks with barnacles like razors.

"It would have had to be someone strong enough to carry you to the porch," Jill said, "though you're so light, most adults could manage that."

"But why go after me at all?" Faith mused. "Obviously, the person—or persons, if there was more than one vandal involved—wanted to wait until I was out of the lighthouse so I wouldn't surprise him in the act. I thought I'd been asleep for longer than I must have been, so there wasn't all that much time between when I heard the footsteps and when I left. My attacker could have re-

236

mained still and I would have never been the wiser."

"That's what's been bothering me, too," Tom said.

"It may have been the plan; then the person realized there was something you'd see, something that would give everything away, so you had to be stopped." As usual, Ursula had hit the nail on the head. "I imagine whoever it was hadn't hidden his car well enough and didn't realize it until you were walking past."

Earl nodded. It was the only explanation that possibly made sense. Not that any of this did. Things like this didn't happen on Sanpere—the spray painting, the fires, the attack.

"Faith, when you stepped out of the lighthouse, do you recall anything that isn't usually here? Lots of cars and trucks park here during the day, but it's empty by the dock at night," the sergeant said. This wasn't an official session. He'd questioned her earlier. Now Faith was surrounded by friends and family. But the officer figured something might jog her memory.

She closed her eyes and was back in the moment, even smelling the night air—the smell before the turpentine. She opened them and shook her head. "What struck me was that everything looked the same as it had when I went in. I had been so terrified that it seemed something in the outside world would mirror that. But it was all normal. The houses, our car."

"What about before you went in?" Jill asked excitedly, "Was yours the only car?" Maybe the blow on the head had been intended to obliterate a memory, not forestall one.

Again, Faith had to shake her head. "Nothing."

There was a knock at the door and Tom jumped up to answer it. More food.

Linda Forsythe crept into the room. She appeared daunted at the presence of so many people.

"I wanted to drop this off." She was holding a basket covered with a bright flowered napkin. "Raspberry scones. My bushes are loaded with berries. . . ." She was as scarlet as a berry herself. "Roland says to tell you not to hurry back, although we'll all miss you." She stopped again and blushed some more, if that was possible. Faith came to her rescue.

"Thank you. I'm sure the scones are delicious, and tell Roland I'll be back Monday. There really isn't anything wrong with me. I was very lucky."

The others in the room were eyeing Linda less charitably, and Earl seemed about to say something, when Linda blurted out the real reason for her visit.

Still clutching the basket, an aging Red Riding Hood, she stammered, "It wasn't just the scones. I mean, I wanted to bring you something, but what I wanted to say . . . that is what I meant to do . . . Look, we didn't do it. KSS had nothing to do with what happened last night. I'm positive. I've spoken to Don . . . to several members, and no one did it—or would have. The spray painting, hitting you on the head—it wasn't us." She looked straight into Faith's eyes.

What to say? Thank you for not attacking me? Thank you for not defacing one of Maine's historical and architectural treasures?

Ursula reached for the basket. Linda loosened the death grip she had on it and handed it over.

"I'm sure we're all very glad to hear what you've had to say, dear," Ursula said. "Now, Faith needs to rest. I was just about to tell that to the others. Please inform Roland that she *may* be back Monday. We'll see."

Faith smiled. Yes, Mother, she said to herself. It felt wonderful to be coddled. It must have been very difficult for Linda to come to the Pines, and she reached out her hand toward the woman. "I appreciate your stopping by to tell me this," she said.

Linda took her hand and Faith pulled her in for a little hug. The others murmured some sort of good-bye. None of them was in the mood for anything remotely connected to KSS.

"Think she was telling the truth?" Tom asked after Linda had left.

"I think she hopes we think so," Faith replied, suddenly exhausted. When she'd taken Linda's hand, it was impossible not to notice the large fresh Band-Aid that stretched across her palm.

"I'm getting on a plane as soon as we reach Vancouver!" Pix Miller was adamant.

"Don't be ridiculous. You'll miss Jasper. You've always wanted to go to Jasper," Faith said, wondering what there could possibly be to eat there.

The sigh that came across the wires was palpable. "I'd feel better about things if I were there with you."

"I know your presence is formidable, especially on Sanpere Island, and that deep in your heart you think if you'd been here, none of this would have happened, but you're wrong. Whatever's happening has nothing to do with you or me. I was merely in the wrong place at the wrong time." Twice, Faith told herself.

Ignoring her friend's implied affront to her ability to control the universe, Pix asked, "Why paint slogans on the lighthouse? Harold is dead, so any plans for opening up a Motel Six are, at the very most, on hold. You do know that Mother wants to buy it from his widow? We have to hope she wants some quick cash and doesn't wait for someone to offer an exorbitant amount."

Faith had a strong feeling that Victoria Viceroy Hapswell wanted both, but she kept her mouth shut. She, too, wanted Ursula to buy the lighthouse. If buyer and seller met, there was a chance a deal could be struck. Ursula, like Pix, was pretty good at getting her own way. Quietly, firmly, but definitely her way.

Pix wasn't getting it now, though. Cutting her family vacation short was out of the question, and Faith was not going to allow her friend to do it. She was pretty good at getting her own way, too, although without the sleight of hand the Rowe women had acquired over the years.

But the lighthouse.

"From what I learned from the Web site Jill and I looked at, these actions are often planned far in advance," Faith said. "The cell members wear disguises—basic black in this case—so they may not know one another, or who to call if a foray is going to be canceled. Earl thinks there was a whole list drawn up months ago—kind of 'Be there or be square.' The state police will be stepping up night patrols here on the island, figuring there will be another one at least before the end of the summer. The sheriff's office is involved too."

"Hmm," said Pix. "It shouldn't be too hard to figure out who will be attacked. I'm sure Earl has made a list, too. He always does. I hope Jill can get him to leave his little notebook home on their wedding day. Anyway, the targets are easy to predict. All you'd have to do would be go to Mabel and look at the figures from the tax rolls."

Last week, Tom had asked Faith to drop by the Town Hall when she had a chance to double-check theirs, since they had to increase their home owner's insurance because of the new addition and he'd left all that information back in Aleford. She hadn't gotten around to it yet.

"It's public information? What everyone's assessed at?" she asked.

"Absolutely. People go in all the time, check on what their neighbor's place is worth compared to theirs, make sure the town isn't overcharging. Or so they say. I think it's plain old nosiness myself."

"Not that there's anything wrong with that," Faith said.

"Now, Faith . . ." Pix laughed.

"Okay, okay. I'll be good. But you finish your vacation. I don't expect to see you here until the thirtieth at the earliest."

"We bought tickets for the play for Friday, and of course Jill's wedding is Saturday. We may be back sooner."

Faith knew this wouldn't happen. The trusty Miller van would lurch in late Thursday or even Friday. They'd take showers, put on fresh jeans, and head off to *Romeo and Juliet.*

"How is the play coming, by the way?" Pix asked.

"The *play* is fantastic, and if Persis ever learns her lines, it will be absolutely perfect. The *rehearsals* have been something else. Becky Prescott's family started sending a family member to keep an eye on things after the Fish 'n' Fritter Fry, when she danced with Ted. The Hamiltons heard about it and started sending their own representatives. It would be funny if it weren't so deadly serious. The lobster war, that is, and all these repercussions. Roland finally had enough, so now all the rehearsals are closed." The Hamiltons and Prescotts who had turned up weren't disruptive, but they'd sat on opposite sides of the auditorium, with arms folded across their chests and such stony faces that it was impossible for the actors to perform. Some days, there was a whole phalanx of these onlookers; sometimes only a few kids—tattletales. The balcony scene had had all the ardor of "kissing your sister," and after numerous equally wooden repetitions, Roland had delivered his ultimatum. It helped that he had taught most of them. There were a few angry shouts about having every right to be there, but in the end, the two camps left. Play duty had been seriously cutting into work time, and as one of the Hamiltons told Freeman, "a little of that Shakespeare fellow goes a long way."

"Poor Roland. He must be sorry he ever got involved in all this," Pix said.

"Maybe, although he has to be happy with the way the play is shaping up, and Linda's sets are beautiful. Still, he has been looking a little frazzled."

They talked a few minutes more and then Faith hung up. Everyone else was at church and she was supposed to be resting. Churchgoing came with her marital territory and, feeling not at all wicked, she was glad for a Sunday off. The call had been a surprise. Everyone had left just before the phone rang. The Millers were heading into Canada and Pix wanted to leave word for Ursula. Arnie, Pix's brother, had insisted on an answering machine several summers ago. Pix had been equally surprised that anyone was at home, it being Sunday morning, and Faith had had to tell her the whole story, eliciting Pix's immediate resolve to be at her friend's side as soon as the wings of man could carry her.

Faith went back upstairs, crawling into the unmade bed. Why was it that this always felt so good? The decadence of it all? Of course a made bed—especially one made up by someone else—with crisply ironed sheets felt wonderful, too, but you couldn't burrow down in them, pull them up around your shoulders, find the comfortable hollow in the mattress from the night before, and fall into a daytime sleep. A made bed was for night—or illness.

She'd pulled up the shades and now the sun filtered through the lawn Priscilla curtains on either side of the window. The room was furnished with bits and pieces from several generations and locales. Faith and Tom had been sleeping in a large spool bed. A Chinese screen hid a door that connected to the next room, the old nursery, presently the quarters of Pix's brother and his wife. An Eastlake dresser took up almost one wall, and a simple pine bookcase—the work of one of the family, Faith suspected—took up half of another. All the books you would ever want to read were there: mysteries, of course—classics by Christie, Sayers, and Stout, and modern ones by Maron, Tapply, Wolzien, and Langton; lots of Trollope, lots of Thirkell; all of John Gould; Eudora Welty—Ursula's favorite; Nancy Mitford; E. M. Delafield; and many much-beloved children's books, covers worn. Faith had picked up *A Wrinkle in Time*. It lay beside her, but before she could pull her arm from its warm cocoon and reach for it, she was asleep.

She was going to the Town Hall to check on the figures for Tom. That was all.

Well, maybe not quite all.

She didn't even have to concoct a story for Mabel, who opened the bottom of the Dutch door that led into her cubbyhole of an office—the top part had never been closed since the day it was installed—and sat Faith down at the table, the ledger conveniently in front of her.

Mabel's plants were also in front of her, each one set squarely on a crocheted doily. Drought was not a problem here, and the carnations, geraniums, and roses bloomed as brightly in August as they did in December, stuck into pots and religiously dusted every week. Photos of several graduates, brides, grooms, and grandchildren, highlighted by blue backgrounds and shiny brass frames, were scattered among the posies.

Duty first. Faith turned to the listing of their parcel of land and noted the valuation, taxes, what they'd paid, footage, everything that was on the page. Then she paused. Who first?

The Classical Wave station was on the radio, soft classical in the background. Mabel was working on another doily. Probably for the fair. Faith started with Harold's holdings and was not surprised to find they were considerable. He had been paying a lot in taxes. Linda was in the same part of the book; her piece was tiny, but she had quite a bit of shore frontage, which raised her rate. What about the Osborns? The only other KSS members she knew for certain. Now, this was a surprise. They owned virtually the entire point of land opposite Sanpere Shores. There were a few holdings in between theirs—the lobster pound was one—but by and large, the Osborns were directly across from all of the future Mc-Mansions. No wonder Donald and Terri were so opposed to it. Faith wondered which came first—KSS or the Sanpere Shores project? That would be interesting to find out.

She was about to turn to Persis's page, when Mabel spoke to her.

"Came back at the crack of dawn. Waiting on the steps for me to open up."

"Mrs. Hapswell?" Who else? Besides, there was that tone in Mabel's voice, that "no better than she should be" tone. Faith had heard it many times in her career.

"Ayuh."

Trying not to get too excited at having actually heard a native utter this word, Faith decided *Romeo and Juliet* could wait. She'd dropped the kids off at camp and had planned on spending only a half hour at the Town Hall before going to the rehearsal.

"What would you say to a cup of coffee and one of Mrs. McHenan's doughnuts?" The IGA was a few steps down the street.

"I wouldn't say no," said Mabel, adding a purple skein to the white ones in her lap.

She'd obviously been dying to tell someone, and Faith was associated closely enough with the island to qualify.

Going for coffee and doughnuts was but the work of a moment.

Mabel stopped tatting at Faith's return. "Her big black car was out in front. I noticed it right away. Mercedes, just like you said. So you could say I *was* surprised and I *wasn't* to see her there in front of me when I went for my keys."

"What did she want?" Faith was enjoying the suspense—and the doughnut. Not greasy, it had a hint of nutmeg and was still warm.

"Wanted to know if I was a notary. Well, of course I am, and I said so. She said I was the right person, then—*that* was some reassuring to hear—and we had to wait for somebody else to arrive. You'll never guess who it was!"

Mabel was certainly getting more than her share of dramatic moments lately. Tempted as Faith was to answer Stephen or Angus King, she settled for an appropriately breathless "Who?"

"Persis Sanford, that's who! She comes along about five minutes later. Meanwhile, Mrs. Who-ever is wandering to hell and gone, picking up copies of the *Town Report*, fiddlin' with the blinds. Then Persis waltzes in and they greet each other like they haven't seen each other since kinder-garten. I'm pretty sure what I'll be notarizing, so I get out my seal and go to my desk."

Faith knew her lines. "What was it?"

"Purchase and sale agreement, of course."

Of course.

"But how could they have one already? The will couldn't have been probated this fast."

"My thought exactly, but I kept my mouth shut. Persis knew what I was thinking, though. 'Now,

Mabel,' she says, 'this isn't a P and S'—that's real estate talk—'it just says that Mrs. Hapswell will be selling the following properties to me as soon as her late husband's affairs are settled.' At least the widow wiped the smile off her face that she'd had since Persis hove in, and put on something a little more dignified."

Faith couldn't help asking; plus, Mabel's words had been her cue. "What was she wearing?"

"Not much, and it was bright red." Mabel apparently felt that described the outfit. "So I dragged the first person off the street I could find, happened to be old Joe Sanford, Persis's mother's cousin, and he witnessed their signatures and I stamped it."

"Did Persis buy everything? Sanpere Shores, the lots in Bonneville, the lighthouse?" Faith was now well acquainted with Harold's holdings.

"The whole shebang, except for one lot excluded from the Sanpere Shores piece."

The dream house.

Faith felt like crying. Sanpere Shores was going to be developed anyway, but the lighthouse! Ursula would be so upset. She was comfortable—although Faith had learned that this word in New England could mean your family had enough for every generation to live in style until the next millennium or that it simply had enough for Locke-Ober's a few times a year. In any case, Ursula, even with money from the rest of the family, wouldn't have enough to meet what Persis would be asking for the lighthouse. Their only hope was pressure from the community. But again, as Ursula had so aptly pointed out, she was a summer person. Persis wasn't. It was hard to predict where the line would be drawn. It wouldn't be simple—or pretty.

And there was no question that Linda Forsythe would be getting new neighbors—and the Osborns a new vista.

Having ascertained that no dollar amount was stipulated in the agreement, Faith left Mabel to her various tasks and drove to the school. Thoughts of how steeped in passion and greed the land beneath her had become plagued her journey.

Roland, normally so calm, was delivering the notes in a frantic manner.

"We open in ten days, people! Remember someone's great idea to have a sneak preview for the dress rehearsal on Thursday night and charge admission? That's two hundred and forty hours from now, and yesterday's run-through was pathetic! Some of you still don't have your lines down and you're going to look pretty foolish come opening night."

Faith knew he was talking in particular about Persis, who was gleefully winging her role, depending on body language for laughs and murdering the Bard's words in the process.

"Now don't blow a gasket, Roly." Persis was the only one who could get away with that nickname. "I'm going to spend the next couple of days doing nothing but learning my speeches."

Since she'd arrived, she'd looked like a cat who had cream for breakfast every day. The others might not know the reason for Persis's glee, but after this morning's chat with Mabel, Faith certainly did. Ms. Sanford was going to make a killing. She'd be the richest woman on the island after developing Harold's properties. The man was not in shape to roll over in his grave, but his ashes must be swirling about like the funnel of a tornado. His widow had retrieved them from the Durgen brothers, restoring their prized view, and announced her intention to inter them in whatever cemetery was closest to Sanpere Shores. No memorial service was mentioned. With all the wheeling and dealing she was doing, Faith reasoned, Victoria was probably too busy to think about something that didn't directly concern her own best interests—interests with a pretty high rate of return.

Persis's words appeared to mollify Roland. "You're all doing a fabulous job, but the days will fly by. That's what I'm trying to say. I need to talk to the stage manager and her crew for a moment now, so why doesn't everyone take ten. Get some fresh air."

Before they had a chance to break up, Kenny Sanford walked onto the stage. He must have come in through the rear door. He was carrying a FedEx envelope.

"Jeez-zuz, Kenny, don't you know any better than to crash into a rehearsal like this?" his mother snapped at him. "What are you thinking of, walking across the stage? Never mind. You don't know how to think. I most forgot that."

He mumbled something about the FedEx might be important and held it out to her, avoiding her eye. She snatched it from his hand and waved him away. She didn't say another word.

Feeling desperately sorry for him, Faith started to follow him out. He didn't look any different from the way he usually did, and she realized he must be used to his mother's treatment. Still, she wanted to say something—to try to take away the sting of those other words. But Linda beat her to it and the two walked toward the door together.

Kenny nodded at something Linda said and Faith was gratified by the shy smile he gave her. Watching the two of them go outside, Faith decided that what Kenny needed was a wife. If not Linda, then there must be other candidates. Faith made a note to speak to both Jill and Pix about it. A steady worker, not bad-looking—a little bumbling maybe—yet still a catch.

When Faith arrived at their house later that afternoon, it was instantly apparent that the miracle she'd been waiting for had occurred. She hadn't seen the work for several days and the house had been transformed. With the cabinets installed, counters and appliances in place, suddenly Faith had her kitchen. All the painting was finished and the paint colors worked. As she went from room to room, her impatience grew. She was tempted to move in and camp again, just to be there. Home.

"When do you think it will be ready for us to move in?" she asked Lyle. Arnie and Claire, Pix's brother and his wife, were coming for the last week in August. Although Ursula insisted there was room for everybody, Faith wanted to be out by then and give them a real vacation.

"Depends on what you call ready," he answered.

She looked around at the detritus—paint-spattered drop cloths, boxes of nails, many soft-drink cans, much sawdust—and decided broom-clean was what she would call ready. She'd do the fine tuning herself.

Lyle figured they should be out by the weekend. There was some grading to be done on the outside and the deck expansion, plus new steps. But this could be accomplished with the Fairchilds in residence.

Faith was envisioning their first party, a housewarming on Labor Day. School started on that Wednesday, and Tom had already declared his intention to stay until the last minute. Their lives would be governed by the school calendar for more years than she cared to contemplate. The new year now started in September, not January. She was happy to stretch out their stay on the island as long as possible, too.

But the house was virtually done. She beamed at Lyle. It was perfect.

"Aren't you happy? You did such a terrific job."

"Looks pretty good," Lyle effused—or what passed for effused Down East.

"Better than that. Take some credit. Your suggestions are what's made it so special. I don't know what Tom is going to do now, though. He's going to have severe withdrawal pains."

"Can work for me anytime. I've told him that. Might get tired of being a preacher."

"Oh, I doubt it," Faith said, although a tiny doubt was nagging at the back of her mind. Tom had been so happy to be away from the pulpit. Too happy? Her mind skipped back to a conversation they'd had last week. They'd taken the Rowes' Boston Whaler and gone a short way down the Reach at sunset. It was a warm night and the sea was calm. As they approached the arching suspension bridge from Sanpere to the mainland, Tom had commented, "Such a fragile-looking connection from here, yet a virtual life-line." Faith had replied, "I feel a sermon coming on," and Tom had snapped back, "Why do you always say that? That's not my whole life, you know." She hadn't pressed him. He seemed to want to enjoy the view quietly, but she had filed it under To Be Continued.

Lyle was packing up his tools. The others had left. Faith just wanted to sit on the deck and look at the view and then back at the house. The kids were running happily from room to room. Ben had peed in the newly installed upstairs toilet and, after the christening, declared it just as good as the downstairs one.

Faith looked at a pile of shavings and bits of wallboard that had been left in one corner of the room. She had a sudden vision of a lighted match being tossed into it and the whole house going up in smoke, like those recently attacked all over the island.

"Now that it's finished, you don't think that crazy KSS group or whoever will attack this house, do you? I mean, we're from away and we did enlarge what was here before. They may think we should have been content with what we had. Small is beautiful." Faith's anxious words ran together.

Lyle stopped what he was doing.

"This little Tinkertoy place? Don't even think about it. Besides, it's not that they're people from away. Gorry, half the island is from away, but it's what they're putting up and the way they're going about it. These aren't people who are real interested in this island, except for the view and the water. They're not going to run for the school board or give money to the Medical Center. They're not going to get paint on their noses making sets for a local play."

Faith reached toward her nose. "Blue, right? I was filling in the sky today."

"Blue it is," Lyle said, and laughed.

Faith felt reassured, a feeling she treasured all the more after her most recent adventure at the lighthouse.

"Just so long as it isn't green," she said.

Lyle's face darkened. He'd been very upset about what had happened to Faith—and the lighthouse.

"Can't believe Earl and the rest of them haven't caught whoever's doing this. Lots of people on the island still think it's kids. You heard that they caught a group of them burning down a shed near the old quarry in Bonneville?"

Faith hadn't heard about this.

"No, I guess it was while I was out of the picture for a bit. What happened?"

"Typical Saturday night—drinking too much—but this time they decided to burn the shed, and someone had the bright idea of making it look like the others. Sprayed slogans on the ledges. Spelled a lot of the words wrong, but that could have been the beers. I never believed it was Don and Terri Osborn, except they are total fanatics when it comes to this stuff. And they hated Harold—and Persis, too—like they were the devil incarnate, out to destroy Sanpere. But Don's way of doing harm is to talk you to death. You should hear him about global warming and wetland preservation. Never takes a breath. Even Kenny, who has to have the patience of a saint, told me he couldn't listen to him anymore."

"Kenny?"

"Kenny caretakes for them, does all sorts of odd jobs Don dreams up—solar panels on every roof, even the doghouse, that sort of thing. They're real close. Have been for years, since Kenny was a kid."

"What's Terri like?"

"As nuts as her husband, or committed to their cause—whichever way you want to look at the whole business. Won't kill a mosquito or wear leather, even shoes. Of course they're vegetarians, too, although Elwell told me he saw Donald at the buffet one Friday night up at Jordan's in Searsport, hitting the prime rib."

Linda Forsythe and the Osborns were soul mates.

Lyle picked up his toolbox and said good-bye.

"Don't worry. We'll be here bright and early. You'll be sleeping in your own room before the week is over."

Faith almost kissed him.

She left the kids with Tom and went back to the Pines to start dinner. I'll never regret the time spent here, she thought, as she turned into the gravel drive next to the house. But it was time to create their own traditions, hang their own photos and the kids' projects on the walls, store up their own memories.

The recent rain had brought forth a modicum of produce, and while she didn't have tomatoes, she had enough other summer vegetables to make a pasta dish that her family loved (see recipe on page 323). She started the grill to smoke some chicken, then set to work dicing peppers, summer squash, a red onion, carrots, and, of course, zucchini. She'd brought fresh rosemary from her very own garden, the one in front of the deck. After she'd cooked some tortellini and combined it with some chèvre, she steamed the vegetables. All she had to do was toss them with a rosemary vinaigrette, add the chicken, which she would cut into bite-size pieces, and mix it all with the pasta.

Ursula came in from the porch, where she had been hard at work on a new sweater for the fair. This time, it was one for a little boy, with a bright red lobster on a navy background.

"Something smells divine! You've spoiled me, Faith," she said.

"I plan to keep on doing so, with your permission. Will you be our first dinner guest?"

"I would be honored." Ursula gave Faith a hug. She'd taken to doing that since Saturday morning. "Now, I think I'll lie down for a little while. The Historical Society is meeting tonight, and Ken Layton is picking me up after dinner."

"Shall I call and invite him to come eat with us? There's plenty of food," Faith offered.

"I'm sure he'd appreciate that, and Ben would enjoy his lighthouse stories. Ken's grandfather was a lighthouse keeper and Ken used to spend summers with him."

Ken wasn't home, but Faith left a message on his machine, then took her book down to the shore to read until Tom and the kids came back.

It was a perfect Maine day—puffy white clouds, Kodacolor blue sky, sparkling sea. Not too warm, not too cool. She could see a small dinghy rounding the next point, getting smaller and smaller in the distance. In the other direction, sailboats of all sizes were gracefully making their way down the Reach to anchor for the night at Buck's Harbor or maybe Castine.

There were a few cars by the dock, and she was surprised to see Persis's big Cadillac. Setting the book down, Faith sprang up, walking rapidly toward the lighthouse. The realtor must be showing the property, showing it before she even owned it! Should I wake Ursula, Faith wondered, and tell her what's happening? Ursula was still hoping the price would be within her means. No, she didn't want to disturb her. Faith could ask Persis herself, client or no client. She found herself getting more and more indignant as she approached the lighthouse. They'd carve windows in the sides and hang cute little nautical curtains in them. They'd put a deck in front for happy hour and serve awful drinks named after lighthouses—the Nubble, the Pemaquid.

The door was open and Faith stepped inside, expecting to hear voices, but there wasn't a sound. Could they be up at the top? The view was the selling point, after all. She was about to climb the stairs, brightly illuminated—Persis must have had the power turned back on—when she saw exactly where the woman was.

She wasn't at the top. She had never left this room. And never would.

Sprawled on her back, her arms stretched out straight on either side, Persis was dead. The coral jacket of her pantsuit was soaked with blood. It had oozed onto the floor, a small sea of red beneath the body. Faith walked slowly over to make sure it was true. She was supposed to do this. Supposed to do this, even though there wasn't the slightest doubt. Persis was dead. Murdered.

Faith started to retch. There was no way anyone could have survived such a savage attack. The woman had been stabbed many, many times. Backing away, starting to run, Faith saw there was a photograph in one of Persis's outstretched hands. Without touching it, Faith tried to make out who was in the picture. There were two people, one a much younger and, yes, very beautiful, recognizable Persis. Next to her stood a handsome young man. It was impossible to figure out where they were. Rocks, sea, sky. Sanpere—or any number of places on the Maine coast. Persis's fingers had relaxed in death and cradled the photo. Trying hard not to see the carnage on the jacket, Faith looked at Persis's face. Her eyes were wide open, staring at sights unseen. Her mouth was twisted in a silent, agonized cry. Had she known her attacker? Her murderer? Who could it have been? Who could have hated her this much?

"I didn't do it," a soft voice said. "She was like this when I got here. I didn't kill her."

Linda Forsythe came out from behind the old mattress, which had been propped against the wall. Her skirt was streaked with blood and she was holding a knife in her right hand.

Ten

Faith screamed and raced for the door. It seemed the prudent thing to do. Linda dropped the knife and followed, moving much more swiftly than Faith would have judged possible. She increased her own speed.

"Faith! Faith! Stop! *Please!* I didn't kill her! You've got to believe me! She was dead when I came in." Linda was gasping between words, but they were clear enough.

"Just now when I heard someone coming through the door, I hid. I thought it was the murderer!"

That made a certain amount of sense, but Faith was not inclined toward reason. They were both outside now, still sprinting. She looked wildly around.

"Go into the boathouse," Faith ordered, pointing toward the small building near the dock where the Lymans and Rowes kept their gear. "Go on. Stay ahead of me and don't try anything."

She realized now that one of the cars parked near Persis's must be Linda's.

Linda headed for the shed and went straight inside. Faith quickly slammed the large door shut and fastened the lock. She suspected it had never been used. It was slightly rusty, but it worked.

"I'm going to the house to call the police," Faith shouted through the thick boards.

Linda didn't reply, but Faith thought she heard the sound of sobs. Without windows, there was no way to check. Sobs of fear? Sobs of remorse? She ran to the Pines with only one thought in her mind. She had to get to Tom before he arrived with the kids.

Having blurted out the unbelievable news and without pausing for his reaction, Faith yelled into the phone, "Just keep away. Tell the kids I'm going to the Historical Society meeting with Ursula and you're going to have a picnic supper and camp at the new house. I'll call as soon as I can. Don't let them out of your sight."

"Faith, Faith . . ."

She hung up and dialed 911, blessing the new convenience that had resulted in names for every road on Sanpere, many that had never had names other than "the road to Dana's" or "the old cemetery path." A lot of people objected to the new signposts and appellations—they knew where they lived and where they were going—but as

262

911 literally saved lives, the opposition faded away. It wasn't saving a life now, though. A life had been taken.

The dispatcher was keeping Faith on the line. She knew she must have sounded hysterical. She *was* hysterical. Persis Sanford was lying dead in the lighthouse, only a short walk away, and the obvious suspect was locked in Ursula's boat-house.

Ursula! Over the dispatcher's objections, Faith hung up and went upstairs. She didn't want her friend to wake to the sound of sirens—and the sirens would be here soon.

She shook Ursula's shoulder gently. The old woman was sound asleep, the steady rise and fall of her chest just barely detectable.

"Ursula, it's Faith. You need to wake up."

Ursula opened her eyes and reached for her glasses.

"What time is it? I hope I haven't overslept."

"No, you haven't. There's plenty of time." Except for Persis, she thought. "There's been an-other . . ." Faith searched for the word. This wasn't an accident. It wasn't a death like the other deaths—Harold's, Helen Marshall's, the others— or maybe it was.

"I found Persis in the lighthouse. She's been murdered. Linda Forsythe was there holding a knife."

She was sitting on the side of the bed and Ur-sula reached for her, holding her tightly.

"I've been afraid something like this would

happen. Things have been so strange all summer, so volatile. I suppose Persis goaded her into it. Terrible that way, despite all the good she did. Oh dear, the island will never be the same without her. Where is the girl now?"

Ursula's tone suggested that Faith might have put her in the living room with a cup of tea.

"I locked her in the boathouse until the police could get here."

Ursula nodded. "Of course. And Tom, the children?"

"They're staying at the house."

"Good." She released Faith and pulled the covers back.

"I suppose we'd better go downstairs and wait."

Faith helped her up. "Yes, it shouldn't be long."

The phone was ringing as they made their way to the living room. By tacit agreement, they avoided the porch, with its view of the lighthouse. Faith answered it on the fifth ring. It was her husband.

"Faith, my God! I've been so worried! Are you all right? I'm going to take the kids to Lisa Prescott's or one of the other sitters. I'm sure I can find someone."

"No," Faith shouted, startling Ursula. The woman was looking at her with a puzzled expression. "I want one of us to be with them at all times until we know what the hell is going on. Linda says she didn't do it. Maybe she didn't. We don't know! There's nothing you can do here. Nothing anybody can do." Her voice caught. She knew she was overreacting, but every maternal gene was marching to the front. She didn't want Ben or Amy out of their parents' sight for even one second.

"It's okay." Tom was speaking softly, calmly. "I understand, sweetheart. They won't leave my side, and we'll all be together as soon as you can get here."

Faith hung up and sat next to Ursula. The sirens she'd heard faintly in the distance while she was talking to Tom were now blaring in the front yard.

It took a while to find the key to the lock on the boathouse. Faith had been correct. It never had been used. The Pines abounded in keys—in drawers, on hooks, and in mason jars. Eventually, it turned up in a Shaker box on the dresser in Arnie and Claire's room. It had been labeled when new and the tag remained readable.

"My father's hand," Ursula noted. "He was very organized, and we all drove him crazy."

By this time, it seemed as if every law-enforcement officer in Hancock County had arrived. There was considerable activity, and confusion.

Kenny Sanford showed up, too. Earl had called him, telling him delicately that there had been an "accident" at the lighthouse and his mother was dead. His old pickup squealed into the yard, leaving deep ruts in the grass. He leapt out, barely turning off the ignition.

"Where is she? *Where's my mumma?*" he cried.

Earl took him aside, but Kenny wasn't having any of it and broke away, running toward the lighthouse and disappearing inside before anyone could stop him. He was out again moments later and threw himself on the grass, pounding his fists on the ground, sobbing. Trained volunteers from the ambulance corps were by his side immediately.

"What am I going to do? What am I going to do?" he wailed over and over.

When they finally got the lock off the boathouse door and Linda emerged, her bloody skirt visible to everyone, it took three men to hold Kenny.

"You killed my mother! You whore! Why? Why? Because of a few fucking trees? Killer! Killer!" His screams grew louder and louder. Linda seemed to be on the point of fainting. She made no protest as her rights were read to her and an officer cuffed her. Faith had moved onto the porch. Ursula remained inside by the phone, which was ringing steadily. In the midst of everything, Ken Layton appeared.

"This looks like some dinner party," he said, coming up the front stairs, but his lighthearted comment gave way to sober grief when he heard what had happened.

"We've never had anything like this happen here before. Poor Persis. She deserved so much better. I always imagined her getting the *Boston Post* cane." He explained for Faith's benefit. "In 1909, the newspaper gave them to the oldest resident in two hundred and thirty-one communities all over their circulation area. A lot of the canes have been lost, but we still have ours." He was quiet for a moment, contemplating this fact or, more likely, the one immediately before him now.

"And Linda! I don't know her well, but I can't believe she had this much hate in her heart."

He relapsed into silence and the two sat watching the scene in front of them. It was surreal. Still a beautiful day, winding down into late afternoon, but now draped with yellow crime-scene tapes. The shoreline was crowded with cars, trucks, and an ambulance. Kenny was sitting in its front seat waiting to go to the hospital. He'd already been sedated and was now quietly crying, his shoulders heaving.

"I don't know what that boy is going to do without his mother," Ken said. "We're going to have to keep a close eye on him to make sure he doesn't do something foolish." He stood up. "Well, being as I am the president of the Historical Society, I have to go to the meeting. I'll see what Ursula wants to do."

Faith remembered the meal she'd cooked, several lifetimes ago, and urged him to go to the kitchen and eat something. He went into the house. She stayed where she was, staring straight in front of her, staring in continued disbelief.

Earl had come over several times, and eventually he asked her if she felt she could answer some questions. He had his notebook out, pen clicked. She nodded. She wanted to talk to someone, wanted to do anything that would stop her from thinking by herself.

"Let's go inside, Faith. I assume Tom has the kids someplace?"

"Yes, they're all at our house." She got up and went through the open front door.

Ursula was hanging up the phone.

"Word has definitely spread," she said grimly.

Faith hadn't thought about the repercussions suggested by Ursula's tone. All she could think about was Persis's face, Persis's jacket, Linda's face, Linda's skirt. She realized with a jolt that the murder would polarize the island as nothing before had. Linda not only was associated with KSS but she was from away, an off-islander, even an out-of-stater. Persis's family had roots so deep in Sanpere, they went below the aquifer into the ocean floor. She had been an active, vital force—a partisan. Faith had a sudden image of more fires, fires on the lawns of people like Linda, the Osborns. The resentment was going to be enormous. She could hear it now: "If only that girl hadn't come here in the first place. . . ."

Earl was talking to her.

"Sorry, I didn't hear what you were saying. I was thinking about how the island is going to explode now."

Earl didn't bother to contradict her. "We'll try to keep on top of it. Try to get the cooler heads talking, but you're right. This will be regarded by a lot of people as a 'them' and 'us' situation."

Ursula brought a tray in. Tea, real tea this time around, hot and fragrant. She poured Faith a cup and added some heaping teaspoons of sugar, then started to leave.

"She doesn't have to leave, does she?" Faith asked. She wanted Ursula by her side—always.

"Of course not. Maybe she can shed some light on this, too," Earl said. "Anyway, walk me through what happened, Faith. Try to remember exactly what you saw before you went into the lighthouse and then what you saw when you got inside."

Faith obliged. As with Harold's death, there wasn't a whole lot to say. She'd spotted Persis's car, gone to the lighthouse all steamed up, intending to make a last-ditch effort to prevent its sale, and found the body. Then Linda had come out from behind the mattress.

"And the photograph. I looked at the photograph. It seemed so odd that she would be holding something like that. As if the murderer had handed it to her just before killing her. Why?"

"What's this about a photograph?" Ursula asked.

"It's no secret, what with the number of people around. Persis had an old picture of herself in her hand. She looked about seventeen or eighteen. I didn't recognize the man next to her, but someone else did. It was Harold," said Earl.

"Harold Hapswell!" Faith exclaimed. "Why would the murderer have put a picture of the two of them there?" As she tried to make sense of it, she recalled how handsome the young man in the snapshot had been and how both figures had faced the camera square-on, smiling, arms entwined, greeting life with full force.

"I can only think that somehow this whole business with the Sanpere Shores development has unhinged Linda's mind and she was leaving a sign that now both enemies of the environment were dead," Earl theorized.

"Then you think Linda killed Harold, too?" Faith asked quickly.

"I didn't say that. I said both were dead."

"But where would she get an old photograph like that?" Ursula asked. "Linda was probably not even born when it was taken." Earl and Faith looked at each other. Where indeed?

If the residents—all categories—had been on edge throughout the summer, Persis's death sent them tumbling over into an abyss. They even took to locking their doors, searching out the keys at the back of junk drawers and in old jacket pockets. Rumors were rampant, and suddenly every encounter between Persis and Linda was resurrected. Resurrected and embroidered. The incident with the Moxie bottle, dismissed as an accident, now became the first attempt. Persis's car trouble became another as residents recalled how handy and mechanical Linda was. Preparing to move into their beautiful house, Faith could not remember feeling this depressed.

Tuesday evening, the family was assembling their IKEA dining table and chairs. The Swedish company made it look like a piece of pastry on the drawings, but the Fairchilds were having trouble figuring out what went where. Ben was enjoying the names.

" 'Jussi.' What do you think that means in Swedish? And why are the bookcases called 'Billy'?"

Tom started to spin a tale about little Billy Jussi, who wanted to get even with the world for making his ears stick out, so he designed furniture and made up the directions, always giving too many little pieces of hardware. That way, people like Daddy would be sure they had not attached something correctly. The kids were laughing hysterically, but Faith tuned out, intent on lining up the holes to attach the leg of her Bror chair. Bror, no doubt, was Billy's brother. This was supposed to be a joyous time. The house was almost finished. And it was wonderful.

She had never felt less like living on Sanpere.

What would Tom say if she suggested selling? After all, it was a ridiculously long drive from Aleford. They could never pop up for a weekend. And then there was the weather; Maine seasons: fall, winter, mud, and July. Why not look on the North Shore or in New Hampshire? Some nice lake. Someplace with no lighthouses.

Linda had refused to talk to anyone; refused a lawyer. She appeared to be resigned to whatever might happen to her. The story was splashed all

271

over the papers as far as Boston. Linda's prints were the only ones on the knife. Like Harold, Persis had been trying to get Linda to sell her cabin, people speculated. It was well known that Harold had offered her twice what it was assessed at. Linda was a thorn in the side of Sanpere Shores.

Tom crumpled the instructions and threw them across the room.

"Get on the other side and let's turn this baby over," he instructed. "Jussi is finished—or Swedished."

Faith smiled wanly.

They turned the table over. It seemed steady and fit into the space in front of the window perfectly.

"You brought dinner, right?" Tom asked, looking at his wife with a worried expression on his face. Normally, a pun of the sort he had just made would have evoked a more dramatic response. But there had been too much drama lately.

"Yes, the leftover smoked chicken and vegetable pasta."

"Yum, yum, right, kids?"

"Yum," said Amy.

"Leftovers?" said Ben, then grinned mischievously. "Double yum."

Sitting down to eat, Faith almost recaptured her equilibrium as they joined hands and Tom said a blessing. It was their first meal in the new house. She *was* blessed. Then all the thoughts came crowding back again. Kenny had returned to work that morning. Faith saw him in the afternoon. He looked terrible. Pale under his tan—a description Faith had read in books with skepticism until now, actually seeing it. It was as if the tan were a body stocking peeled on for appearance' sake. She had tried to find some words to comfort him. What was there to say? "I'm sorry I found your mother's body"? "I'm sorry your mother was killed"? Instead, she settled for just "I'm sorry," and he nodded, then blew his nose on a raggedy red handkerchief.

With both his stage manager and one of the leads lost to the production, Roland Hayes was distraught, although not in complete despair. He called a special meeting of the cast Wednesday evening. Faith thought she'd skip the meeting and go over to the house and put some Billy bookcases together, but Ursula's "You're not going to Roland's meeting?" sent her scurrying for her car keys. Duty first.

"Some of us talked about canceling the play," Roland said. "I know the joy has gone out of it, but there are two things to consider. The pool project is an important one. We're sold out Saturday night and are close to it for the other two. That's a lot of money, and we have an angel who is matching whatever we make, remember." Faith looked at the sober faces gathered around the director. Becky and Ted, Romeo and Juliet, looked so young, so innocent. This would be a summer they would never forget, a summer filled with too much tragedy.

"Then the other consideration is what Persis

herself would have wanted, and I have no doubt she would have wanted us to go on."

"Maybe we can dedicate the performance to her," Becky suggested tentatively.

"What a splendid idea," Roland said. "It would mean a lot to Kenny, too. I asked him how he felt about having us do the play without his mother, and he said as far as he was concerned, it was the best thing to do in her memory."

People relaxed a bit. It was settled. Roland continued.

"Fortunately, the sets are almost finished and the crew knows what needs doing." He shook his head, and the message was as clear as if a cartoonist had drawn a bubble from his mouth: Linda Forsythe, artist, stage manager, murderer?

"And Persis's understudy has indicated her willingness to play the role."

Lady Capulet—Sharon McDonald—stepped forward. She'd need more than a little padding, but Faith knew that Sharon had all the lines memorized. She'd fed them to Persis when the older woman had been at a loss. If this had been a question of a broken leg, theatrical history would be about to be made, a star born. But the circumstances did not allow for any pleasure, although pleasure was what Sharon was probably feeling in her heart of hearts. She had thrown herself into the other role with passion. Her husband's misgivings about the bank clerk and the boards may have been prophetic. Sharon had been waiting for her shot at playacting all her life.

It felt right to rehearse after Roland's talk, and it went smoothly. They were doing it for Persis.

"Faith, it's Earl. I wonder if I could ask you to do us a favor?"

"Anything," Faith replied. "More allergic relatives? Need some new hors d'oeuvre ideas?"

"Not that 'us.' " He cleared his throat. "The police. I'm in Ellsworth."

Oh, that "us," Faith thought, and replied slightly less enthusiastically, "Of course. What do you need?"

She'd gone over Monday's events, starting with her visit to the Town Hall, several times with several different "uses."

"It's Jill's idea. She said you'd gotten close to Linda Forsythe while working with her on the play."

"I wouldn't exactly say 'close.' " Faith was beginning to wonder where this was going, and the choices were not great.

"Closer than anyone else on the island, except for the Osborns and others in that group, and they're not exactly what we have in mind right now. The problem isn't just that the woman won't talk. She won't eat, either, and we're on the point of having to hospitalize her. She's getting dehydrated, for one thing. She sleeps. That's about all she does."

Faith wondered what she could do about the situation. Force-feed Linda one of Louella's pies?

This, as it turned out, was very close to what

Earl had in mind. They wanted Faith to come with a basket of goodies and try to get Linda to eat some of them, thereby loosening her tongue for a full confession.

Faith felt uncomfortable with the role, to say the least. "Doesn't Linda have any family members?" she asked Earl.

"Apparently not. Parents dead. Only child. A few cousins in New Jersey. We contacted them, and the ones who remembered her didn't want anything to do with this. Not sure they know where Maine is anyway."

Now was the time for a New Jersey joke, but Faith wasn't in the mood. Besides, Jersey girls are tough, she reminded herself again, and Linda is a Jersey girl. She'd need all that toughness now.

"I'll put together some food and talk with her, but she has to understand that anything she tells me isn't in confidence. I don't want to trick her."

"We generally frown on things like that in the law-enforcement business," Earl said dryly. "Entrapment, First Amendment. You know."

Faith was feeling feisty. "Alst I know, Earl Dickinson, is that for you guys, it's fish-or-cut-bait time."

She was going pretty native herself.

Faith ended up taking two baskets and a cooler. The pie basket held one of Louella's strawberry rhubarb pies. Faith didn't tell Louella where it was going, although there had been a surprising amount of sympathy for Linda, and the island had not exploded as Faith had feared. Smoldered, but no pyrotechnics. The general opinion was that the woman was stark raving mad and needed to be locked up for a very, very long time. The other basket held blueberry muffins, still warm and fragrant, fresh from the oven; some baguettes from Lily's; two dozen Comfort Cookies; brownies; and a small zucchini bread. Remembering Linda's garden, Faith had gone to the house and harvested several varieties of tomatoes, sugar snap peas, peppers, lettuce, carrots, raspberries, strawberries—wild and tame—plus pungent basil. She had a hunch that Linda would find it difficult to resist the fruits of her own labor. The fruit and vegetables were in the cooler along with dressing, tarragon chicken salad, hardboiled eggs, chutney-cheese spread, a chunk of rat cheese—the sharp Cheddar the IGA sold—tabbouleh—Linda seemed the type—iced tea, and lemonade. At the last minute, she'd sacrificed some of the Côte d'Or dark chocolate bars she'd brought for her family's picnics. Struggling under the weight of the feast, Faith entered Linda's cell. This was by far the most unusual event she'd ever catered. Linda was sitting on the narrow bed. She had refused to bathe, but fortunately she was not too ripe, although her hair had taken on an unpleasant oily sheen. It was scraped back from her face in a tight ponytail. The orange prison jumpsuit was definitely not Linda's color. She looked up as Faith entered, then down again.

Faith had been rehearsing all the way to

Ellsworth. Tom had wanted to drive her. She'd refused his offer, preferring to be by herself. And besides, she had no idea how long she'd be. Linda might be in a secure facility, but Faith still wanted one of them with the kids whenever they weren't at camp.

"Linda? Oh, Linda! This is all so crazy. I have no idea what to say to you, but you have to eat something. They'll take you to the hospital if you don't, and that will be horrible, even more horrible." It wasn't what she'd thought to say, yet it would have to do. Methodically, she began to unpack what she'd brought. When she took out the bowl of Sweet One Hundred cherry tomatoes, Linda burst into tears.

Faith put one in her hand and Linda popped it into her mouth, chewing slowly, tears continuing to irrigate her cheeks.

Faith gave her another. She'd asked Earl to find out what might be the dangers if Linda did decide to eat and stuffed herself. He'd gotten back to her and said to try moderation and liquids first. Linda wasn't in danger of starving and she had been incarcerated only since Monday. Dehydration was the main concern.

"Lemonade?" Faith offered her a cup. "I hope you don't mind, but I made it with some of the lemons from the trees on your deck."

Linda shook her head and between sobs told Faith that she did the same thing herself.

They sat like this for a time. Faith made Linda a chicken-salad sandwich. Linda ate it. Faith passed her the strawberries and the brownies. She inhaled those too.

"I didn't do it," Linda whispered after the strawberries were gone.

Faith *had* worked this one out. She'd figured if Linda did talk to her, this would be what she'd say. It was what she'd said at the lighthouse. The only thing to do was go with it.

"Okay. Then why were you there?"

"Persis left a note for me, telling me to meet her. She had a client who wanted to commission two paintings. One of the lighthouse and another of the view from the top. She said we'd split the sale."

"Where is the note now?"

"I left it on the kitchen table. It was stuck in my screen door."

Faith hadn't heard anything about a note. Linda's cabin had been searched thoroughly. One thing to tell Earl, anyway.

"And she didn't phone you, because . . ."

"As you know, I don't have a phone."

Exactly.

"So, she told you to meet her at the lighthouse. Had she ever asked you to do this sort of thing before? Do a painting and split the proceeds?"

"No, but I thought it was very nice of her to throw some work my way."

"I thought you two didn't get along!"

"That's what's funny. I thought so, too. I mean, she practically accused me of trying to murder her when she drank the turpentine." Linda's face flamed as red as the berries she'd eaten.

"Still, you went."

"There was no reason not to."

Faith wished everything Linda had said didn't make so much sense.

"Did you know that Persis was buying most of Harold's property from his widow, including Sanpere Shores?"

Linda looked totally aghast. "I didn't even know he was married, and I certainly didn't know Persis was going to buy the property! How would I?"

Obviously, Linda was not part of the island grapevine, but then again, she wouldn't be—especially not this particular vintage.

Faith reached in the cooler and poured more lemonade for Linda, grabbing a few cherry tomatoes for herself.

"What was your relationship with Harold like?" A new scenario was taking shape, but Linda quickly erased it.

"I knew who he was, but we never had much to do with each other until he bought the land. At first, he told everyone it was just an investment and he was going to leave it the way it was; then he began buying up everything he didn't already own. It was terrible. I'd even had him to dinner once; then he made it so Adelaide—my nearest neighbor—had to move. She was worried about her medical bills, and so instead of staying in the farmhouse where she'd been born, she moved in with her daughter and her husband, plus their three kids. They all live in the house they bought with the money from the farmhouse. It's no palace, no Sanpere Shores." Linda bit into a carrot vehemently.

"But you didn't sell."

"No, and I never will—or I guess that's *would* now. I'm going to prison, aren't I, Faith?"

"I think you need to get yourself a lawyer," Faith said. She ate some more of Linda's food. "So was Harold putting a lot of pressure on you to sell, too?"

"Absolutely. Offered me another shore lot over near Granville—tidal. Not that I don't like the tides, but it was nothing compared to my place. He got pretty ugly. I think he had somebody who wanted a big piece but would only buy if it included mine."

And presumably Persis knew about the somebody, too. Faith pictured her going through Harold's papers with the grieving widow and planning how to make all their dreams come true.

But none of these things added up to a motive for Linda to kill Persis; more likely, one for Persis to get rid of Linda.

Persis and Harold were enemies of KSS, however. Just how involved was Linda—and how crazy?

Faith took a deep breath.

"I understand you're a member of Keep Sanpere Sanpere." She just couldn't say the acronym. The place was all wrong.

"I am. What's happening to the island—and it's not just the developers—is a crime. In ten years, it will be Bar Harbor." Linda was recovering fast.

"I agree with all this, but not with the kinds of things you do," Faith said. "Destroying property . . ."

Linda burst into tears again. She wasn't as tough a Jersey girl as Faith had supposed.

"Maybe we went a little too far in the beginning," she said, trying to collect herself. "But we stopped. Or at least I did, and I'm pretty sure Terri and Don did, too."

"Tell me about it. When did you stop and what had you done?"

"We wanted to make a statement. Sanpere doesn't realize what's happening. They just think that these people are going to bring in tax money, but they're not taking the longer view. I mean, after the first year, the money goes mostly to the state, and then—"

Faith interrupted the diatribe.

"What did you do, Linda?"

She looked at the floor and mumbled, "I spray-painted the slogans on that big house going up in Bonneville. It was last May. And I . . . well, I helped set a fire, a very small fire, in an oil drum on the site. How could we know it would get blown over and spread to the trees?"

"Was that it?"

"Almost. I was doing some more spray painting one night in June. I told Don no more fires, and he agreed. It turned out I was the only one there. I don't know why the other people didn't show up. Don said later that I had the wrong night. Well, that's possible. I do lose track of time, especially in the summer. . . ."

She lost track of her train of thought, too, and Faith pulled her back on the rails.

"What happened that night?"

"Someone caught me and I said I'd never do it again. I wasn't comfortable with it anyway. I mean, I thought speaking at meetings and writing articles for the paper made more sense. I guess I was glad I got caught, because I told Don it was just too dangerous and I wasn't going to do it anymore."

"Who caught you?"

"Kenny. Kenny Sanford."

Kenny—Persis's son. This was getting as tangled as the pile of old line next to Freeman's shed. He kept meaning to sort through it one of these days. Unlike the rope, this knotty mess had to be sorted right away.

"What did he say to you?"

"Not much. He's not a big talker, but he said he wouldn't tell anyone, and I'm sure he didn't. Otherwise, I'd have known about it."

This was true, Faith realized, but if he'd told his mother, it might explain why she was so sure Linda and KSS had doctored her Moxie.

"What about the Osborns—did they stop, too?"

"They said they did, but things kept happening. The place on the old quarry road . . ."

"And the dummy with a knife in its heart," Faith added, finishing for her.

"That was definitely not KSS. None of us would do anything like this—and none of us attacked you, either." Linda's voice had recovered some strength and she sounded stubbornly sure.

"But do you know everyone who is a member?"

"Most of them. We had meetings in the beginning—to strategize. Don ran them. He told me a few weeks ago that some of the summer people had joined, but I don't know who in particular, because we'd stopped the meetings."

Faith remembered Linda's telephone conversation backstage after Hapswell's death.

"I happened to be in the hall when you got that call the day after Harold died. I overheard you arranging to meet someone at nine o'clock to get your stories straight. You said, 'If they came to you, they'll come to me.' What was that about?"

Linda's face flushed. "Nothing to do with Harold. The timing was a coincidence. The state police had been looking into the arson at Seth Marshall's work site and they'd questioned Don. He figured they'd come to me, too, and wanted to warn me. Terri is wicked jealous, though she has no reason to be. Don is crazy about her, always has been. But he didn't want me coming to the house. When we had KSS business, we'd meet on that beach where I saw you and your kids. We were there that night, too—the night Seth's office got torched—and Don didn't want the police to know. He was sure Terri would find out that he was with me and misconstrue things. He'd told them he was in Ellsworth—which he had been earlier, before driving straight to the beach—and I was to say I was home. Which I was—mostly."

Faith thought about Don Osborn—stocky, Brillo hair and beard. Not her first pick for Lothario of the island, yet it appeared he was to his wife. And Linda? Trysts on the beach. She was finding it hard to believe that all the meetings involved KSS and not kiss.

"I'm very fond of Don, but he's not my type." Linda was chatting confidentially now, as if she and Faith were having a slumber party. She'd be asking Faith to do her hair and nails soon. Not that Faith wouldn't love to see Linda with a semblance of a hairstyle and nails less ragged.

Faith sighed. She was no closer to getting what Earl wanted than when she'd entered the cell. True, Linda had broken her fast, but they hadn't touched the real main course.

"Linda, let's say I believe you. Believe you were framed for Persis's murder . . ."

"I was!"

"Okay, let's accept that as a fact. Then who did it? Who framed you? Who killed Persis?"

"I haven't got the slightest idea," the woman said dismally. "I guess you'd better find me a lawyer."

The Fairchilds were finally able to move into their house. They worked all day Friday, assembling the rest of their furniture and nesting in general. As Faith made beds and improved on Lyle's idea of broom-clean, she ran through every possibility she could think of that didn't include Linda as Persis's murderer. The Osborns had the best reason to want both Harold and Persis dead. Sanpere Shores would spoil their view. People have been known to kill for less, Faith thought. Plus, they were ecofanatics. With Linda as prime suspect, they could easily be thinking they would get away with it. Of course the note from Persis that Linda had described was nowhere to be found. Earl searched the cabin and surrounding area. The Osborns were a short kayak or canoe trip away. Easy to leave the note; easy to retrieve it. They went out almost every day, she'd heard, so no one at the lobster pound would think anything of seeing them on the water. Either craft could put in anywhere, then a quick dash to Linda's. Did Terri frame Linda, believing she was having an affair with Don? Did Don alone frame Linda to thwart the developers' plans? Linda hadn't heard about Victoria Hapswell's plans to sell to Persis, but that didn't mean the Osborns hadn't. It was simply a question of being in the IGA or post office at the right time on Monday. But supposedly, these people didn't even kill mosquitoes. Then again, they seemed to believe very strongly that the end justifies the means and they may have treasured insects more highly than Persis. What did she contribute to the web of life, after all?

Faith kept thinking about the photograph. Why was it placed in Persis's hand? Or had the murderer handed it to her while she was still alive?

She thought for a moment about Kenny. Was Harold Kenny's father—or Don Osborn? Both men were the right age and both had been among Persis's summertime beaux. But this was the kind of gossip that would be common knowledge on Sanpere, since both men lived here. And Ursula didn't know who Kenny's father was. By extension, that meant the Sewing Circle didn't know. She stopped scrubbing the tub and sat back on her heels. Don had always taken an interest in Kenny, employing him as a caretaker. The two were close. Could Persis have just now revealed to Don he was Kenny's father? Earth Mother Terri looked so calm, but according to Linda, she was a tigress when it came to her man. Did Don kill Persis to save his marriage?

It was the only thing that made sense. When Tom arrived with fish sandwiches—each one appeared to contain an entire deep-fried crunchy haddock filet with lettuce, tomato, and plenty of tartar sauce—he had news that clinched it.

"Don Osborn is going to buy Sanpere Shores from Hapswell's widow. Apparently, the 'intent to sell' document was a valid agreement only between Persis and Victoria. Even if Kenny wanted to pursue it, which I seriously doubt he'd ever want to do, it wouldn't apply to him, even as Persis's heir."

"What about the lighthouse?" Faith asked immediately.

"I didn't hear anything about that. I only heard this because someone at the take-out counter was mentioning that he thought KSS would be start-ing a fund to help with Linda's legal bills. The woman next to him laughed and said she thought the only real money any of the KSS people had would be tied up now, because Donald was going to buy Butler's Point."

The rest of the afternoon Faith debated whether to call Earl and tell him her theory. That night, falling asleep for the first time in her new bed-room—looking straight out into the night sky and the dark pines, feeling as if she were perched in a very comfortable tree house, she decided there was someone she needed to talk to first.

She didn't have to invent an excuse. She wanted Kenny Sanford to make them a chest of drawers, hoping he'd have time now that he wasn't work-ing on their house. She hadn't been able to find one that would fit below the long windows in the bedroom. The cabinetry he'd done—enclosing the sinks in the bathrooms and some finishing work—showed he was up to the job. In any case, the chest she wanted was a simple one. Saturday afternoon, on the spur of the moment, she drove to the Sanford house outside Granville, armed with measurements and a rough sketch. Tom had gone back to the Pines with the kids for a sail with Arnie Rowe. He'd arrived the day before with his wife and planned to spend as much time on the water as possible, as he did every year.

She was disappointed not to see Kenny's truck in the driveway at the end of the dirt road that led to the house from Route 17. Persis's big Cadillac had been returned, though, and Faith felt her throat close over as she thought of the vibrant presence who would never get behind the wheel again. Persis had loved everything she did, from selling houses to playing Juliet's nurse—and driving her Caddie at breakneck speed. It was true: The island wasn't the same without her.

About to get back into her own car—a Honda with relatively little personality—Faith decided to leave Kenny a note. Easier for him to get in touch with her. She'd leave the drawing and dimensions. She went around to the back door, which was open, as she'd expected. In the last day or two the island population had returned to normal—leaving their latches up. Persis and Kenny had probably never locked theirs in the first place, though. Persis had not been afraid of anything—and she should have been.

The kitchen was small and spotless. There was a glass, one plate, and knife and fork in the dish drainer. A bowl of plastic fruit graced the kitchen table, plus an array of baked goods, which indicated the women of the island had sprung into action. No doubt the fridge and freezer were full, too. Persis's funeral was scheduled for Monday. The table was Formica from the fifties; it would bring a fortune in New York City. The linoleum was much older than that and the pattern had been almost obliterated by frequent scrubbing. She stepped into the living room. It was crammed with an incongruous assortment of furniture—a

La-Z-Boy in front of a very large TV, surrounded by several uncomfortable horsehair pieces. Small tables, one with a marble top, impeded movement, and a huge china closet took up half of one wall. Doilies abounded; either Persis and her mother had had the knack or they'd been regulars at the Sanpere Stitchers fair. A lamp in the shape of a lighthouse sat on a round table that had been placed in front of a big plate-glass window facing the ocean. The Sanfords had a view, and someone had installed this window to take advantage of it, replacing what must have been a small three up and three down like the others in the room. The only book in the room was a photograph album on the table. Telling herself it made sense to wait a little while for Kenny, Faith opened the book and started leafing through the pages. Each picture was meticulously identified in the beginning, starting with a formal wedding shot of Persis's parents and moving quickly to Persis at birth and every step of the way thereafter. She had been a beautiful baby, and her beauty bloomed throughout her childhood. She was an only child, and her doting father was the photographer, appearing in a few rare shots. But her mother was in many, her arm around her daughter, whose long curls had been brushed into shining ringlets. Teenaged Persis appeared at clambakes, holidays, and notably as queen of the prom. There were several more, but they weren't labeled. Faith remembered hearing that Persis's father had died when she was a teenager. That probably explained the drop in the number of photos and even the lack of captions, some of which had been of the "Aren't I cute?" nature. Her mother would not have felt like it. She turned the page and saw an empty spot. A photo had been removed. Judging from the corners left in the album, it was exactly the same size as the one that had been found in Persis's hand. Faith examined the others on the page. They were of another clambake. So the photo had been taken on Sanpere here. Taken one summer when Harold and Persis were an item. How had her mother liked that? She kept turning the pages, expecting the whole process to begin again with Kenny—Kenny at birth, first steps, and so on. But there were only two pictures of Kenneth Sanford in the rest of the book. She checked again. One was taken on Santa's lap—a pale, terrified-looking four-year-old—and the other a solemn graduation shot. All the rest continued to be of Persis—Persis at various community functions, four pages for each Fourth of July parade where she'd been the Grand Marshal. Faith turned back to the page with the missing picture, studying the empty space.

"Guess you know where it went," Kenny Sanford said, coming into the room. Quiet. He'd always been quiet. His face didn't look particularly vacant now, though—or frightened. He looked thoroughly in command.

It had been staring her in the face all the time. Matricide.

"Why?" she asked.

He smiled and motioned her toward a small rocker next to the table.

"Thought that would be obvious to a smart city woman like you. Hated her. Hated her from before I can remember. And she hated me right back. I was a mistake. The only mistake she ever made. Thought he'd marry her, since she was up a stump, but he wouldn't. How did he know it was his? 'Get rid of it,' he said, and she tried, but it was too late."

Faith thought of the album, those two pictures. She thought of the life he'd led with those two women in this house, a life glimpsed only in the public humiliations she'd witnessed. Kenny Sanford had lived in a hell she couldn't begin to imagine.

"Why didn't you leave? Get work on the mainland?" As she spoke, she knew what his answer would be.

"She wouldn't let me. Somebody had to do the chores. And I couldn't leave the island. Didn't know any other place. I guess I was too scared. Scared to stay; scared to leave. It got worse when Gran died, though her tongue was sharper." He stared out the window, and Faith thought he'd almost forgotten she was there. It was as if he were talking to himself. Thinking out loud. Getting to say what he'd kept in for thirty years or more.

"She started having me do things for her. 'Take this tonic down to Mary Ellen. She's been poorly.

Tell her I made it myself from the dandylions. Make sure she drinks it.' 'Take these doughnuts to Helen. Those doctors don't know what they're talking about. She needs a treat now and then.' My mother was an evil woman, Mrs. Fairchild, and the Lord has used me as an instrument to strike her down."

He laughed.

"Wish I believed that. The Lord had nothing to do with it. I wanted her dead myself. She made me kill my own father, as well as the others."

"What!" Faith half-rose out of the rocker. Kenny nodded for her to sit down, and she did.

"Mr. Hapswell. She told me he was going to the police. That he'd seen what I was doing. The spray painting. Torching the houses. First time, I'd caught one of those loonies doing it. She left and then I gave it a try. Felt real good. Always did like to set a bonfire. This was a lot like that, and I kept going. No reason to stop. My mother thought it was funny. She found the paint cans in my pickup. I'd forgotten to heave them in the water when I left one night. She said Mr. Hapswell had seen me and was going to have me locked up. I couldn't be locked up now, could I? She told me where to find him, what to do, and I done it. A week later, she got drunk and started laughing fit to kill. She'd finally gotten even with him, she said. Him—'your father.' 'Killed by his own bastard,' she said. So I got even with her. She was flying high, buying his land and everything. Wanted me to remodel the lighthouse into a bed-

293

and-breakfast. It was worth it to see her face when I took out the knife and shoved the photo in her face. I wanted it to be the last thing she saw, and it was, 'cept she grabbed it and I couldn't get it out of her hand in time. I knew Linda was coming and I had to get clear. Took my skiff, just like the other time."

He looked over at Faith.

"Wish I had that picture. It was the only one. He was a nice enough guy. I did some work for him now and then. My own father, and I never got to know him. He never let on, neither."

Faith slowly let out the breath she'd been holding.

"I'm so sorry, Kenny—Ken." She resolved to stop calling him Kenny. It was obscene. The whole situation was.

"That is, you've had a terrible time." She searched for the words that would get her out of the house and found none to hand. "I just dropped by to ask if you'd build a chest of drawers for us." Perhaps if she pretended that the man in front of her had not just confessed to being the protagonist in a Greek tragedy, she could slip out.

"I'm some sorry, too—sorry you happened by today," he said sorrowfully.

She was with him there, Faith said to herself, and tried to stand up again. A look from Ken made her sit down abruptly, rocking back and forth. It reminded her of the hammock on Ursula's porch.

"You were outside the lighthouse that night! You knocked me down!"

"I was afraid you'd see the truck. But I didn't want to hurt you. What were you doing wandering around at night like that anyway?" he said in an accusatory tone, then kept talking. Ken Sanford was monopolizing a conversation for the first time in his life.

"I've been going out to the lighthouse a lot. Mr. Hapswell gave me a key. He wanted me to do the work, too." Kenny gave a short laugh at the coincidence. "Always wanted to live in one. I've got quite a bit saved up, and I thought I might be able to buy it from Harold. Told him he wouldn't get his money out of remodeling it, just to lead him astray, you see. I still plan to get it from his widow. Hear she's selling everything fast. It's going to be all built-ins, cherry. Stay here until I get it done; then maybe I'll torch this place." He smiled in anticipation. The bonfire to end all bonfires, followed by a lighthouse bachelor pad.

"But"—he gazed fiercely at her—"I can't do it with you blabbing about this all over the island."

Faith hastened to reassure him. "I won't say a word to anyone. Not even my husband, and he's a member of the clergy."

If she hoped to kindle some feeling of possible remorse by the mention of a man of God, she was mistaken. Kenny went into the kitchen. She followed him, planning to make a run for the door.

He'd opened a drawer and was pulling something out. She ran, but, without moving much at all, he stopped her with one hand, grabbing her elbow and pulling her back. There was no fat on his body; muscle and years of hard work had produced the same effect as a daily workout with a personal trainer. Kenny was as strong as an ox. He pushed her into one of the kitchen chairs and bound her wrists tightly together with duct tape. Sanpere homes usually had a roll close at hand, and the Sanfords' was no exception. Also like most locals, they had a yard that was a sea of bright blue tarps covering woodpiles, old traps and pot buoys, rusty machinery, and anything else you wanted out of sight, out of mind. Faith began to panic as she realized she could be joining this motley assortment, never to be found.

She tried again. "Kenny, even if someone does find out, you'll never be convicted. There are all kinds of abuse and your mother definitely abused you; maybe your grandmother, too. This wasn't your fault. I'll help you. So will Tom and all your friends on the island." Convicted, no. Locked up in whatever place Maine had for the criminally insane, yes, yes, yes.

He waited patiently for her to finish.

"Nope, I planned this out perfect. They've got Linda, and not a soul suspects me. I was a little afraid she wouldn't come, though she's the kind of girl who does what people tell her to. Ma and her were never what you'd call friends, but she went. Even picked up the knife, I heard. Nope, this is my chance. Now, let's go."

"Where?" her voice was shaking. As soon as they were outside, she'd scream her head off.

Sound carries over water, she thought. And she intended to create some very high decibels.

He closed the kitchen door behind them. The house was well off the road, so no one would have seen her car. She wondered what he planned to do with it. Another blue tarp? He was a lot smarter than anyone thought.

"Make one noise and I'll do you right here," he said matter-of-factly, producing a large Buck knife, exactly like the prop from the play. Faith opened her mouth, willing to take her chances. He couldn't butcher her in his own yard; there was no way he could avoid leaving evidence. Evidence. Her blood. She started screaming. Almost immediately, he wadded one of his red bandanna handkerchiefs into her mouth and tied another over it. He seemed to have an endless supply in the pockets of his work pants, pulling them out the way a magician pulls silk scarves from a top hat. They smelled and tasted of turpentine. She gagged and swallowed the bile rising from her stomach. He pushed her along the small dock in front of the house to his skiff, lifted her in, and pushed off. There were no other boats in sight. The fishermen had gone home long ago, but where were all the summer people? Where were all the sailboats? Especially Arnie Rowe's?

Kenny Sanford rowed easily, smoothly. It was the same skiff he'd been keeping at the Rowes' dock. The same one he'd used to get away after both Harold's and Persis's deaths. Unremarkable. Part of the Maine landscape. She could see they were headed for open water. Still no other boats. Luck was with him—just as it had been when he killed Harold. Just as it had been when he'd murdered his mother.

He reached into the bottom of the boat and from the mess of Clorox-bottle boat bailers, bits of bait, hooks, and line, he moved a large rock tied to a long line closer to his feet.

Faith was going to "drown." He started toward her, an oar raised over his head. At least he was doing her the kindness of knocking her out before he tied her to his anchor and cast her overboard. There was only one thing to do. Throwing all her weight to one side of the boat, she dove into the water. It was so cold, she thought she would die. Wanted to die. Every inch of her body ached with pain. The water closed over her head and she started sinking. She shut her eyes and let her body plummet. Somewhere in her numbed brain, she heard Pix's exhortation: "Swim like hell; get your blood going. You'll be warm as toast." She opened her eyes and looked up at the daylight filtering through the water, then began kicking frantically, using her arms as a kind of piston to get back to the surface. She crashed through and breathed through her nose, coughing into the gag as the salt water seeped into the cloth. A very distant cousin to a sense of warmth and well-being took over; she was alive.

She could hear Kenny shouting behind her. She was about to dive down again, out of his sight, when she realized he was in the water, too. He'd been standing when she leapt out, and the movement must have sent him over the other side. He was flailing madly, begging her for help.

"I can't swim! I can't swim! Push the boat this way, Mrs. Fairchild! I promise I won't hurt you!"

The boat had been quickly carried by the waves out of his reach and toward Faith.

Faith stopped trying to make any progress away from him and attempted to get to the boat, but it was moving too fast. She didn't know how she could hold on to it even if she did reach it, so she concentrated instead on treading water. The gag loosened and fell off. Kenny's cries continued. She shut her eyes and wished she could put her hands over her ears. He didn't last long.

Eleven

Mrs. Earl Dickinson had floated out of the Congregational church, the perfect image of love's sweet dream, in a cloud of tulle. She and her groom were gently pelted with rice, followed by their young attendants, who had all marched straight up the aisle without parental assistance. After storm clouds in the morning and a few drops of rain, it was now glorious—a perfect Maine day.

George and Lydia Johnson, old friends of Jill's parents, had offered their large home in a spectacular South Beach site to the young couple for the reception. Wedding guests were consuming the hors d'oeuvres and champagne, happily crowded on the deck, enjoying the view.

Bubbly in hand, Faith walked to the railing, where she was immediately joined by Pix, who had scarcely let her out of sight since she'd arrived on Thursday and heard about Faith's first—and last, she averred—swim in Penobscot Bay.

"This is an incredible house," Faith said, looking down at the rock-strewn beach far below and out across the water to Mount Desert Island rising majestically from the sea many miles to the north.

"Perfect for a party," Pix agreed. "It was built in the sixties by an architect who did several houses in the area—Scott Day. This is my favorite. The Johnsons commissioned him and got exactly what they wanted. You know there's no electricity in this section?"

Faith did know and wondered what the allure was. It had some sort of cachet on Sanpere—look at Linda—that escaped her. The Johnsons had a generator and solar panels for this, the main house, succumbing to conventional electricity, wires and all, for the guest houses and her studio. She was a potter.

"Jill looks radiant, as well she should," Pix continued.

"And Earl looks stunned." Faith laughed. "I think he can't believe he finally got her to say 'I do.'"

"Are you sure you're not getting tired?" Pix asked anxiously.

"Yes, Mother, I'm sure," Faith replied emphatically. It was nice to be cosseted, but a little was starting to go a long way.

She had suffered no ill effects from her plunge into the Gulf of Maine. Soon all kinds of boats had begun passing and she had been able to hail a small speedboat with the improbable name *The Bronx* on its stern. The skipper promptly got in touch with the Coast Guard, and the police were waiting at the Granville wharf, along with Tom, Ursula, and just about everyone else on the island. Kenny's body washed up on Great Spruce Head Island several days later.

It was over.

"Samantha looks beautiful. All your kids look great, but Samantha seems to have changed the most this year," Faith said.

The Millers' daughter had just finished her sophomore year at Wellesley. Tanned and fit from the "Westward ho" trek, she was wearing a long, simple buttercup yellow silk slip dress.

"Sam's still not used to his little girl as a young woman. As we were leaving for the church, he pulled me aside and asked if that was all she was going to wear. 'Doesn't it have something that goes on top?' " she said, mimicking him.

"Tom will be exactly the same," Faith said. "He was at the high school last spring for something and came home wondering how the guys ever got any work done or could pay attention in class with all that female flesh exposed. I told him they were used to it and he told me I was nuts."

Faith was looking beautiful herself in a soft green Prada sheath, her hair loose. The sun had lightened her hair to a very agreeable shade— somewhere between hollandaise and lemon curd. She'd bought the dress for the wedding the last time she'd been home—in the city, that is. It had been a gift from her grandmother, and Faith was extremely happy she'd gotten the chance to wear it. There had been moments on Saturday when she'd had her doubts.

Tom was talking to the Osborns inside the house. She could see them through the two-story glass windows, angled together like the prow of a ship. They formed the front of the house, which was really one very large open space, with a fully equipped kitchen at the opposite end from the dramatic windows. Honed black granite counters had been cleared for the trays of hors d'oeuvres, and the rest of the space was taken up by round tables, set for dinner. After dinner, they'd be removed and the same swing band that had played the night of the Fish 'n' Fritter Fry would play for an evening of dancing. The late-afternoon sun eliminated the need for illumination, but Faith had noted the rows of votive candles and oil lamps on narrow shelves on the walls and along the windowsills. The generator was for the kitchen appliances, the pump—and, tonight, the band.

"I said that the play was fantastic," Pix said. "What are you thinking about?"

"Nothing much—this place, getting some more champagne, eating another of those smoked trout and endive spears. But yes, the play has taken the island by storm. They've sold standing-room tickets tonight, because so many people were disappointed that they weren't going to get to see it."

They moved inside, joining Tom and the Osborns. They were talking about the play, too.

"I'm so glad it . . . well, um, worked out, so Linda could take a bow, so to speak." For once, Don was at a loss for words.

Linda Forsythe had been released immediately on Saturday, and the first thing she did was drive straight over to the Fairchilds' and throw herself into Faith's arms—or rather, across the bottom of Faith's bed, where Faith had been lying, insisting she was fine, really fine, then falling asleep again. Linda had returned on Sunday with a package. Faith, who had graduated to a chaise on the deck, had greeted her warmly.

"I don't know how I can ever thank you," Linda had said. "But that night when you came to dinner, I kind of thought you liked this."

When Faith had removed the brown paper from what was obviously a painting, she saw that it wasn't just a painting, but the painting she had indeed wanted—wanted very much. It had reminded her of Gauguin, yet the subject matter was far from Tahiti—pines, rocks, the purple shadows of sunset. She'd been overwhelmed, and very happy to have it.

The shadows were lengthening here at the nuptial feast, too, and everyone was peering at the place cards.

"I'll find out where we are, honey," Tom offered. Don Osborn hastily told his wife the same thing.

It was the opportunity Faith had been waiting

for. There weren't many loose ends, but there was one that was bothering her the way a sore in your mouth does. Try as you might, you can't keep your tongue from straying to it to see if it still hurts, and it always does.

Terri looked Faith straight in the eye and snagged two more flutes of champagne from a passing waiter. "Let's go out on the deck."

The air was cool but not cold, and welcome after the body heat inside. Family and friends had added up to an extensive guest list.

"You probably thought it was us—or one of us, right? You don't have to answer. I would have thought so, too. We have been a little crazy since we heard about what Harold was going to do with Butler's Point. We'd have bought it, but things change so slowly here that it never occurred to us that it would all be sold—and developed."

Faith nodded. "I guess that was true at one time. People held on to what they had, but it's not true now. Not with the kind of prices off-islanders are willing to pay to get deep water and a view."

"They were friends growing up, you know. Harold and Don. Summer boys. Pretty wild, from what I understand."

Faith couldn't think of anything appropriate to say.

Terri kept talking. Champagne didn't involve cruelty to anything but grapes, and Mrs. Osborn had clearly taken advantage of the fact. "Don and Persis had a fling. I know all about it. On and off for a while, but it ended when he went to college. When we came here to live, there were a lot of rumors that Don was Kenny's father. Persis made it worse by totally snubbing Don, acting as if he'd jilted her, left her with a kid to raise alone. But it wasn't Don. He told me it wasn't, and I believed—believe—him. Not just that." She smiled a little wickedly. "The timing was wrong. Don was an exchange student in Portugal one summer—*the* summer. I checked Kenny's birth date, and unless Persis belonged in the *Guinness Book of World Records* for shortest or longest pregnancy, it would have been impossible."

"What about Harold?" This was the end Faith was trying to tie up—Kenny's father. Persis had wanted Harold out of the way, and she was abusive enough to tell Kenny a lie later just to torment him.

"Don and Harold only fell out when Harold started buying and selling land. Before that, we saw a lot of him, and he told Don that Kenny wasn't his. There was someone else Persis had met up in Northeast Harbor that summer. Very wealthy. A Rockefeller type. Harold said most of the summer, Persis wouldn't give him the time of day; she was always going up to see the other boy. Persis liked money, even then, and she wanted off the island. Don was going off to college, and Harold . . . well, Harold was a hippie—not much cash."

"What's going to happen with KSS?" Faith asked.

Terri gulped down the rest of her drink. "We'll never give up, but we are renaming ourselves, and Don is going to run for the Planning Board. The only way to stop this sprawl is through zoning—and educating the people who live here."

With her flowing fuchsia print, beads, and hoop earrings, Terri looked an improbable Boadicea. Faith wasn't sure the people who lived here needed the kind of education Terri was talking about, but dinner was being served, and it wouldn't do any good to try to argue with the woman anyway.

"What are you going to do with the land? Give it to the Island Trust?" Faith asked idly as they went back inside.

"Heavens no! We're going to develop it ourselves. Fewer houses, of course. Very tasteful, hidden from sight, and no pools, or tennis courts. Like this one. You can't see it from the water, because of the way they left the trees. You don't have to stick a house out in the open to take advantage of all this." She waved toward the water and islands fast disappearing into the dusk.

An environmentally friendly Sanpere Shores. They'll make a bundle, Faith thought ruefully. She hoped Linda would get to keep her little slice. And as for Victoria Viceroy Hapswell—they'd tie her up in so many delays for permits if Don got on the Planning Board that she might as well give in now. Perversely, Faith hoped she wouldn't.

Living on Sanpere was as complicated as living anywhere else, despite the claims of the Department of Tourism brochures. Up and down the coast, the same thing was happening. Communities that had been relatively static for a long period of time were experiencing sudden seismic change. So what to do? Tom, Ursula, Arnie and Claire, Sam and Pix, Nan and Freeman were all waiting at one of the tables, waving at her. For the moment anyway, she'd go with the flow—and did.

Faith couldn't believe she was on Sanpere. It was ten o'clock and the party was still going strong. Earl had to be at work the next afternoon—they'd wanted a winter honeymoon anyway—and the newlyweds seemed as loath as anyone else to call it a night. Perhaps because it was such a magical night. The moon was almost full—full enough for Faith to comment on it and be corrected by all the Millers and Ursula in unison. The candles and lamps had been lighted, sending a soft warm glow over the dancers. Faith understood why they had opted for them instead of lightbulbs. The soaring cathedral ceiling was in darkness and the walls shimmered. She wasn't tempted to cancel their account with Bangor Hydro, yet the lack of electricity suited this place, giving it a timeless quality. The Johnsons were dancing together, steps smoothly synchronized, as were many other couples, joyously dipping and swirling to the familiar beat of Ellington's "Take the 'A' Train." Faith was dancing with Arnie. The swing dance classes he'd been taking with Claire had paid off, and Faith was having a great time. The man could dance.

"Did Ursula tell you our news?" he asked.

"I don't think so. What news would this be?" Faith asked.

"We've made Hapswell's widow an offer for the lighthouse and she's accepted."

"That's wonderful!" Faith was thrilled for them, and she knew that under the Rowes' ownership, the lighthouse would go back to what it had always been, a beacon from the past, an intrinsic part of the landscape.

"The best part of all is that it isn't going to cost us much."

"What? I can't believe she'd let it go for anything under market value, and you know what that is these days, just for the location alone."

Arnie chuckled. "I made sure the purchase and sale included the contents. She had no objections, and apparently her lawyer is as eager as she is to make a killing quickly. Oops. Sorry, Faith."

"Don't worry. I've been saying the same sort of thing myself. But stop being so mysterious and tell me what you did." Arnie was always very clever when it came to making a profit. Pix had all sorts of tales of lemonade-stand entrepreneurship in their youth.

"The lens. The original Fresnel lens. It's worth a fortune and we're selling it to a maritime museum. A win-win situation."

That's exactly what it was. "Promise me one thing."

"Anything," he said, pulling her back after a very smoothly executed step.

"I never made it to the top." She shuddered slightly. "I'd like to see it in place before you have it removed."

"Done. Just let me know when you want to come over. We'll have a party. Make an occasion of it. Mother will like that."

Looking over his shoulder, Faith saw the side door burst open. Roland and some of the cast appeared, flushed with success. They poured into the room, and Roland, wearing a scarlet-lined cape and top hat, strode over to the band. He waited until the number ended, then grabbed a glass, tapping it with the bandleader's baton.

Expecting another toast, people reached for glasses and moved to the chairs along the walls.

He bowed and removed his hat with a flourish. "Good folk, you see before you a man totally stunned. A man who has been in said state only once or perhaps twice before, if memory serves." He was grinning broadly. "Some of you may have seen our modest play. . . ."

Shouts of "Bravo" and "Hear! Hear!" greeted this remark.

"Thank you, thank you." He bowed. "Yet, it is not as the director that I come before you, but, rather, as a messenger, a Mercury." He was clearly enjoying himself. "You'll never guess in a trillion years what happened tonight at the end of the show." He dropped his theatrical manner and reverted to good old Sanpere vernacular.

"We were taking a second curtain call, when Romeo—Ted Hamilton—and Juliet—Becky Prescott—stepped forward and held up their hands for silence. I blushingly admit I thought they were going to make some reference to my own poor but adequate effort, or perhaps Linda's. Instead, they asked their parents to come up onstage, which, after much hemming and hawing, they did. Becky turned to hers, holding Romeo's hand, and said, 'Mom and Dad, Sanpere isn't someplace in Italy, and Ted and I want a happy ending. Everyone has been wicked foolish this summer, and we decided to put a stop to it. You're looking at Mrs. Theodore Hamilton. We got married last week.' "

Roland waited for the room to calm down. Hamiltons and Prescotts in name or by marriage were present and they started roaring questions; plus, there was a more general outcry of sheer surprise.

"Then Ted said something to his parents about ending the feud and the whole place was as quiet as the grave. I was thinking of ducking out to call Earl, except I remembered he'd be in no condition to enforce the law, should one get broken. Becky and Ted are both of age, so no problem there. Becky's father was as red as any makeup artist could make him, and he took a step toward Ted; likewise Ted's father toward Becky. Can't imagine what he had it in mind to do. Then the two men looked at each other, and damned if they didn't start to laugh their heads off. Tears were running down their cheeks, and if they had slapped each other's backs any harder, they'd have broken a bone. 'I guess they got us!' Hamilton said, and everyone headed over to Sam's place to pick up appropriate comestibles—fortunately, he never closes—and there's another marriage celebration going on down in Little Harbor right now. Mazeltov to both couples! Maestro." He handed the baton back and the band immediately began to play "Love and Marriage." People sang along, and Faith noticed a few duck out, obviously headed for the other party—making a doubleheader of the night. The most exotic offerings on Sam's shelves were the new Doritos Extremes, but they went well with cold Bud.

"You were right," she said to Freeman, who came to claim a dance once the sing-along ended. "The feud ended just the way you said it would, although even you couldn't have predicted this."

"Oh no? Who do you think drove them to Ellsworth? Course, I was going up there anyway. Didn't want anyone to know they'd been off island, so they left their cars outside the school on one of the rehearsal days."

Between Freeman and Ursula, a girl could never get ahead, Faith conceded to herself.

"Wait a minute. What about the turpentine? Do you know about that, too? I don't see how Kenny could have gotten to it. And besides, it was before he knew about Harold. Before Harold was even dead."

"I expect one of the Prescotts is just about drunk enough now to confess to Ted that he didn't mean any harm, thought it wouldn't hurt him, only meant to scare him away."

Faith twirled out under Freeman's arm. She'd known she was right. It *had* been meant for Romeo.

The band packed up at eleven o'clock, right after "Good Night Ladies" and "Auld Lang Syne." Jill threw her bouquet; Samantha caught it, and her father almost snatched it from her hands. They'd been hearing a little too much about someone named Nick on the trip. She gave him a kiss. "Don't worry, Daddy. I'll always be your little girl."

Choked up, he called to the rest of the family that it was time to go home. At the door, Samantha turned and winked at Faith, who winked right back.

The Miller vacation had been a great success— and they'd had the best meal of the trip in Jasper. Sam had been raving all evening about the Alberta beef he'd had at a place called Becker's.

"We'd better be going, too, sweetheart," Faith said. Ursula had left after Roland's startling news, getting a ride with the Marshalls. Lisa Prescott was sleeping over at the Fairchilds'—the first occupant of the guest room.

"The first of September. It feels like fall," Tom said as they walked toward the meadow where the cars had been parked. "What a night."

"I wish we could do it all over again—the dancing, the food, all those wonderful people."

"You may get your wish. The Johnsons were talking about doing it cooperatively same time next year—'The South Beach Dance Club.' "

A new tradition to replace all the traditions that were slipping away. The summer was over, but Faith would never forget this one. One that had brought her so close to losing her life—the life she cherished because of the people in it. She didn't want any of it to change, although it would, and for a moment she felt a stab of fear, but the full moon—no, make that almost-full moon—shining steadily overhead pulled her anxiety from her like an ebbing tide. She squeezed Tom's hand hard.

"What is it, Faith? What's wrong?"

"Absolutely nothing," she said.

EXCERPTS FROM
HAVE FAITH
IN YOUR KITCHEN
BY Faith Sibley Fairchild
A WORK IN PROGRESS

CORN PUDDING

2 cups fresh corn, cut
    from the cob, or 2
    cups canned, frozen,
    or cooked corn
2 large eggs, slightly
    beaten
1½ tablespoons unsalted
    butter, melted

2 cups scalded whole
    milk
1 teaspoon sugar
1 teaspoon salt
⅛ teaspoon pepper

Preheat the oven to 325°F. Mix all the ingredients together and pour into a buttered baking dish. Set it in a pan of hot water (the water halfway up the sides of the dish) and bake until firm, approximately 45 minutes. Best with fresh corn, yet still a good side dish for a winter evening, when elephant's-eye-high stalks are but a dream. Serves 4 to 6.

CRAB CAKES

½ cup mayonnaise,
  preferably Hellman's
1 large egg, slightly
  beaten
1 tablespoon Dijon
  mustard

1 pound fresh lump
  crabmeat, drained
1 cup crumbled saltines
  (25 to 30 crackers)
Vegetable oil

People have very strong feelings about crab cakes. They're like barbecue—beef or pork? Catsup-based or mustard-based sauce? With crab cakes, the debate starts with the crab—Maryland, Louisiana, and Maine devotees weighing in on one coast; Washington on the other. Faith loves all and any crab, but she is partial to Maine's peekytoe crab because she lives there. Then, breading, crackers, or potato as binding? Worcestershire sauce, Old Bay, Tabasco, or all three to complement the crustacean? Celery? Onions? The following is the recipe Faith's family prefers, after having made many happy trials. The Fairchilds like their crab cakes crabby, with as few additions as possible.

Combine the mayonnaise, egg, and mustard. Mix well, then fold in the crabmeat and saltines. Faith puts the saltines between two sheets of waxed paper and rolls them with a rolling pin to crumble them. Let the mixture stand for about 3 minutes before shaping it into patties. This recipe makes 12 patties. Put them on a baking sheet, cover with waxed paper or Saran wrap, and refrigerate for an hour.

Fry the cakes in vegetable oil, about 3 to 4 minutes on a side, until they are golden brown. Drain on a paper towel and serve. Do not fry the cakes in olive oil or any other oil with a strong taste. Faith uses canola oil.

For spicy cakes, add ½ teaspoon of hot sauce to the first three ingredients. Faith often serves her crab cakes with a dab of mayonnaise mixed with Old Bay seasoning (to taste) on the side.

BLUEBERRY MUFFINS

2½ cups flour
1 cup sugar
2 tablespoons baking
 powder
¾ teaspoon salt
1 teaspoon nutmeg,
 preferably freshly
 ground

¾ teaspoon cinnamon
2 large eggs
1 cup milk
¾ cup unsalted butter,
 melted
2 cups blueberries
Butter for greasing

Preheat the oven to 400°F. Sift together the dry ingredients: flour, sugar, baking powder, salt, and spices. Lightly beat the eggs, milk, and melted butter together. Add this to the dry ingredients and mix. Fold the blueberries into the batter and fill each cup in the muffin tin completely, not ¾ full. Faith learned this trick from Lori Boyce, by way of Kyra Alex's cookbook, *Lily's Café*. Makes 2 dozen muffins.

PASTA WITH SMOKED CHICKEN AND SUMMER VEGETABLES

4 pounds skinless, boned chicken thighs and/or breasts
2 cups diced carrots
2 cups diced zucchini
2 cups diced summer squash
1 cup diced yellow or red onion
1 red pepper, diced
1 large sprig fresh rosemary
1 cup vinaigrette with 1½ teaspoons fresh rosemary leaves
16 ounces tortellini, dried or fresh
5 ounces fresh chèvre
Salt and pepper

Smoke the chicken on the grill, using hickory chips, apple wood, or any flavor you prefer. While the chicken is cooking, dice the vegetables and make the vinaigrette, using your own recipe or Faith's—1 part balsamic vinegar to 3 parts olive oil, plus ⅛ teaspoon Dijon mustard and a pinch of salt and pepper. Add the rosemary leaves and shake well.

Steam the vegetables with the sprig of rosemary until soft, but not mushy. Remove the rosemary and toss the vegetables with the vinaigrette. Cook the tortellini according to the instructions on the package, drain, and then add the chèvre, mixing it thoroughly.

Cut the cooked chicken into bite-size pieces and add to the tortellini. Add the vegetables and mix gently. Salt and pepper to taste.

This is a wonderful dish to take to a party, as

Faith does, garnishing it with nasturtiums from the garden. It should sit for about an hour and be served at room temperature. It can also be served over greens as a salad. Serves 8 to 10 at least.

COMFORT COOKIES

2 sticks unsalted butter
at room temperature
1 cup brown sugar
¾ cup white sugar
2 large eggs, slightly
beaten
½ teaspoon vanilla
extract
2¼ cups all-purpose
flour

1 teaspoon baking soda
1 teaspoon salt
1½ cups semisweet
chocolate chips
1½ cups butterscotch
chips
1 cup coarsely chopped
walnuts

Preheat oven to 325°F. Cream the butter and sugars together by hand or with an electric mixer. Add the eggs and vanilla extract. Beat until fluffy. In a separate bowl, combine the flour, baking soda, and salt. Add this to the butter mixture and stir or mix well. Stir in the chips and walnuts. Drop golf-ball-size portions onto a nongreased cookie sheet. Bake for 15 to 20 minutes. They should be golden brown. Use the longer time for a crisper cookie. Cool on brown paper or racks. Makes 2 dozen cookies.

You can substitute the chips and walnuts with whatever comforts you or your family and friends enjoy—other chip varieties (they now have Reese's and M&M chips), raisins, other kinds of chopped nuts. These cookies are especially comforting when they're still warm and the chips haven't hardened. This is a variation of Kyra Alex's extremely comforting chocolate-chip-cookie recipe, again from Lily's Café in Stonington, Maine.

Note on recipes: Substitutions can always be made: Egg Beaters, margarine, low-fat mayonnaise, and 1 percent, 2 percent, or skim milk, for example.

Author's Note

On the morning of September 11, 2001, I was
driving to a neighboring town for a reason I cannot now recall. I turned on the radio and heard
what I first assumed to be a review of some dis-
aster movie, but soon realized, fighting disbelief,
that it was an actual news bulletin. I stopped at
once and turned around.

What I do clearly remember from the short
drive is what a beautiful day it was. At the moment I heard the news, I was looking at the Flint
Farm fields stretched out on one side of the narrow road, the barn and farmhouse on the other—
all under a cloudless blue sky. The farm dates
back to the 1640s, and Flints are farming it still. It
will always be farmland; the family has given it to
a trust. It will always be there. Growing up in
New Jersey, approaching New York City so many
times from across the river, I watched the Twin

Towers go up and become a part of the familiar skyline. We thought they would always be there, too.

Returning home, I ran into the house, unable to say anything to my husband except "Turn on the television." We watched in horror as the second plane struck. Then, in what seemed like a very short time, we saw the towers fall to earth. Footage of two young women crouched behind a car appeared over and over again throughout the day. They were clinging to each other, looking up; then one pulled the other to her feet and they ran, shoeless, disappearing into the cloud of ash and debris. From their faces, you could tell they were screaming. There was no sound. I see their faces still.

There were no degrees of separation on September 11. Everyone knew someone affected. The first tragic news was that the mother and stepfather of one of the administrators at my son's school had been on the plane that went down in Pennsylvania. She has taken comfort from the knowledge that those passengers were able to prevent something even worse. A friend's brother didn't make it out; another friend's son did. We didn't try to make sense of it all, but we went to a town vigil; prayed at our church, open all day and night; and then finally attended the service and silent march the high school students organized. It was impossible to keep back the tears at the sight of all those youthful faces as the students quietly walked toward the bleachers at the football field. They could not, still cannot, know how different their lives will be.

And I was writing this book. I'd started it in July and was immersed in Faith's world. I wasn't able to get back there for many weeks. I talked with writer friends, some experiencing the same difficulty, others finding solace in their work.

Instead of writing, I read, cooked, cleaned closets—and my husband, my son, and I went to Maine. Especially that first weekend, it was the place we wanted to be. Away from CNN and the other stations for a while; the three of us together. As we drove north, every car displayed a flag. Turning off the turnpike onto the back roads to "Sanpere Island," we saw that every yard had a hand-lettered sign, more flags. It was Indian summer. We sat watching the tides, the osprey still in her nest on the opposite point, and broke bread with friends, cherishing their company.

When I got back to this book, I rewrote the few post–September 11 attempts I'd made. I'd lost the rhythm of Faith's life, just as my own had been so disturbed, but it came back. The book takes place in the summer of 2001, ending on September 1 with a wedding. I think back to that summer, and it now seems like some kind of Camelot, my own uncomplicated days very different from Faith's. As I wrote, I found myself giving her some of those moments, as well—moments removed from the plot, times when she watches her children and husband, wanting to remember the secure, serene feeling forever. Just as many of us date things from before the Cuban missile crisis and before the assassinations of the Kennedys and Martin Luther King, Jr., we have another "before." Yet, once I returned to it, this book was a joy to write, as they all are. I recalled the answer British mystery writer P. D. James gave when asked why crime fiction is so popular. She said, "These novels are always popular in ages of great anxiety. It's a very reassuring form. It affirms the hope that we live in a rational and beneficent universe."

This hope was affirmed in countless ways immediately following September 11 and continues to be in ways large and small all over the globe. This hope is my wish for you, dear reader.

Turn the page for a peek
at the next thrilling installment
in the Faith Fairchild series,

THE BODY IN THE ATTIC

Available now wherever books are sold.

"It's big. Yes indeed. No problem there. But . . ."

"But what?" Tom asked anxiously.

They were standing in Dr. Robinson's living room. The weak January sunlight struggled to find chinks in the yews and hemlocks that had grown up over the windows. Their branches pressed against the frost-covered panes. Faith snapped on a lamp. The damask shade barely permitted any light to penetrate through.

"It's dark. It's very dark," Faith said, shivering slightly. It was cold, too. The heat had been turned down after Dr. Robinson's friend left.

"We'll bring our own lamps. No problem. And I doubt we'll be spending a lot of time in this room."

Faith doubted it, too, although she could immediately see its possibilities. It was the size of the parsonage's living room and dining room put together and then some. A fireplace surrounded by an Adam mantel and surrounded by black marble shot with gold faced a series of leaded-glass windows overlooking the front yard, which was screened from the prying eyes of passersby on Brattle Street by a solid fence. It was painted brown to match the brown-shingled house. Dark. Everything was dark. Were this house hers, she'd take the wooden fence down, plant a living one, and pull up all the shrubs around the house's foundation. She'd paint the living room walls a warm color—Longfellow yellow or the rosy red of cream of tomato soup. They were covered in what had once been much brighter William Morris wallpaper, faded now to a uniform sepia, the willow pattern barely visible. There was a lot of furniture—piecrust tables, chairs from Shaker to Sheraton, and a large hairy-paw Chippendale sofa. Much was slipcovered in burgundy damask, and the overall effect was an *Antiques Roadshow* dream, but not user-friendly.

Tom crooked his elbow through his wife's. "Come on, let's look at the rest of the house. There's supposed to be a library back here." He opened a door on one side of the fireplace.

It was a library—and it was dark, too, but the walls glowed with the deep rich colors of bindings—row upon row of leather-bound books. As in the living room, an Oriental rug covered the floor, but this one was brighter—reds, golds, bright blue, and even orange. The one in the living room was intricate and somber—dark blue and rose.

"Better, but still not a place where the kids can hang out," Faith said.

Tom was lovingly running his hand across the top of the mahogany desk.

"It seems like a sacrilege to put a computer on something like this," he murmured.

Faith laughed. "You were born in the wrong century, love. Okay, let's see the rest."

The rest was a formal dining room. No problem entertaining, but they'd have to shout at dinnertime or cluster down at one end of the table. Eating in the kitchen was out. It had been constructed for a cook and a maid to wait on the table. The butler's pantry was almost as large as the kitchen itself. Faith was glad to see that the stove was a gas one and had been updated. There was a dishwasher and a new refrigerator—but no place for a family of four to eat. The dining room it would be. Gracious living. The bell panel on the wall above the sink in the butler's pantry attested to it.

On the second floor, there were five bedrooms and two baths. There had been a half bath at the foot of the back stairs, off the kitchen.

"We'd better put Amy in the small bedroom that shares a bath with this one, which we can use," Faith said. "I can imagine her wandering around, trying to find the other bathroom, and getting lost on her way back to bed."

"Whatever you say." Tom was determinedly upbeat. It wasn't hard. He was looking forward to this time in a completely new place as he had looked forward to few things before in his life. He sat on the bed and patted the mattress. "Feels fine."

It probably is, Faith thought. The whole house was well maintained and comfortable. The Victorian bedroom sets in each room were back in fashion again, and there wasn't even a scratch on any of the marble tops.

"We can use the room across the hall, in the front of the house, for the kids' playroom. Put their things there and maybe a television."

"Don't forget the top floor. Maybe there was a nursery there. An old hobbyhorse or two." Tom was a fan of E. Nesbit and A. A. Milne.

"Let's go see."

The stairs to the top floor were not as elaborate as the main staircase, and no niches lined the wall. Faith had been relieved to note that the professor had had all his porcelain packed away himself and that the niches were blessedly empty, as well the living room shelves and the dining room sideboard.

Unlike the rest of the house, the third floor was warm—airless, but warm. Dust filtered through the light as the Fairchilds opened the doors, which revealed a totally different way of life: tiny bedrooms for the servants, an antiquated bath, and small kitchen that dated from the forties at least. One door opened into the attic. It was filled with packing crates—the porcelain and other items Dr. Robinson had had placed out of harm's way. Faith stood in the doorway. There were old trunks and piles of newspapers, a dressmaker's dummy, an empty birdcage, chairs whose seats needed caning, bureaus with chipped paint. On the bureau nearest the door, someone had long ago affixed gummed red-bordered paper labels on the drawers. In a spidery hand, someone had written "Gift wrap, tissue paper, and string" on one. The next read "Dust cloths, mending yarn," and the last said "Ornaments, tree lights." She knew exactly what each drawer contained: wrapping paper ironed to be used again, tissue smoothed, string too short to be saved, threadbare cloths, carefully tied snippets of yarn, ornaments that needed hangers, and lights that needed bulbs. It was the quintessential New England attic. It could have been her in-laws', right down to the smell of cedar. She closed the door, feeling happier than she had downstairs in the land of wealth and privilege. Up here, the servants had been free, or at least freer. Their rooms were small and the mattresses straw—she'd tested one—but when they'd come up here the day's work was done.

At the opposite end from the attic, a door did indeed lead into a nursery.

"See, I was right. Look at the toys. Wow, this Lionel train must be worth a fortune! It looks brand-new, but it has to date from the fifties, or even earlier."

There was a window seat that stretched beneath the windows overlooking the front yard. White pines towered above the house and their branches beckoned to any child brave enough to go out the window and climb down. Ben was that kind of child, but that wasn't what made Faith decide to locate the children's playroom down a flight and make this floor strictly off-limits.

What decided this was the feeling she got as soon as she had opened the door—a feeling so palpable that she was sure Tom must share it, but from the look on his face as he examined the train, it was clear he didn't. It wasn't just the air, which had an acrid shut-off smell from the room's obvious disuse. The feeling was coming from something she couldn't define. She shook her head in a vain attempt to get out from under it, but, like a blanket during a nightmare, it smothered her.

Something horrible had happened here. She was certain—and she was afraid.